WITHDRAWN

THE LIGHT OF

COMMON

~~~DAY~~~

BY JOHN HERMAN

The Weight of Love

The Light of Common Day

John Herman

THE LIGHT OF COMMON DAY

NAN A. TALESE

DOUBLEDAY
New York · London · Toronto · Sydney · Auckland

Published by Nan A. Talese
an imprint of Doubleday
a division of Bantam Doubleday Dell Publishing Group, Inc.
1540 Broadway, New York, New York 10036

Doubleday is a trademark of Doubleday, a division of
Bantam Doubleday Dell Publishing Group, Inc.

All of the characters in this book are fictitious,
and any resemblance to actual persons,
living or dead, is purely coincidental.

Two stanzas of "Mariposa" by Edna St. Vincent Millay. From *Collected Poems*,
HarperCollins. Copyright 1921, 1948 by Edna St. Vincent Millay. All
rights reserved. Reprinted by permission of Elizabeth Barnett, literary
executor.

"Do Not Go Gentle Into That Good Night" by Dylan Thomas, from *The
Poems of Dylan Thomas*. Copyright © 1952 by Dylan Thomas. Reprinted by
permission of New Directions Publishing Corp. and J. M. Dent.

Book design by Ronnie Ann Herman

Library of Congress Cataloging-in-Publication Data
Herman, John
The light of common day / John Herman.
p.   cm.
I. Title.
PS3558.E6815L5   1997
813'.54—dc20   96-24268
CIP

ISBN 0-385-48318-X
Copyright © 1997 by John Herman
All Rights Reserved
Printed in the United States of America
May 1997
First Edition

1   3   5   7   9   10   8   6   4   2

This book is for my daughters

THE LIGHT OF

COMMON

DAY

∿∿∿ He was climbing upward. He ascended swiftly, feeling his way along the bars in the dark, his hands doing most of the work, never relinquishing contact with the rough, cold metal that he could not see; and, as he ascended, the dark fell away with the tree line and he emerged into the liquid purple of the sky.

He couldn't say when he had started to climb. It had been automatic, an extension of mounting the hill, as if the crane had been placed behind the school precisely for him, and he was partway up before he gave thought to what he was doing, walking along the diagonal bars the way he always knew he could, moving upward into the night. It was easy.

Because he had always been able to climb. There was no rock he couldn't scale. As a boy he had climbed any tree, any fence, shinnied rain pipes up the face of buildings. He had even essayed the rock face of the gym building on the upper field. He wasn't afraid of heights. He could stand at the edge of a cliff and look down two hundred feet into the sea. He had always known he could climb the crane where it towered behind the school in the lot where the new library was being constructed.

Now as Paul Werth emerged above the wall of trees he could see far below the dark of the Quad with its last few lights, the last sounds of the dance floating distantly like stray fireflies, the last couples moving off into the night; and then, as he climbed, that too dropped away and he could see out across the tops of the trees into the sleeping suburbs and, above that, twinkling in the fragrance of the dark June sky, the stars.

His father had taken him out at night as a child to see the stars. He could never remember the constellations except the Big Dipper and then the North Star. He would stand close to his father and smell his odor and listen to the excitement of his voice as he identified Orion, Draco, Pegasus, Cassiopeia.

"Look," his father would explain, "that's the Milky Way. That's our galaxy, millions and millions of light-years long. It's like a great saucer extended horizontally through space. Our solar system is at one edge. We're looking across through the saucer. The shining of all those stars in the galaxy is what makes the Milky Way."

His father lay with his hands on the sheets. The room smelled of medicine. In the corridor he had passed an old man with a bottle on a rack that he pulled and a tube descending into his black shriveled vein. The old man was wearing slippers and a white hospital coat open at the back. And he thought, I've been here before. I've seen this before. I will be here again.

"I don't want you to deal yourself out," his father said.

He was almost at the top of the crane. He must have climbed without thinking, trusting to the skill of his body; and now, when he looked down, the earth beneath him was a well of darkness. The crane swayed slightly under his weight.

A breeze had come up. The lights had been extinguished in the school, and the sleeping suburb, a breathing lake stretching to the horizon, was distinguished only by an occasional light that fluttered upward through the leaves. He was alone except for the hum of the great city in the distance. It seemed to him an absolute good to be sitting at the top of the crane watching the stars. He tried to imagine a light-year but he couldn't. A plane passed overhead, distant and blinking. Beneath him the leaves rustled, sighed vaguely. He could feel the steel of the crane gripped between his knees. He was no longer even holding on.

And he thought, the blackness stretches forever. Day is only a kind of illusion, the merest fingernail of light. He imagined the earth below him, a small globe whirling in space. Trivia, really. *To cease upon the midnight with no pain!* And a voice whispered in his ear, "Cast yourself down!"

Alarmed, he shifted his weight, testing his purchase with his knees. But when he looked, all he could see was blackness. And it seemed that he was entirely alone.

1

Philip Richards leaned against the gym wall and removed a pack of Camels from his breast pocket. The boys huddled in the March cold at the top of the hill where they couldn't be seen. Their breath plumed damply in the air, coming in puffs like the steam from young horses. They had fifteen minutes between classes.

"Well, our dandy principal really outdid himself today," Richards said. He had sardonic blue eyes and his mouth was pulled into a small, sardonic grin. He invariably wore a blue business suit and black business shoes and his blond hair was slicked back in a single line to the back of his head. His hand shook slightly as he lit the cigarette.

"Jesus!" Jeb said in some awe. "Drugs!" He was a pudgy, pale-looking boy with freckles and earnest, serious features, and he stared at the others now with a frown. "I mean, I'm not even sure what drugs *are!*"

Paul Werth turned away. He too was uncertain what was signified by *drugs*, but he kept this to himself.

"Our Great White Leader doesn't know what drugs are either," Richards observed. "He's just whistling 'Dixie.'"

"But aren't drugs *addictive?*" Jeb continued. "I mean, heroin and that sort of thing? Can't they kill you or something?"

"Sure they can kill you—if you don't know what you're doing," Richards said. "That's not the point."

"So who would use them? I mean, if they are going to kill you."

"Don't be such a sap, Jeb. Marijuana's not going to *kill* you. It's not going to make you impotent or give you pimples."

"Marijuana?"

"Yeah—weed. Grass. Don't you guys know anything?"

The other boys maintained an uneasy silence.

"So who's dealing drugs?" Jeb asked.

"I couldn't say," Richards said, regarding Jeb from under his brows as he dragged on his cigarette, "but I'll tell you this—he must be one dumb son of a bitch. You've got to be dumb to deal drugs, *bambini.*"

The boys heard someone approaching up the hill and, startled, they cupped their cigarettes behind their backs. It was Craig Lewis.

"I thought I'd find you here," Lewis said. He was a tall, thin boy with bushy eyebrows and a broad, heavy brow dotted with painful-looking pimples. Lewis was the brainiest boy in the class.

Paul and Jeb nodded in greeting but Richards merely scratched with his shoe in the earth.

"I think we ought to discuss what Mr. Bates said."

Richards shot Lewis a look, half amused, half impatient. "What's to discuss?"

"Any of you guys know anything about this?"

"Whaddaya mean, Craig?"

"I don't think there should be drugs at Highgate. It screws us *all* up."

Richards snorted with amusement. "You worried you won't get into *Harvard?*"

"Maybe I am," Lewis said. "I'm not ashamed of that. I don't want my chances loused up by some jerk selling drugs. You should feel the same," Lewis continued, turning to Paul, "and you too, Jeb. Don't you want to go to Yale?"

Paul and Richards looked at Jeb, who frowned as if trying to agree and disagree at the same time.

Down the hill the warning bell for the next class rang. The wind had come up, sweeping the trees. From somewhere in the distance a first bird offered a tentative cry. The boys stubbed out their cigarettes.

"Well, if I find out who's pushing drugs, I'm going to Bates."

"Bully for you," Richards said.

"We're the leaders in this class," Lewis continued, turning to the other two boys. "You guys shouldn't even be up here *smoking*."

Richards merely laughed. "Here, Craig," he said, "have a cigarette. It will do you good."

"We could put an end to this if we wanted," Lewis said. Then, turning on Richards: "I wouldn't be surprised if your friend Berger knew something about this."

"Oh? Why don't you ask him?"

"I don't know why you hang around with this guy," Lewis said to Jeb and Paul in disgust.

"Get lost, creep," Richards said good-humoredly.

Paul Werth and Philip Richards descended the hill together after the others had left.

"You think Berger really *does* know something about this drug business?" Richards asked.

"How should I know?" Paul said. "*I'm* not his friend."

They had reached the Quad; crowds of students pushed and hurried around them in the last minutes before class. Werth and Richards turned left toward the far doors where the junior and senior lockers stood.

"But I don't think it's Berger," Paul added.

"No?" Richards looked at him with casual interest, lifting his eyebrows in his peculiar fashion so that his forehead almost disappeared. "Why not?"

"Because I know who it is."

"No kidding!" There was always a note of amusement in Richards' voice. "So who is it?"

"It's the jocks—Hillman and Pursy and that bunch."

"Yeah?" Richards was only paying partial attention. "Why do you think that?"

"I dunno. The way they act in the locker room, I suppose. It's just something I know."

Richards looked at Paul and his blond eyebrows again went up in amusement. "Something you *know*? Do you always put so much faith in your insight?"

"Yes, I do," Paul said, drawing back into himself, his feelings hurt, for Paul always trusted his intuition, it was his surest way of interpreting the world.

Richards only laughed. "So what do you propose to do, *caro mio*? Turn them in?"

"Of course not!"

"Aren't you worried about getting into *Harvard*?" But noticing that Paul was pained, Richards changed tack immediately. "No, of course not. Your brother's there already, right? As for myself, I could burn the place down and they'd still have to accept me. My family helped found the shithouse."

The boys paused at the door before entering the school corridor.

"So you think it's Hillman," Richards said.

"Yes—I know it is."

"Well, you're probably right!" And he patted Paul on the shoulder. "Take care now, *bambino*," and he turned off toward the senior hall. "I'll see you later. *Ciao!*"

Paul came into the junior corridor and immediately he was surrounded by students heading for class. He could feel his nerves tighten. His chest contracted as though he couldn't breathe.

Stopping at his locker, he caught sight of Nicole Swann, dressed in a yellow sweater and standing down the corridor among a crowd of girls. Her back slouched softly like a cat's. Then she was swept onward with a stream of students into the next corridor and carried out of sight.

The French class was strangely hushed when Paul entered. March sun poured through the windows, heating the back desks and glowing in oily smudges on the tarnished wood. A column of dust danced heavily in the still light.

Paul took a seat in the back row.

Craig Lewis sat in the front with his head down, checking his homework; even from this distance Paul could see the dandruff on the back of his shoulders. In the middle row Jack Wheeler shared wisecracks with Chipper Jones.

Outside the window a branch swayed slowly, glided

upward, moved beyond ear-reach in perfect dreamlike stasis.

Then Mrs. Wagner entered. The class came to attention, Paul could feel his stomach tighten.

Mrs. Wagner was a stout, handsome woman with bulbous dark eyes without demarcation between iris and pupil. She invariably wore a brown tailored suit and a brown sweater that accentuated her large bosom. She was a European woman, ironic and disabused, who spoke with a slight accent; her soft, dark mustache, visible from the back row, was unsettling but not—surprisingly—disfiguring.

"So! You hear what Mr. Bates says," Mrs. Wagner announced briskly. "Wery serious! Wery serious!"

Her eyes darted about the room as if in anticipation of roasting some culprit.

"I vant to remind you that I am a member of de committee Mr. Bates has selected to inquire into this matter of droogs. If any of you knows anything about droogs, you can speak to me at any time. Whatever you say will be held in strictest confidence, I assure you. Strictest confidence!"

And Mrs. Wagner snapped a piece of chalk between her fingers.

"Now—what do we have today!"

She sat down at her desk facing the class and opened her text with irascible alacrity. Paul too opened his text and regarded it with distaste; he had neglected to do his homework.

Craig Lewis raised his hand.

"Yes, Craig—what do you want?"

"You asked us yesterday why we should learn French, and I want to answer."

"Ah, of course! Well, please instruct us, Craig. I'm sure the class will be most interested!"

"I think we should learn French," Craig said, "so we can read the French classics. I believe that Racine and La Fontaine are among the world classics, but we can't read them unless we know French."

"Racine and La Fontaine are among the world *bores*," Berger whispered to Paul.

Paul hadn't noticed that Berger was sitting next to him, and now he leaned away; he didn't want to attract Mrs. Wagner's attention.

"How well you put that," Mrs. Wagner said dryly. "Racine *is* one of de world classics."

And closing her eyes, she leaned back in her chair and started reciting from memory.

> "O toi, qui vois la honte où je suis descendue,
> Implacable Vénus, suis-je assez confondue?
> Tu ne saurais plus loin pousser ta cruauté.
> Ton triomphe est parfait; tous tes traits ont porté!"

When she finished she opened her eyes, and it took an instant for her to recognize where she was.

"There," she said, straightening and looking about the room. "That is poetry!"

"Could have fooled me," Berger whispered.

"What?" Mrs. Wagner snapped. Her eyes darted around the class and bore into—Chipper Jones, seated immediately in front of Berger. "What did you say, Alfred? Do you have something to share with de class?"

"No, Mrs. Wagner," Chipper said dolefully, not lifting his eyes. "I didn't say anything."

"You didn't? Are you sure you didn't?"

"Yes, Mrs. Wagner."

"Don't stutter, Alfred. Speak up! Tell the class what you have to say. Don't slouch there like some kind of duffel bag! Do you think your parents pay all this tuition for you to be a duffel bag?"

Chipper eyed Mrs. Wagner stolidly, his lower lip depending like a basset hound's.

"My goodness, Alfred, you *are* a specimen. Come to the front of de class. Come along now—don't shuffle! Come to the front of the class and help us with the homework."

Chipper stood up, and he did resemble a duffel bag. He shuffled down the aisle behind the row of students.

Jack Wheeler administered a surreptitious noogie as Chipper passed.

"Well, class, isn't this nice!" Mrs. Wagner said. "Alfred is going to do the homework for us on the board! Look alive, now, Alfred! You don't want to make a fool of yourself before the class! Write the answer for *numéro quatre* on the board."

Chipper shifted uneasily on his feet, ducked his head, dug with his index finger into the cuticle of his thumb.

"Alfred, I'm talking to you!"

"Sentence number four, Mrs. Wagner?"

"That's what I said. Aren't you awake dis morning?"

"Yes, Mrs. Wagner, only . . . I didn't *do* number four."

"What's that?"

"I didn't do number four, Mrs. Wagner."

"Why not, Alfred?"

"I dunno." And Chipper began repeatedly ducking his head as if in the hope that he might disappear. "I must of gotten the assignment wrong."

The slightest suggestion of a smile crossed Mrs. Wagner's mouth.

"Got the assignment wrong? How *extraordinaire!* Did anyone else get the assignment wrong? Brigit, what was the assignment for today?"

"To do sentences one through fifteen, Mrs. Wagner."

Chipper glanced quickly in Brigit's direction and then dropped his head.

"One through fifteen! *Précisément!* Now isn't that *remarquable,* Alfred, that Brigit got the assignment correct, but you didn't? However, that doesn't stop us from doing the assignment *now,* does it?"

Chipper hung his head in sullen resistance but didn't say anything.

"Please do sentence *numéro* four for us, Alfred."

Mrs. Wagner opened her text and read the sentence out in English.

" 'Hardly had de trip started when I became seasick.' "

Chipper gazed stolidly at the blackboard. He was a lumpy shapeless boy with large features and rumpled hair and his lower lip protruded as if it had been bruised by a stone. He stared at the board and did nothing.

Craig's hand went up in the front row.

Le voyage . . . n'est guère . . . commencé, Chipper wrote. Then he stopped and considered what he had accomplished. Mrs. Wagner looked at the class and smiled.

Chipper continued: *quand je . . . me suis . . . devenu . . . malade.*

There was a moment of stunned silence. Craig's hand went down.

Paul thought he was going to laugh. He looked at Chipper with new-won respect: he couldn't have done that!

"Excellent, Alfred, excellent!" Mrs. Wagner exclaimed, and her voice was not unkind. "You can sit down now. You see, that wasn't so hard! Didn't Alfred do vell, class? Let's see if the rest of you can do so vell! Open your books to page fifty-four *s'il vous plaît!*"

Paul opened his book to the appropriate page. Mrs. Wagner had already started asking students for answers; she invariably began in one corner of the room and snaked through the rows from left to right, and a simple computation allowed Paul to approximate which questions might be his. These he now began trying to answer.

Outside the branch tapped at the window, rose like a wave, distant and beautiful, then receded. Paul tried to concentrate on his work.

"Hardly had the trip started when I became sick." "Tous les étudiants aiment ce professeur." "Le médecin rédigera une ordonnance."

He looked up: eleven minutes had passed. Eleven minutes since the start of the class. Eleven minutes out of fifty. He felt his back break out in perspiration. "Tous les étudiants aiment ce professeur."

Hardly had the trip started when I became seasick.

Between classes Paul stood in the long corridor with his backside pressed against the radiator; the air was raw with

March dampness and the radiator steadied his nerves. Students whirled about him, opening lockers, getting books, comparing homework. Girls passed in brightly colored shoals, dressed in plaid kilts with oversized safety pins at the thigh and starched white or pink oxford shirts. Young men lounged in groups, laughing and joshing nervously.

Highgate stood on the side of a wooded hill in a suburb a half mile from Paul's house. The main buildings were built of granite and feldspar quarried upstate at the turn of the century and floated downriver, and the face of the buildings retained the irregular rugged look of the unsmoothed stone. The body of the school consisted of a series of buildings, irregular in shape and coupled together like freight cars, which described the three sides of a rectangle. This space constituted the Quad, a great open pool of light and lawn ascending from the lowest building to the crest of the hill, crossed at midsection by a single walkway. At the base of this lawn against the lower buildings there rose a stand of hemlocks, lofty and dark-needled, whose branches swept down to touch the ground: here in winter the branches held the snow in great frozen avalanches; and in summer, when the heat was up, the trees harbored the air like tents.

Some of the other kids at Highgate lived in the suburb like Paul, but most commuted from the city by car or bus or subway.

Now Jack Wheeler, a short, wide-hipped boy with sandy hair and a lively, crooked face as if it had melted slightly in the heat, separated from the mass of students and drifted into Paul's vicinity.

"Hey, man, what's up?" Wheeler inevitably used a kind of bebop jargon that matched his image as a cool cat.

"Nothing special. What's new with you?"

"Oh, I dunno. You heard about Berger?"

"No, what's up with Berger?"

"I hear he's betting on the basketball finals—can you dig it?"

Paul looked at Wheeler for a moment. Jack and he were not particularly friendly, though they had been classmates for years.

"Berger is an idiot," Paul allowed himself, though he saw immediately that this displeased Wheeler.

Wheeler shrugged. "I was just wondering whether you were going to bet—that's all."

Keith Firman approached and stood looking at them out of large, soulful brown eyes.

"You talking about Berger?"

"Yeah—you heard about it?"

"Of course."

Keith sounded disgusted. He couldn't play sports because of a childhood injury, but he acted as general manager for various varsities, including basketball.

"He shouldn't be betting on the teams," Keith said. "It isn't right."

"Hey, man," Wheeler said, "Berger would bet on which taxi would reach the end of the block first."

"Did you check out Nicole at the game last Thursday?" Keith asked, changing the subject.

"Yeah, I saw her."

"So what did you think?"

"She's okay," Wheeler answered nonchalantly. "What's the big deal?"

"What's the big deal? She's only the most beautiful girl in the class, that's all. What do you think?" Keith asked, turning to Paul.

"About what?"

"About Nicole Swann. Don't you think she's a knock-out?"

"Keith's got this thing for Swann," Wheeler explained, looking at Paul and lifting his eyebrows. "It's like he's conceived this passion—dig it?"

"Oh? And is it returned?"

"You kidding?" And Wheeler laughed, poking Keith in the arm. And the three boys laughed together.

Paul had conceived his passion for Nicole Swann that past autumn at a party in the city. He had rarely spoken with Nicole before, but at the party they began a bantering flirtation and after a while he asked her to dance.

They were playing "In the Still of the Night," and in the darkened room he pressed his leg against her until, with the heat of her through the silky smoothness of her dress, he felt something melt inside him.

They left the party together, and though he couldn't think of anything to say, he feared that if he didn't think of something soon, he would lose his opportunity forever.

"So which way are you going?"

She looked at him languidly, a dark girl with flat, rather high cheekbones and large brooding eyes. Her body looked full and slightly swollen.

"Oh, this way, I suppose. You want to walk with me?"

"Sure!"

They started westward, trailing under the autumn

leaves, and the air, still fat with the autumn heat, carried the throb of the city.

"You look like Tony Perkins," she offered after a bit.

"Do I?"

"Yeah—that kind of thin, nervous look. Have you seen his new movie?"

"No, what's his new movie?"

"*Psycho.* They say it's incredibly scary!"

He wanted to ask her to go to the movies with him but he didn't have the nerve. They came into the light of an awning, the doorman dressed in a dark green coat with polished buttons, then continued into the dark.

"You're in Mr. Lemming's class, aren't you?" she asked. "I tried to get in but they wouldn't let me." She wrinkled her nose. "That's the genius class, right?"

"Hardly genius. Actually, Lemming is something of an old lady."

She smiled at that. "Don't you read Dostoyevsky?"

"Yeah—*Crime and Punishment.*"

" 'Everything is permitted!' " And she laughed as if that tickled her. "Why haven't you spoken to me before?"

"I thought you only spoke to the older guys."

She shrugged impatiently.

"Well, I'm glad you spoke to me tonight."

They had stopped at a curb, and he could see into the swaying shadows of the park. He wondered whether he dared ask her out.

"Weren't you on the baseball team or something?"

"Yes, last year. Did you ever see me play?"

"I can't remember. I didn't know there were sopho-mores on the team."

"Just me." And he laughed, trying to make it sound nonchalant; but she looked at him seriously and didn't smile.

"You going to win the championship again this year?"

He wondered how she knew about the championship, and he felt his throat tighten.

"I dunno, I hope so. Will you come and watch me play?" He attempted to make it sound like a joke.

"Well, who can say—spring is a long ways off. But sure! Why not?" Then she reached and straightened his collar.

"Your collar's all screwy."

The gesture thrilled him.

"Listen," he said, "about that movie."

"Which movie?"

"You know—the one with Tony Perkins."

"Oh, yeah. Well, what about it?"

"Well, I was wondering if you wanted to go. With me, I mean. If you're not too *scared*."

She looked at him.

"Scared of you?"

"No, of course not! Of the movie."

"Sure," she said after a moment. "Why not?" But then she added, "But let's make it in the afternoon, okay?"

Midway through *Psycho* he nerved himself to take her hand. It lay limply in his but it wasn't withdrawn, and it excited him so that he lost all track of the movie: during the famous shower scene he was unmindful of what was happening on the screen, he only knew that the small, soft object that sweated in his palm was suddenly galvanized, caught at his fingers with urgency, and clutched with a strength that pained as much as it pleased.

"But wasn't he in *drag?*" she insisted when the picture was out and they had issued into the sticky heat.

"Yes, I guess he was."

That excited her. She leaned against him, and he could smell her closeness in the autumn evening. A taxi passed, its heat bleeding into the city. He was still holding her hand.

"We can't go back to my place," she said, disappointed. "My parents are there."

So *that* was why she had made the date for the afternoon, so she didn't have to invite him to her apartment.

She walked beside him for two blocks, still under the spell of the movie. He could feel her against him, her body moored to him in the heat. They passed a small restaurant, a middle-aged couple arguing, a man walking a dachshund—and Paul's heart beat in his throat.

Impulsively he dove with her into a brownstone; and it was there in the foyer, holding her against him, kissing her, that he was sucked in by the astounding sweetness of her lips.

When Paul arrived home after school he let himself in the front door and stood listening to the silence of the house. Late March sun fell through the foyer window. A pale lozenge of light fluttered against a wall. His nostrils filled with the warmth, as intimate as the murmur of his own blood.

Paul went upstairs and paused for a moment at the top,

and he remembered how he had sat there weeping. It had not been immediately after the death of his father, nor a month nor even two months after. Weeping was then a daily occurrence, a release from pain so severe that its onset did not even provoke shame. Nor had it been six months after, when there was some relenting, not of the pain, which he held with stubbornness and pride as if it was a measure of his love, but of any public display (for tears were a thing to be shown only under duress, and in proportion to that love which hurt so terribly). No, it had been a year and then some that had elapsed when, returning to the house and mounting the stairs toward his father's room, he had again been staggered by the weight of his loss, and falling to his knees, he had wept in anguish and incomprehension.

Now Paul passed his brother's room and turned into his own at the end of the hall. His punching bag hung from the doorframe. The hi-fi he had assembled with his father stood in a corner. Paperback books, none of them for class, littered the floor. The light over his desk was still on.

Paul threw his book bag down and surveyed the place; then, sighing, he walked to the window and stared absently into the top of the spruce that guarded the front of the house. The tree had been his constant companion since childhood and he knew beyond effacement the pungency of its odor, the moan of its branches, the rustle of its needles.

He should have been studying. His father had explained that his homework constituted his duty, just as his, his father's, duty consisted of his work.

That was during one of the little conferences he used to have periodically with his father. His father would call him to the den, or to the garden, where during pleasant weather he passed much of his time. Because Paul loved his father, he listened respectfully, knowing that the words were not really the point, knowing that his father was unhappy, that he hated his work, that he was trying to pass on to Paul something that was already inadequate. And he saw that his father knew this too, though he did not admit it—even to himself. Perhaps especially not to himself. And so Paul did not bring it up.

His father had been a lawyer. Every morning he arose at six and took the seven thirty-three into the city; every evening he returned at eight or nine or ten, tired and irritable. He had been a great student, his father, had gone to Harvard, both as an undergraduate and for his law degree. Often when their grandmother visited, she would recount anecdotes about how clever he had been. Paul was proud of his father and listened to the anecdotes patiently, even when he had heard them before, but he didn't believe in them any more than he believed in the advice his father offered during their talks together. Secretly he didn't approve of the anecdotes. They had nothing to do with his love for his father.

Something had gone wrong with his father's career. It wasn't discussed in the family, but it was the sort of thing that Paul knew. His father's firm had merged with a larger firm and his father had fallen out with one of his colleagues. Because his father had known this man for many years, he could not bring himself to say what he really thought, but Paul thought that his father's anger was killing him. Paul didn't know for sure what the issue was, but he knew the other man was part of the cause.

But Paul also knew that the anger was older and more ingrained than that. He didn't know enough to put it in words, but it was as if something had taken over his father's life long ago and had slowly usurped his father's birthright, squeezing him until there was no living space left that was his own, where he could laugh and breathe and be himself the way he had been when Paul was a child. Sometimes it seemed to Paul that his father's true space had been reduced to the size of his garden, a small strip of carefully tended flowers in the back of the house where his father would spend what remained of his free hours. Here he would be on Sundays—he worked all day Saturday—bent lovingly, absorbedly, above his plants like a surgeon above the open heart of a patient.

Sometimes Paul thought that his father should have been a gardener. All the anecdotes about his father's cleverness missed the point. His father should have given it all up, thrown it all over, moved to a warmer climate, begun his life anew. But of course that never happened.

Instead he had a heart attack.

He had gone for a regular checkup, his physician had discovered a spot on an X ray, they had decided to perform exploratory surgery. (*"Exploratory surgery?" his brother had exclaimed. "What jerk permits exploratory surgery?"*) The surgery proved negative, there was nothing on his father's liver, only a shadow on the plate of the X ray. Then, during his recovery in the hospital, he suffered a heart attack.

A stay that should have lasted five days had been protracted to as many weeks.

Paul's mother held an important position in the city, to which she commuted each day in her Dodge from the suburb where they lived. Paul would hear the wheels of the car on the gravel when she returned home in the late afternoon; then he would hear her moving around in the kitchen preparing dinner. He would go down the back stairs to meet her.

"Did you visit Dad?"

She would look up but she didn't pause with what she was doing.

"Of course."

"Is he okay?"

"Yes, he seems fine. All the nurses love him."

They shared a look of amusement.

He observed the familiar ritual as his mother put away the groceries she had picked up, the bread in the bread box, the vegetables in the bottom bin of the refrigerator, the cereal in the cupboard over the sink. This was his favorite time with her, the time when it was easiest to talk.

Absently he picked up one of the empty paper bags and began folding it.

"How was school? Did you finish your English paper?"

"Yes, Mom."

"How is it?"

"It's fine, Mom."

"Do you want me to look at it?"

"It's upstairs."

"Well, I'll be glad to look at it if you want. This is an

important year for you, Paul. It's important that you do well."

Sometimes he tried to talk to her about the things that worried him, but her solution was always the same.

"Just be true to yourself. Be true to Paul Werth and everything will turn out fine."

He hadn't discovered that being Paul Werth made anything so fine.

"Well, I'll have to get dinner going," his mother said. "It's just the two of us again, Paul."

He watched her move swiftly about the kitchen.

"I worry about your father," she continued. "I wish your brother was here. I'd tell him to come home from Cambridge except he has to study. But I can't help wishing he was here."

Paul didn't see why his mother wished his brother was there. All his brother did was get angry at his father. The two had fought for as long as Paul could remember. His father needed his brother the way he needed a fall down a flight of stairs. Was his dad worse than his mother was letting on? Or was it just that *she* wanted her son, her firstborn, the apple of her eye?

His brother found all skills easy. If he wanted to sail, he read a book and taught himself to sail. He taught himself tennis and beat the captain of the Highgate tennis team. He was the best stickball player in the neighborhood. In his senior year he was captain of the baseball team. He knew by heart the statistics of every major league baseball player since 1950. Everything electric interested him: electric trains, electric radios, the wiring of lamps, toasters, televisions. He was unassailable at hearts, bridge, poker, canasta. He was a Merit Scholar. All things were easy to him but himself. He was afraid of girls and kept a secret collection of girlie magazines at the back of his closet. He had not allowed anyone to kiss him since he was six. He hated their father; if their father touched him he went to the bathroom and washed.

Matthew was Paul's hero. He could re-create Matthew's room with his eyes closed: The nautical map of Bailey Island on the wall, the advanced math and physics books by his desk, the china horse head Matthew had won as a boy at a county fair, the complete set of Rick Brandt mystery novels Matthew had collected when he was twelve. Paul knew the history of every object his brother owned, from the Indian blanket he had purchased when he was in fourth grade to the senior yearbook with the much thumbed picture of Elizabeth Stone. The thought of his brother filled Paul with pride and love and despair.

And Paul recalled how his brother and he had invented a game called "Digging in Aunt Jemima's Hiney," the name suggested by the grinning, beturbaned countenance on the pancake mix box. They had invented the game when they were very young while playing in the cliffs across the road where the school property began. The game consisted of digging with sticks in the rich earth, interrupted only by sudden, unexplained barks of laughter.

It was not that either had been scabrous, unwholesome, scatological—quite the contrary. But they had shared cubhood together, they had shared rooms, toilets, sheets, scuffles, bites, jokes, illnesses, private words, bad odors, mornings, shames, secrets, guests, holidays, toys, aunts,

cousins, sleep, voices, summer, light through curtains, the
intimation of death. They had shared the sound of their
father, the tobacco smell of his breath, the hair on his
arms and chest, the way he placed his keys and change at
night on his bureau. And they shared their mother, her
words and gestures and flesh, her odor, the shape of her
smile, and the secret of her womb hidden somewhere like
the source of the Nile.

Now, in his room in the early spring of 1962 when
John F. Kennedy was still the thirty-fifth President of the
United States and Paul was a junior at Highgate, when
boys still wore their hair short and the United States was
not at war in Vietnam and America had not yet heard of
drugs or rebellion or failure, exactly fourteen months after
the death of his father, Paul Werth, leaving the window,
gazed vacantly at the pile of work he was supposed to be
doing and then, picking up his leather jacket, the much
loved one with the pockets on the sleeve, he went out the
door.

Once outside his spirits lifted. Night was gathering but
the evening still burned in the sky, the west a brilliant
swirl of red and orange. The air smelled cold and, invigo-
rated, Paul zipped his jacket as he walked.

Paul lived north of the city in a suburb along the banks
of the river. He had lived in the suburb all his life and had
gone to elementary school there and then to prep school
at Highgate, where his brother had gone before him. The
suburb had changed in Paul's sixteen years, but it was still
rural by comparison with the city, and Paul knew every
street and backyard, and sometimes, it seemed, every tree.

Now, as he crossed the highway, he faced the high-rises that lined the bluff, cheap-looking buildings with balconies stacked on top of one another like saucers at an Automat. When he was a child there had been nothing but the indigenous tangle of bush and brake that commenced west of the highway and fell helter-skelter in jungle profusion to the river. Here lay the estates of the wealthy, properties that stretched for a mile at a time and bore the names of some of the great families of the country, mansions surrounded by lawns and stately trees standing guard against the abundant, encroaching luxuriance of the undergrowth.

Slowly the estates had been broken up and sold off to the aspiring brick.

His father had hated to see the community change; every high-rise, every bulldozer, was an affront to his sense of beauty and order.

"The whole country's going to hell in a basket," he would say. They would be sitting at the table and his father would be reading something in the newspaper. "Believe me, we'll live to see a time when there's no wilderness left. Why, our own little community is being parceled up and macadamized over. Do you remember the pond up by Tank Rock?"

"The one where we used to hunt crawfish?" Paul asked.

"Precisely. Well, they're leveling the hilltop to build a high-rise."

"That's terrible!" their mother exclaimed.

"We'll see the top of the building when we go out the front door."

"You mean they're filling in the pond?" Paul asked incredulously; it seemed an impossible thing to do, like vacuuming up a cloud.

"That's right, son—filling it up and plastering it over."

"But—how can they do that?"

"With a bulldozer, I suppose."

"But can't they be stopped, Dad?"

"No way that I know of. They want to make money, son. Everybody wants to make money."

"There's the community to be thought of, also," their mother said.

"Yes, they've thought of the community all right—of developing it. The developers have control of the city council—you'll live to see a time when this community is swallowed up in the city."

"We used to take the children there when they were young, to see the pond."

"Well, now we'll take them there to park the car."

Now at sixteen, as Paul came over the crest of the hill, he saw the river. He could never explain why it affected him as it did, riding below him, its gray gunmetal waves catching the sun. If he could put it in words, then he could have it and keep it, but he never could. It was something outside him, coiling in power, changing with weather and light, never at rest, never less than lordly, and he came to it every day if he could, always deeming it worthier than whatever else he had to do.

If you were a native and knew how to negotiate the remains of the great derelict estates, you could still thread your way all the way to the river through wood and high-grassed meadows without ever quitting wildness. Descending the hill, Paul would sometimes start a pheasant, its explosion of wings jolting his heart to momentary frenzy. There were still raccoons in the area, skunks, rabbits, an occasional fox; he could not account for the presence of such creatures, but there they were in the suburbs of metropolitan America in unbroken succession stretching back to the Indians before the Europeans arrived to take possession of the land.

It was to the river that Paul went to escape. And it was there that once, coming abruptly over a knoll, he surprised below him in the tall grass a pair of autumn lovers.

The woman, fleshy and aging, lay on her back, her skirt hiked to her waist. She was dark, with heavy eyebrows and an inexpensive floral dress, and as she rested on the ground she stroked the back of the man, whose face was averted, so Paul could see only the balding spot at the back of his head, and who, as he lay in the woman's lap, pumped in and out, in and out, in what to Paul was a preposterous fashion.

Paul remained frozen. The man was unaware of him; but the woman, looking over the man's shoulder, caught the boy's gaze in a long, sad, unwavering stare that, remarkably, made her beautiful.

All the time she continued stroking the man.

Paul backed away; once out of sight he turned and ran. He could still see the eyes of the woman looking at him. But what he most carried with him was the absurd, the astounding, the unheralded spectacle of the man's buttocks, naked, pumping out and in.

Certainly *he* would never look like that!

2

Paul was thankful he hadn't been home when his father suffered his first heart attack. He couldn't think of his father as ill, he couldn't think of him as anything but strong and healthy.

That was in September of the previous year, when Paul had been in Cambridge visiting Matthew.

"It's nothing, it's really nothing," his mother had said on the telephone. "It was a very mild attack. Daddy doesn't want us to make a fuss."

"Should we come home?"

"No, that's all right. Finish your visit with Matthew."

"Tell Daddy I love him."

"Of course. You can call him this afternoon and tell him yourself."

Paul had been staying in Matthew's room in Eliot House, sleeping on the floor in a blanket in the corner of the large untidy space that Matthew shared with his roommate. It was already cold in New England and when he woke at first dawn he lay on the floor watching the light point among the bright trees in the New England autumn outside the window.

He was only staying with Matthew for three nights, "To get a taste," as his mother explained, "for Harvard."

Harvard was a big deal in their family, though they were too polite to say so. Paul was expected to go to Harvard like his brother and dad.

Matthew started his day by studying. He would roll

out of bed and into the chair by his desk and begin reading where he had left off the previous evening. He was majoring in chemistry and studying German and Russian, and he applied himself to his work with the determination those nations had used to subject each other.

Before the telephone call from their mother they had spent much of the weekend criticizing their father.

"He's a loser," Matthew explained lucidly, as if summing up a physics problem. "I mean, the guy doesn't know anything. He used to quiz me on science during dinner, but I soon saw I knew more than he did. He's just a phony."

Paul squirmed under these imputations, but Matthew believed in his own superiority and became angry when contradicted.

Paul limited himself to saying, "You don't understand Dad," whereupon the two brothers glared at each other, the memory of their own history of violence—the time one had broken a stick across the other's shins, the time one had threatened the other with a knife, the time one had chased the other into the bathroom with a baseball bat—vivid between them. But Paul hadn't journeyed to Cambridge to revive such sanguinary contests, and he backed off.

Matthew frowned and bit his lip, struggling with his black moods, which frightened and depressed him and over which he could exercise little control. He looked at Paul and half smiled, and Paul felt his love for his brother surge.

"Let's get some breakfast," was all Matthew said.

They sat in the cafeteria and ate pancakes and sausages and laughed about the time one summer when their uncle had tried to fix the car and had dismantled the motor and been unable to assemble it again, and they remembered how they used to sneak out at evening and let themselves into the lake, the water as sweet and tepid as syrup, and swim noiselessly along the shore under the boughs of the trees where the surface was alive with mosquitoes; and, reminiscing, the two boys seemed completely at one.

Throughout the morning Paul accompanied Matthew to his classes; in the afternoon they returned to Eliot House, where Matthew studied while Paul read *The Stranger.*

Paul was reading his way through Hemingway, Faulkner, Eliot, Dostoyevsky, Camus. He wanted to be a writer. He didn't know what that implied exactly—except that it meant to create sentences as startling as those he read in the authors he loved, sentences that took you inside people and made you understand how they worked and felt.

"What are you reading?" Matthew inquired somewhat brusquely. He had closed his books and come over to Paul.

It was dark now beyond the window and the air looked cold.

Matthew took the paperback from his brother's hands and inspected it briefly, then, shrugging, flipped it back into Paul's lap.

"Any good?"

"Yeah, it's great."

"Yeah?" Matthew sounded skeptical

"What I don't get," Matthew said, pursuing his own train of thought, "is this modern poetry stuff. Do you dig it?"

"What modern poetry?"

"Oh, you know—Eliot and that stuff. We had to read *The Waste Land* for Humanities 6. Do you dig *The Waste Land?*"

"Yeah!"

"You do? What's so great about it? Can you show me?"

"Yes!"

"You can? Here, let's see."

Matthew took down an anthology and rummaged through it until he found what he wanted.

"Okay," he challenged, bringing the book to his brother, "show me. It's gobbledygook to me."

Paul took the book and glanced at *The Waste Land,* and the familiar lines affected him immediately. He leafed through the pages.

"It's not what the poetry *means,*" he said after a while. "It's the language itself. Either you see it or you don't. Here, look at this."

Matthew picked up the book and read the lines to himself while Paul watched.

"The genius," Paul said, "is in that word *bumped.*"

Matthew stared at the poetry. Then his face softened and his jaw shifted to one side.

"I see," Matthew said. And he handed the book back to Paul.

And he *had* seen—Paul saw that his brother had seen.

And he felt great pleasure, because for once he had shown his brother something.

That evening they attended a party off campus. The apartment was crowded, with undergraduates milling about and drinking white wine out of chipped irregular glasses. Left to his own devices, Paul wandered from room to room observing the Radcliffe girls, all of whom seemed to glitter brilliantly as they laughed or straightened a strand of hair or a loosened blouse.

"Oh, Hegel—Hegel is just a justification for the Prussian state."

"I'm going to Washington to have a meeting with Bundy."

"Wiesel spoke the other night but he wasn't as brilliant as Kosinski."

"Aren't you Matthew's brother?" a tall, thin blonde asked. She had large teeth and large, striking brown eyes and she had appeared suddenly out of nowhere.

"Y . . . yes."

"I can see the family resemblance. It's something about the mouth."

He smiled, half pleased, half embarrassed.

"Are you Gail?"

"Yes, that's me! And you are . . . let's see. Paul! I knew I'd get it. So, Paul, how are you enjoying Cambridge?"

"Very much, thanks."

"Oh, how polite!" He blushed under her mockery. "But you should come in the winter when the snow is piled over the cars. That's less jolly!"

"It gets pretty cold back home as well."

"Oh, not like Cambridge! Nothing's like Cambridge! What are you interested in, anyway, Paul?"

"Well, I dunno. English, I suppose. Writing."

"Oh? Not another scientist? Good! A book person, like me! So tell me, have you read Kafka?"

"Kafka? No, I've never read Kafka."

"Oh, you've *got* to read Kafka! *The Metamorphosis.* I'll lend you my copy."

"No, I can get a copy, thanks." And he determined to read all of Kafka.

"Listen," Gail said, laughing, "you'll get a kick out of this. You know, after Harry Levin finished writing *The Power of Blackness,* Marvin Peck saw him walking one evening in the Yard, and he said to him, 'Excuse me, Professor Levin, but could you tell me, just how powerful *is* the Power of Blackness?'" And she gave a hoot that caused the wine in her glass to jiggle.

"Hullo," Matthew said, "here you two are. Are you getting along?"

Matthew looked flushed and happy, as if he was actually having a good time for once.

"Oh, we're having a little chat," Gail said, and she took Matthew's arm and pulled him to her.

"You okay, Pauli?"

"Sure, I'm fine."

"Your brother's neat," Gail said. "Why didn't you tell me? We should have him come up and join us in Cambridge."

Paul's head was swirling when they returned to Eliot House. He lay on the floor listening to the groan of the pipes, the occasional passing of a car, the laughter of students returning from some undisclosed glamorous entertainment, and his heart swelled with longing and rue.

The next morning their mother called about their father's heart attack.

The boys walked by the Charles and leaned against a bench staring out into the cold river.

"It's so stupid," Matthew said. "It's so goddamn stupid of Dad."

"What do you mean, stupid? How is it his fault?"

"Of course it's his fault. How many men get heart attacks at fifty-two? It's the stupid way he lives, the way he leads his life."

Paul would have punched anyone else who spoke this way about their father.

"How does he lead his life? What does he do but take care of us? Is that what you call stupid?"

"Yes, I do, if it makes him so goddamn unhappy. Who ever told him he had to take such good care of us?"

"Don't be stupid."

"Well, who ever said he had to be so responsible? Where does it get him?"

Paul looked at Matthew, thinking that responsibility would never be Matthew's problem; but he saw tears in his brother's eyes, and Paul looked away.

They spoke to their father that afternoon; it was their father's voice all right, calm and reassuring, but it sounded emptied of some dimension.

Paul took a walk by himself, and as he passed along the narrow diagonal paths of Harvard Yard he studied the trees and the students, and they seemed like actors in

another drama, happy and absorbed and entirely irrelevant.

He thought of his father in a hospital room three hundred miles away, and his head swam.

If I were sick, Paul thought, Dad would come to me.
And immediately he knew what he had to do.

"I'm going home," he said to his brother as soon as he
was back in Eliot House.

"What for? You heard them say that everything is
okay."

"I don't care, I'm going home anyway."

"Well, suit yourself," Matthew said, and again he
sounded angry.

The hospital with its sleek, seamless lines appeared like
a battleship run aground in the middle of the suburb. Paul
followed his mother through the automatic sliding glass
doors into the cavernous neon-lighted reception area, and
the air felt smudged and used.

They walked down a corridor and into a large elevator
designed to accommodate gurneys, and Paul concentrated
on not breathing the odor of the hospital, a smell compounded of medicine and overheated air and the suggestion of cafeteria food and the elusive, unmistakable reek
of human beings.

When they came out onto the fifth floor Paul saw the
sign for cardiac patients, and suddenly he felt dizzy. His
mother passed through two large black swinging doors,
and Paul saw the nurses' station ahead, the nurses dressed
in white uniforms with small white hats, their heads bent
over charts and telephones, and his heart raced.

"We'll be there in a moment," his mother said. She looked at him intently. "Are you all right?"

"Yes, I'm fine."

"Do you want to sit down for a moment?"

"No—I'll be okay."

They turned into his father's room.

His father lay propped up in a hospital bed in one of those white hospital shirts with large short sleeves and no collar and white narrow strings that tie in the back. He was himself as white as a raw plantain. His hair hung about his face lifeless, and his face was taut and drawn as if he had lost ten pounds. From his nose there depended a transparent plastic tube attached at the other end to a complex system of tubes and cylinders.

Paul watched his father for an instant before he was himself seen: his father reminded him of an old man on some park bench surrounded by pigeons. Then his father caught sight of him and his face lit grimly.

"Well, hello, Paul. Look what your old man has done."

"Daddy!"

"Come here, son. Let me see you."

Paul went to his father's bedside and took his hand, now strangely gaunt and hesitant, and he felt his heart wrenched by love.

"Pretty stupid, eh?" his father said, and smiled—and instantly Paul knew everything would be all right.

His mother patted the pillows behind his father's head.

"Matthew would have come," she said, "but he has his first classes."

"Of course, of course. I wouldn't want him rushing down for nothing. Let's not make a big deal over this." And he began to cough. His head came up off the pillow and his handsome features pulled into a mask of pain as his chest shook under the dry, insistent wheezing. Paul looked at his mother, and he read in her smooth, pleasant features outrage and fear.

The weekend his father returned home he looked tired and frail, but he came under his own steam, walking up the garden path and entering the front door with the old familiar sound.

"Well, Pauli—east, west, home's best."

"It's great to have you back, Dad."

"It's great to be here. You miss your old man?"

"You bet!"

"What a revoltin' development, eh?"

"Well, it's behind us now," his mother said. "The main thing is that you're home safe and sound."

"Well, home, at any rate." And his father gave his familiar chuckle.

They set him up in his bedroom, but he was soon wandering about puttering with this and that—he could fix any lamp, any piece of furniture, and he loved to be busy with his hands. When Paul woke at night he heard his father downstairs in his old familiar manner, sighing and pacing like some ancestral ghost.

"I don't know what to do with you, Ed!" his mother said in the morning. "You've got to get your sleep. Didn't you take your sleeping pills?"

"Oh, I've had enough of Carter's Little Liver Pills. I think I'd better call the office."

"You'll do no such thing! That can wait till Monday."

"Ah, yes—Monday should see a great improvement!"

Paul went walking with his father and he was frightened to see how winded is father became at even the slightest incline.

"I've become an old man," his father gibed.

"Don't say that, Dad. We'll go out walking every day. You'll get better soon."

"Well, we'll see. How's school, Pauli?"

"Oh, it's okay."

"Is it? Mommy worries about your grades."

Paul felt himself stiffen.

"Does she?"

"Not your *grades*, Paul. I said that the wrong way. She worries because you're preoccupied."

"I'm fine, Dad—truly. You don't have to worry."

"I know this has been a tough time for you, Paul. It's been a tough time for all of us. It's been a tough time for your mother."

"She's okay, Dad."

"I just want you to know that if you're worried about anything, you can always come to me."

"I know that."

"Well, will you promise me that you will? Come to me, I mean? If you ever have to?"

"Yes, Dad—I promise."

Philip Richards lived with his mother in an apartment in the city; but Richards' father lived in the suburbs in a white colonial mansion overlooking the river, and sometimes after school when Richards' father was at work, he and Paul would go and sit in Richards' room in the mansion while Philip expostulated in an amused, friendly manner on the nature of the world.

Richards had attended a prestigious boarding school in New England, where he had studied Greek and had been expelled under circumstances that remained cloudy but which redounded, it was understood, to Richards' superior *savoir vivre*. Richards was a year older than Paul; they had met in the Advanced Humanities course taught by Mr. Lemming, with its mixed enrollment of juniors and seniors, and Paul had liked Richards immediately. Richards was handsome in a strange, satyrlike manner, with pale blond skin and blond pointy eyebrows and amused, superior blue eyes. He always dressed like a businessman, which was peculiar, since he professed to despise them— his father was a businessman—and he knew about jazz and call girls and about late-night spots in the Village. In fact, Richards seemed to know something about everything.

"What D. H. Lawrence is really writing about is homosexuality," Richards explained. "He writes all those rhapsodic books from the point of view of a woman because he is just imagining getting laid by a man."

Paul was astounded. He had been reading D. H. Lawrence with great excitement and absorption and what Richards now said worried and perplexed him, though it did not strike him as entirely wrong.

"How can he be writing about homosexuality," Paul asked, "if it seems so right to *me*?"

"I couldn't say." Richards shrugged, giving a slight laugh. "I've never been able to read Lawrence myself.

Now if you want to try a *real* writer, why don't you read this."

And he handed Paul a dog-eared paperback of *Naked Lunch*.

Paul opened the book but he couldn't get the hang of it and decided he would have to try it at home.

"Pretty good, eh?" Richards asked. He had been observing Paul from where he lounged on his bed. Paul looked up from the chair.

"Yeah, cool."

Richards gave a snort of approval.

"See, *caro mio*? You're full of potential but you'll have to let me take you in hand. We don't want you to turn into another *bourgeois*."

Paul didn't know exactly what Richards meant by that, but he acquiesced vaguely. Richards employed all sorts of phrases that were foreign to Paul's usage: *caro mio* and *bourgeois* and, for that matter, *getting laid*.

"Now as for *pornography*," Richards said, as if it were pornography they had been discussing, "I can put you on the right track there. Here, let me see what we have." And, turning on his bed so his body was corkscrewed, he began rifling through a stack of books.

"Is that all pornography?"

"That's not my *real* collection. I keep my real collection downtown where my father can't get his paws on it. Pornography is a subject for connoisseurs, not for dirty old men like my father."

"Here!" Richards exclaimed, pulling a book from the stack. "Why don't you start with *that*. That'll put *Lady Chatterley's Lover* in its place!"

He handed Paul *The Story of O.*

Paul held the book gingerly between his fingers.

"What's this all about?" he asked uncertainly.

"Sadomasochism, *bambino.* Obsession. All sorts of good things they don't tell you about at school. It's about a woman who puts a ring through her clitoris."

"Her *clitoris*?" Paul said. "Why does she do *that*?"

"Because her boyfriend tells her to—dig it? It's an act of *submission.* Don't you know anything about sex?"

"Sure!"

"Oh, yeah? What's a clitoris? Do you know? Have you ever seen one?"

Paul didn't say anything.

"Listen, *caro*," Philip said, dropping his voice and leaning forward solicitously. "It's okay. *I'd* never seen a clitoris till last summer. A clit is like a girl's prick. It's her hot spot, dig it? It's this little thing right between her legs. If you press it you drive her wild."

Paul felt dizzy. He hated this conversation—yet he was eager to learn what Philip had to divulge.

Sometimes the two boys walked by the river and Richards would affect a kind of black, stiff-rimmed sombrero such as Paul had never seen before save in Mexican cowboy movies—*Zorro*, perhaps. Richards wore the hat at a rakish angle above his business suit, and he would grow rhapsodic at the sight of the river, reciting passages from Greek, which he chanted aloud to the sky in a singsong voice, his arms spread wide to embrace the clouds.

*"Mānin aēde, Thea, Pālāiadeo Aksilāos
Oolomenān, hā muri Aksaiois alge ethāken!"*

"Ah, Greek!" Richards would exclaim, pursing his lips and shaking his head as if savoring a specially beneficent species of wine; and Paul wished that he too understood ancient Greek and could whisper to himself such incantations, for the language did indeed sound rich and strange and bountiful of all learned mysteries.

"Now a place like Highgate could never teach Greek," Richards explained. "Highgate is a school for turkeys. Even if they offered Greek, which of course they don't, it wouldn't be *Greek*. And do you know why? Because Highgate could be defined as a place that is *non-Greek*. I mean, that's like its definition, the very sine qua non of the joint. Dig it, *bambino*? How could Bates or Lemming or any such person teach *Greek*? All they can teach is gobble gobble gobble."

The boys had been walking by the river and the wind came up and licked their hair. In midstream a boat lumbered against the current, its bow throwing off flakes of fire as it pitched and strained, moving northward.

"And what is Greek?" Richards pursued, speaking with a kind of haughty, amused arrogance. "Greek," he said, "is to perceive beauty in every moment. Greek is to be above the petty and mundane. Greek," he concluded, gesturing grandly, "is to burn at all times with a hard, gemlike flame!"

Paul didn't know much about burning with a hard, gemlike flame, but he knew he loved to come to the river. He loved to come alone, without Richards (even though Richards and he were now friends), and watch the freight trains shuffle past. The tracks lay parallel to the river, and the commuter train ran, sleek and hissing, approximately every hour; but there were always freight cars parked on the sidings, and Paul could climb them and contemplate the opportunities for riding them, as he had witnessed countless times in movies or had read about in books.

As a child he had lived for a summer by the river in one of the houses on a hill with a great lawn and an attic and a pantry and birds that built a nest in a tree in the backyard. His mother had shown him the eggs, sky blue, and they had watched every day until they hatched and offered up gawky-haired chicks that squirmed and opened and shut their beaks like turtles. He had loved the birds and had been a little afraid.

At night he would lie awake listening to the trains passing in the dark. Friends were living with them, Stephen and his two beautiful sisters, older girls with braids and freckles, both so attractive that he was in love with both and could not tell them apart. They taught him mumblety-peg and cartwheels, and sometimes when they did cartwheels their dresses hiked up and he could see their panties.

That was the summer he learned to put on his own sandals.

Stephen and his sisters were wealthy, but their parents were Quakers, which meant they didn't show off their wealth, and Paul's mother approved of this very much. Paul's mother was great friends with Stephen's parents, who were away in Europe.

Paul's father was away at work.

Paul's mother had said to them, "You children can play any place you want on the lawn or in the back of the house, but you can't cross the road or go into the thicket by the tracks. It's not safe by the tracks and sometimes there are men there."

Later, when they were alone, Stephen, who was a year older than Matthew, said, "Sometimes there are tramps by the tracks."

"What are tramps?"

"Tramps are men who live outdoors all day and who stay outdoors all night."

"So what's so bad about that?"

"I dunno. I guess they don't wash. I guess they smell a lot."

"Oh," Matthew said. He didn't sound convinced.

Paul listened to this without saying anything. He wasn't anxious to have anything to do with tramps.

Later that summer Matthew and Stephen crossed the road and played in the tangled bushes and even ventured down to the tracks where the trains passed, but Paul preferred not to go. Matthew was three years older than Paul, Stephen four, and they both qualified as Big Boys.

Paul went to play by the stream with the two sisters and he fell in and got wet and Melinda only looked at him coldly but Virginia took him in her arms (though he wasn't unhappy), and then he knew it was Virginia he loved.

But it was he who saw the tramp. He had wandered up the road in the direction of the Horse Pasture, beyond where he was supposed to be, all the way to the great field that stretched on the left toward the river.

The field swayed with the wind. He looked, and the long grass was fretted with flowers, blue and white and yellow, bending under the movement of the air. He stopped and stared in wonder.

Then he started back. He was afraid now because he had come so far, and because he had to cross through the wooded area where the road bent down toward the tracks and the large oaks overhung the road with shadows. He was always apprehensive when he crossed this area, even with his mother, and he had crossed it safely this way only because he had been daydreaming and had passed unnoticing.

As he came down into the shadows he could feel the fear up and down his spine and he thought of running but he didn't. Coins of light danced by the side of the road. He could smell the forest now, cool and damp and not the bright, blank smell of the sun. He observed the ants and sticks as he walked and the oak leaves with their green familiar shapes and the acorns with their small brown caps. Then he saw the man come out of the shadows.

Fear stopped him. He saw the man, who was dressed in a brown baggy suit and who appeared tired and unshaven and sad, look at him and then look vacantly away and then look back again. Paul didn't move. He might have run save that the man, who was a tramp, and who was carrying a soiled paper bag in one hand, and who had holes in his shoes and, Paul now observed, at the elbows of his brown baggy suit, stood between him and any place he knew to go.

Then Paul began to walk. He walked as far to his side of the road as he could get, his small feet shuffling in the leaves, and as he walked he kept his head down, though he was aware of the tramp in every part of his being. He was passing closely now, and he felt the fear like a sickness, a tightening in his stomach and throat, a pounding. The tramp stood and watched him vacantly.

Then Paul ran. He ran with great speed, his small body hurtling through shadow and light, his heart racing within his narrow chest, and, as he raced, he heard behind him the man call out, although he could not make out what the man said, it was just words he did not stop to hear.

Then he was again in sunlight. He had traversed the difficult place and he was again where he could see the house on the top of the large lawn where his mother would be, and his brother Matthew, and Stephen, and Virginia, whom he loved. He was again safe.

Somewhere behind him in the forest he had left the tramp.

He slowed to a stop. He didn't want anyone to see him running. He didn't want to be asked what had happened. Because he had gone where he shouldn't be.

And then he remembered the tramp's words. He remembered them after the fact. It was as if he was only hearing them now, like an airplane that has already passed, and he knew what the tramp had said. "Don't be afraid," the man had called, "I won't hurt you—you don't have to be afraid!"

3

Paul observed Nicole Swann from his classroom window. Nicole, Nicole, Nicole! What is in a name? And he recalled the heat of her leg through her dress that night of the party.

He hadn't spoken to her since October, though it was now already March; he would pass her in the hall without saying a word. And yet he *knew* she liked him.

He watched her standing in the Quad surrounded by a group of girls, her back bent softly beneath her sweater, her underlip pouting as if it had been bitten by a bee.

"Paul? Paul, could you please read to us from Chapter Eight?"

"What?"

"Chapter Eight, Paul. Where are you?"

He was in Miss English's class, everyone was watching him.

"I'm sorry," he muttered, feeling himself color. And he turned the pages, looking for Chapter Eight.

She was in the Quad again at three that afternoon speaking with Brigit Bloom.

As he approached he averted his eyes. Then as he passed a wave of self-disgust assailed him, and without stopping he turned and heard himself say,

"Did you ever read that Dostoyevsky?"

She looked up, startled, and Brigit was looking at him

as well and frowning. He stopped and turned halfway round and his heart was pounding in his chest.

"Dostoyevsky?"

"Yeah, remember? *The* . . ."

". . . Oh, of course I remember!" And she laughed. "*The Possessed*. Yes," she said. "I read it. I wanted to ask you about it."

"Yes—isn't it great?"

"It's so—I don't know!" she said. "It's so *cool*."

It made him laugh, but he was aware of Brigit standing between them and watching.

"Why didn't you talk to me about it?" she said, but she was saying something else, for he had not spoken to her in four months, ever since she had refused to go out with him.

He merely shrugged.

"Nobody knows who *Paul* is going to speak to," Brigit said, and there was an edge to her voice. "He's a mystery."

"Well, now you'll have to talk to me about it," Nicole said, but already she was slinging her books over her shoulder. "But now I've got to run."

"Maybe I'll call you," Paul said.

"Yes, call me. I have to talk about Dostoyevsky!"

He called that evening, though his hands were sweating and he feared his voice would break. His heart gave a lurch when Nicole picked up the receiver.

"Oh, Paul, I'm sorry, I can't talk right now," she said, and her voice sounded wrong. "I've just got too much to do."

"Oh, yeah? Well—maybe tomorrow."

"Yes," and her voice brightened slightly, "maybe we

could meet after school. Do you want to meet in the Quad?"

"Sure."

"Okay—tomorrow then. I'm sorry I can't talk now—really I am!"

She was waiting for him the next day on the other side of the Quad after his last class. The air was raw, but there was a suggestion of spring in the breeze, a lifting and lightening. The black branches clicked above him as he hurried toward her.

"Hi!"

"Hi!" He hadn't been sure she would be there.

They mounted the hill in silence and crossed the wet fields to the tennis court. Evening was settling and the horizon had turned luminous; as they passed the plot for the library he saw the crane towering like an exclamation point into the sky.

She stopped and leaned against a tree, and he could make out the softness of her body underneath her clothes.

"Why haven't you spoken to me for all these months?"

"You made it clear you didn't want me to."

"Did I? Well, you didn't have to believe me."

He made a gesture of exasperation which caused her to smile. Her front teeth were slightly too large, but their effect was only to pout her lip further, and suddenly he remembered the sweetness of her kisses.

"At any rate, I'm glad you spoke to me yesterday. You're so *difficult!*"

"Difficult?"

"Yes—touchy. I'm always afraid you'll take offense at something I say."

She lowered her eyes, and he was shaken again by her power over him.

"I've missed you," he said grudgingly, in confusion and embarrassment. He felt himself color.

"I've missed you, too. I've missed talking to you."

"You could have talked to me anytime."

"Well, we're talking now. But you're so intense!" and she laughed.

He scowled into the gathering dark.

"I like it," she added. "I like your intensity. It's like— Raskolnikov! But it's getting late," she added. "I've got to go."

"Are you going to the basketball game on Thursday?"

"I might."

"Why don't you come. It'll be fun."

"Maybe," she said, though she was already moving away. "Maybe I'll see you there."

The basketball court smelled of wood polish and perspiration, and the shouts of the crowd mixed with the sound of the ball as it hit the floor or rebounded off the backboard. Paul watched a forward dribble downcourt, pivot, jump shoot from the corner—and the ball whooshed through the net. A small explosion of applause and the ball was again in play.

He paused to survey the bleachers. He had been looking forward to this moment all day; but standing in the gym he was suddenly seized by melancholy, for she wasn't there.

Philip Richards huddled in a far corner with Keith Firman and Berger. Paul approached slowly, half watching the game: a player dribbled, fired downcourt, another shot—and the ball swooshed through the net. Again the bleachers exploded; Highgate was winning.

"Hi, Philip."

"Paul!" Richards spoke with his peculiar high-pitched nasal drawl, his voice shooting up in ironic, good-natured greeting, his forehead disappearing as his eyebrows rose and his blue eyes rounded in mock surprise. He had a way of suggesting that you were the one person in the world he most wanted to see.

Paul smiled broadly.

Firman looked at him, and Paul was aware of some unspecified hostility. Berger offered his mocking, younger-brother smile.

"We've just been setting the odds on Saturday's game," Richards explained. "Keith here thinks we're going to lose to Woodtown and I've been asking him for the odds."

"I think it stinks," Keith said.

"What stinks, Keith?"

"Betting against your own team."

"That's a worthy sentiment, Keith. It does you credit. But let's be reasonable—it's not my team."

"That's typical," Keith said, and he turned and gave Paul a hard stare.

"What about you, Werth? Are you betting against the team?"

"I don't give a shit about the team," Paul said quietly.

"Oh, yeah—I forgot. You're too big to care about the team, right?"

Keith turned away, angry and sarcastic, and Paul remembered when they had been friends.

"Come on, Keith," Richards said, jollying him. "It doesn't affect anything if we bet on the game. We're not the goddamn Rosenbergs, for chrissake!"

A shout went up from the court. Paul watched the ball pass from player to player and then, arching, whoosh through the net; and for a moment he sensed in his own hands the kinetic satisfaction of the basket.

Highgate had scored again. Paul glanced into the stands: on a steel girder high in the rafters a damaged pigeon shivered in the cold.

When Paul looked down, he could see Hillman and Doyle standing by the gym door.

Three times a week Paul worked out in the gym preparing for baseball. Often he would go in midafternoon when it was easier to obtain the weights; he would change in the upper locker room and have the downstairs workout room to himself.

He was supposed to use a partner when he worked out, but he rarely did. Between sets he sat by himself or stood at the end of the bench staring out through the double doors, across the cinder track and the field, to the wall of trees, still gaunt and leafless in the March cold. Only the forsythia evinced a tentative smudge of yellow against the dull gray of the landscape.

He enjoyed the chink of the barbells and the odor of

the metal as he worked; exercising reminded him of the previous year when he had been the only sophomore on the baseball team and had changed by himself in the lower locker room.

Sometimes Hillman would be in the workout room with Doyle and Pursy, seniors who exercised seriously, belching and sweating while they spotted one another. Doyle and Hillman would greet him, but the lines were drawn: Paul was tolerated only because he was a varsity teammate and a letter winner.

Robbie Doyle was the captain of the baseball team. Off the field he seemed a dim bulb, vacant-eyed and stutter-tongued; but on the field he could play any position, make any play, and was a formidable competitor.

Highgate was divided between jocks and intellectuals, but there was never any question where the allegiance of the school lay: the prep school was dedicated to getting its students into prestigious colleges. True, the most popular girls—the glamorous seniors who existed in some vague mythical elevation like Olympian goddesses—dated the jocks; but the jocks were a resentful bunch nonetheless.

One day when Paul was in the locker room changing into his street clothes, he looked up and saw that Rick Flask had entered. Flask was a white-faced busybody who had made himself known by the causes he espoused: Ban the Bomb, Keep the Rec Room Clean, Support the Honor System. He was an earnest self-important kid with hair combed back from his forehead and pens protruding from his pocket; but he was no worse than others, and seeing him now Paul gave him no thought.

Paul had stayed later than usual working out, and most of the other boys had departed; only Hillman and his crew were gathered at the farther end of the room. Paul wasn't paying attention when Flask drifted into Hillman's wake; what caused him to look up was the sudden silence.

Paul had known Hillman all his life, and even in third grade he had known enough to give him plenty of room. When Paul was in fifth grade Hillman, a grade above him, began jogging around the Highgate cinder track, something Paul had never known a lower grader to do. Sometimes when Paul was in class staring out the window while he was supposed to be listening, he would see Hillman, a handsome, not particularly large boy, jogging doggedly around the immense high school circuit. Paul had no idea how Hillman had obtained permission to accomplish this, but there he was, a small, persistent figure leaning slightly forward, his arms and legs moving rhythmically, his head slightly down, running in a manner that was unprecedented to Paul. By the end of that summer Hillman's size seemed to have doubled.

Hillman was now a senior and the captain of the football team and the unquestioned king of the jocks. There were many stories about Hillman and the things he did and the girls he dated, and most of these set Paul's teeth on edge. Hillman would hold court in the upper locker room, bragging and belching and snapping his towel, telling tales about how he had scored with this or that girl, Suzanne Pratt or Betty Rollins or Laura Kinski, and the other large-muscled jocks would crowd around, naked and leering, their skin flushed from the shower, their faces pocked with acne and blackheads, eager to learn whatever they could from Hillman's scabrous braggadocio.

When Paul looked up, Flask was surrounded by a group of these large boys, most of them naked except for a towel wrapped about their midriffs, at the center of which sat Hillman, lowering and smiling and sneering like some species of dandified crocodile set upright at a banquet.

An unwritten rule held that only varsity members could use the upper locker. It was impossible to enforce this completely, since one had to pass through the upper locker to reach the upper gym; but the lowly lingered at their peril.

"What is this little chickenshit doing here?" Hillman now inquired of no one in particular, casting glances at his myrmidons while he worked his alarming muscles.

Flask looked at him and blinked his eyes; the dimensions of his predicament had not yet dawned on him.

"What's your problem, Ned?"

"My problem? Dig this guy, will ya? He wants to know my problem. You're my problem, Flask. Your little ass is my problem."

The tone of voice was enough to give Flask pause. He blinked at Ned Hillman as if Hillman were a large beast which had suddenly crossed his path.

"You know what you are?" Hillman said, his voice a mixture of humor and ill intent. "You're a little fart, that's what."

Rick Flask laughed nervously.

"Sure you are," Hillman said, and he pushed Flask slightly but enough to set the smaller boy staggering.

The other boys had formed a half circle about Flask and were laughing quietly. Doyle stood to one side with his chin protruding, a fierce pimple tipping it.

"Do you know how to fart?" Hillman pursued. He was smiling faintly.

"What do you mean?"

"Fart, fart—you know what I'm talking about! Here!" And by suctioning his palms, Hillman produced a farting sound.

"Go to hell," Flask said in disgust.

"Ooo!" Hillman turned to the others in mock horror. "You hear that, guys? Flask wants me to go to hell!" He turned back to Flask.

"What's wrong, Flask—don't you know how to say your own name? Here," he said, addressing one of his companions, "teach Flask how to say his name."

The other boy looked at Hillman puzzled.

"Fart for him," Hillman explained. "Teach Flask how to fart."

"I'll fart *at* him," the boy said delightedly. He was a large, rubicund kid, pimply and dull-eyed. Concentrating, he scrunched up his face until he turned a darker shade of red. Then, bending his knees and easing the chap of one buttock with his hand, he emitted a resounding fart.

"Hey!" There was general laughter and applause.

Rick Flask smiled with distaste; he was looking uneasy.

"There!" Hillman exclaimed. "That wasn't so hard, was it? See how he did that? Now it's your turn."

"Fuck you," Flask said—but he had blurted it out inadvertently, and now he looked scared.

The other boys grew quiet.

"What did you say?" Hillman asked. His voice had lost all pretense to amusement.

"Nothing."

"Sure you did," Pursy said. He was a lean, mean-looking boy with a black wispy mustache, and he now pushed Flask hard from behind.

"I don't take it kindly when someone says 'fuck you' to my friends," Pursy said, and he pushed Flask again, harder.

Paul had stood up, he didn't know when. His breath was constricted and his mouth had gone dry. He knew that Flask was in trouble but he didn't know what to do. He wished he wasn't there.

Doyle caught Pursy by the shoulder.

"C . . . come on, Ralph. Leave him alone."

Pursy turned around slowly and looked at Doyle; Pursy was a mean kid and, unlike the others, he was smart. He now looked down at Robbie with a kind of drawling stare.

"Who taught you to talk, Doyle?"

Doyle treated it as a joke; Pursy would be no match for him in a fight.

"I'm going to bury his head in the towel bin," Pursy said, indicating Flask. But the moment of crisis had passed.

"Doyle's right," someone said after a pause. "Leave the poor shit alone."

Pursy hesitated, sensing he had lost the momentum. Then Hillman turned away, deciding the issue.

"Run along, shitface," Hillman said to Flask. He had regained his thuggish good humor. But he called out when Flask was a few yards away,

"If I ever see you up here again with the big boys, I'm going to make you suck my dick!"

Another explosion of general laughter.

In the Quad, Paul caught up with Doyle. Robbie seemed in a gay mood.

"What's wrong with Hillman?" Paul blurted out. He was still shaking from the incident.

"Whaddaya m . . . mean?"

Paul looked at Robbie. "You know what I mean."

"You mean Flask?"

"Yeah. What's going on?"

Now Doyle looked at Werth, and it was as if he really didn't know what Paul was talking about.

"You're r . . . really such a little shit," Robbie said good-humoredly. "Do you know that?" And he walked away.

Paul had gone out for baseball the previous year. His brother had been the captain of the team when he was a senior at Highgate, but Paul had no expectation of making the varsity in his sophomore year.

"You've got to be *hungry*, gentlemen," Scotty would say. He would be pacing back and forth in front of them in the March air, his blue sweat pants bagged to his knees, his head down and his forefinger gesticulating emphatically, pacing in his strange jerky manner as if he had already counted out his footsteps and had now to retrace them exactly; and Paul, sitting among his teammates on the lower field with his knees pulled up to his chest, could see behind them the evening sun flare on the bricks of the gym building.

Paul was excited about trying out for baseball, though he didn't admit this even to himself. He would sit in the lengthening evening shadows while Scotty harangued them, and for the first time in years at Highgate, he would be happy.

"Now, Doyle is hungry," Scotty continued, "but Doyle *stays within himself.* That's why Doyle is the captain, gentlemen. Isn't that right, Doyle? We can't all be captain. But we *can* all stay within ourselves—and we can all be hungry!

"Now, I want to see you do these wind sprints, and I want to see you be *hungry!* I don't care if you puke your guts out afterward. I want to see you break a leg."

The boys stood up in the gathering darkness and shook their arms and legs as they snorted with nervous energy. They milled loosely at the starting line. Then Scotty yelled "Sprint!" and they sped off down the field, their spikes digging into the soft earth, their elbows pumping fiercely. Doyle established the lead. After fifty yards Scotty called "Jog," and with a great expiration the pace slackened: for twenty yards they could jog.

"Sprint, gentlemen! Sprint! Bust your guts. Break a leg. Move your sorry tails."

Paul's chest burned and his mouth tasted of pennies. He fixed his eyes on the back of Bower, the first baseman, and made himself keep pace.

"Sprint, you sorry bastards! Harder! Harder! Run, Bower. Run, Werth. Stay up with Bower. Run like your brother!"

Paul Werth lowered his head and sprinted. He felt his feet hit and push, hit and push, his knees working like pistons. He experienced a sudden spurt of exhilaration and, lifting his head, he saw that he was even with Bower: in front now there was only Doyle.

But the reason he made the varsity that year was a boy named Babits. Babits was a stocky, muscular Hungarian of chronic indiscipline. He was supposed to be a power hitter and he could indeed clobber the ball, but something was wrong in his head. He strutted onto the field like a bantam cock. He played second but he tried to cover shortstop as well; and at bat he wouldn't take the signs.

Scotty, who fancied himself a strategist, was driven wild. He would pace up and down the sidelines muttering and swearing, kicking the dirt into explosive little clouds.

"What is that crazy Hungarian doing? What the fuck does he think he's doing?"

Then one blustery April afternoon they were behind Westfield two nothing and Scotty was pacing back and forth, gesticulating and muttering to himself while he issued commands to Keith Firman, who acted as his assistant manager and relayed his instructions to the field.

"Tell Babits to close that gap! Tell that crazy fucking Hungarian to move away from second. If I wanted him to play shortstop I'd have ordered him a new pair of hands. Can't he see that this kid is going to drive the ball into the hole? I mean, Jesus, he's opened a fucking bowling alley on the right side of the field!"

Then, no longer able to control himself: "Babits, you idiot!" he bellowed, the veins standing out dangerously in his neck. "Move over to your left so you can stop the ball!"

Babits blinked at him and didn't move. He bent over from the waist and pounded his glove with his fist.

"Play ball!" the umpire called.

The batter, a muscular kid with an angry carbuncle on the side of his neck, stood ramrod stiff with his bat poised like an exclamation mark. Then Wolf, the pitcher, delivered and there was a clean, solid crack and the kid had hit the ball through the hole into right field for a single, driving in a run.

"Jesus!" Scotty hit his forehead with the heel of his hand. "That's it! That's fucking it!"

He surveyed the bench with flashing eyes.

"Werth! Get in there! Get in there and tell that idiot Babits to get out!"

Paul's heart beat so violently that he ran onto the field forgetting to remove his jacket; he had to throw it backward toward the sideline. The distance seemed to him immense; he was breathless by the time he reached Babits.

"Scotty says you're to come out."

Babits glowered at him but didn't move.

Far away, as if in another dimension, Scotty was gesticulating in furious pantomime. For a long moment nothing happened.

Doyle trotted over from third base.

"What's going on?"

"Scotty wants me in for Babits."

"Come on, Nick," Doyle said.

For another moment Babits didn't move. Then, dropping his eyes, he trotted away, his head jerking back and forth, his legs working in stiff, small movements like a warthog's.

Then the batter was up and Wolf surveyed the infield and went into his motion. Paul, pulled to his left and standing ten feet behind the base line, felt a fluttery lightness in his stomach; then he saw not heard the crack of the ball and without thinking took the hit on a hop and even had time to steady himself before firing it to first for the out.

After that the noise came back with a rush and he could hear.

But when he was up at bat he was nervous for real. He took the first pitch for a strike. The pitcher was a tall, skinny kid with long arms and a protruding Adam's apple, with great sting to his throw. The next pitch was another fastball high and away and Paul figured the kid didn't have much control. The next one was a curveball outside and the count was two and one and Paul planted his feet and waited for the fastball. He knew that if he got a fastball he could hit it. Then the pitcher went into his motion and it was a fastball all right and Paul punched it over first base into the hole. With his speed and with Bower running toward home it was an easy double.

He had driven in a run.

After that he was a regular. At first they used him as a utility replacement, but after a while he was the starter at second: during the huddle before a game when Scotty called out the names of the starting players, he would wait to hear his name, and every time he would shiver with excitement when it came.

"Second—Werth."

Then they would put their hands together and give a cheer and trot out onto the field.

They won the divisional championship that year.

Doyle was at third. Wolf was the starting pitcher. Bower played first, Boom-Boom Teller was the shortstop. And Paul, at second, was the only sophomore.

At first he batted sixth, but after a time Scotty put him up second: he could get his bat on the ball almost anytime. He wasn't a power hitter, but he could switch-hit, he could bunt, and he had good speed.

He loved the sound of his spikes as he ran out onto the upper field for a game. His lungs filled under his jersey, pungent with his own perspiration, and as he ran his eyes adjusted to the quality of the light, now watery, now unguent, now flaming against a distant building. The light excited him like the sentences he read alone in his room when he was supposed to be doing homework—Camus, Faulkner, Hemingway. It seemed to hold some promise he could never quite define, something implicit in the strength of his body, the exhilaration of running, the excitement of leaping down the stone stairs two at a time to the lower field and loping onto the grass, past the thin crowd of spectators, the few adults, the bevy of girls in their sweaters and kilts and penny loafers.

Paul would never forget the smell of grass in the spring air, the sound of a ball pounding into a mitt, the thwack of a bat connecting squarely. The odor of his glove (part conditioning oil, part new leather), the clatter of the ball into the fence behind home plate, the click of bats carried in the training bag or thrown down on the lawn, the feel of the turf under his spikes, the adrenaline rush as he took the field—these would come back to him vividly long after the intricacies of the particular games had faded beyond recall.

Perhaps because he was the youngest, he never got to

know the other boys well, though they treated him with good-humored neglect—which suited him just fine.

After a game when the juniors and seniors went upstairs to shower, he'd stay downstairs alone. Sometimes he'd go upstairs to shower with his teammates, but the upper locker room was shared with the track team, with Hillman and his goons; and though Paul had known these kids all his life, he kept his distance.

"Did ya date Suzanne Pratt last night?"

"Yeah."

"Wachya get?"

"Two."

"Two! No shit!"

But on the field it was different. On the field a guy like Boom-Boom Teller was serious and impressive—and even friendly.

At the banquet at the end of the season Scotty gave a speech and Doyle even got up and stuttered some words. Paul sat in the second row and smiled and looked at the floor and thought Big Deal! But he was the only sophomore to go to the podium to collect a letter, and as he stood staring out at the auditorium and looking uncomfortable and pleased in spite of himself, he couldn't foresee that this moment marked the high-water point of his high school career.

He wished his father was there.

When Paul was little his family would drive to the country on Sundays. His grandparents had bought a house during the Depression, and though it was hardly more than a cottage, the family loved it. The trip was long and boring, but the expectation invariably excited Paul.

During summer vacations the family traveled to Maine. They would pack the night before, and when Paul awoke he would hear his father outside loading the car. For an instant Paul wouldn't be able to recall why he was waking so early; then it would come back with a rush, and running to the window, he would look down into the driveway, where his father would be closing the trunk, pulling the ropes taut across the roof carrier.

Paul loved the odor of the morning and the color of the air, still dark though luminous now with the first tinge of day; he loved the sound of the motor idling under his window, the car covered with dew, tracked like the face of waters; he loved the rustle of his mother and father moving quietly in the farther rooms so as not to disturb Matthew and him; and for the rest of his life he would associate these things with those early-morning departures.

By the time they started the sun would be rising and its brilliant orange would almost blind them, making the trees stand out like silhouettes against the horizon. Later the journey would decline into the light of common day; Paul would grow restless and tired and curl up in a corner and fall asleep; but he never forgot the magic of those mornings.

His father drove and his mother sat on the front seat next to him. The two boys sat in the rear; but as Matthew got older he wanted to sit in the front too, where he could keep an eye on his father in case he required his assistance; so he moved between his mother and father, leaving the back seat for Paul to stretch out and dream.

His father was never happier than during those trips. He improvised an extended story about a character named Lon Buffalo, a buffoonish but lovable creature who outwitted—but never vanquished—an opponent named Mr. Badbadbadbadbad (the name could be extended depending on just how bad Mr. Badbad had been). Mr. Badbadbadbadbad was responsible for all manner of catastrophes, but especially for car accidents; and whenever they passed an old car lot with a pile of dilapidated jalopies, the first to see it would cry out, "Mr. Badbadbadbadbad has been at work!"

For reasons unknown to any but himself, their father had christened their car the Mabel, and he improvised songs and snatches to celebrate her accomplishments.

Oh, Mabel,
So capabable,
No one so able
As sturdy Mabel!

Their mother was the greatest appreciator of these ditties; she was the official Navigator (until Matthew assumed these responsibilities later on), and she would sit poring over maps (of which their father was particularly fond) with a concentrated half frown.

Their father would sing to her.

K-K-K-Katie,
My beautiful Katie,
You are the only g-g-g-girl whom I adore!

A Dairy Queen stood on the left side of the road halfway to their house, and despite the pleading of the boys, their father would usually drive past, for he frowned on "junk food." Sometimes, however, it happened otherwise.

The first time this occurred it was alarming.

As they approached the Dairy Queen their father said in a worried voice, "Something is happening to the car!"

"What's happening, Ed?" their mother asked with concern. "What's wrong?"

"I don't know, it's acting strange—it seems to be pulling to the left."

"Could something be wrong with the tires?"

"I don't know, it could be—I'm having trouble holding it on the road."

"Oh, dear!"

"It's swerving to the left! I don't know whether I can hold it in place!" Here he threw his weight to the right and seemed to wrestle with the wheel. "The car is mysteriously turning to the left!"

The boys watched with consternation as their father fought the car to the right. Nonetheless, the Mabel turned slowly to the left, crossed the road safely, and came to a stop in front of—the Dairy Queen.

Thereafter this mysterious occurrence would happen periodically—though never predictably.

When they arrived at the cottage the boys would jump out of the car and tear about like wild animals; then their grandmother would come out to greet them and they would have to help carry things into the house.

The cottage was low-ceilinged and cool and smelled of the silk-covered pillows that lined the couch. They entered through the kitchen, where their grandmother would have lemonade and cookies waiting. She would

kiss Paul and would attempt to kiss Matthew, who resolutely eluded her, and then the boys would run outside
into the sunlight and roll on the grass.

The women would prepare the afternoon dinner while
their father mowed the lawn. The boys embarked on their
ritual exploration of the property: circling the lawn, trac-
ing the stream, visiting the swimming hole with its thin
waterfall and its large black snake (there was also a snake
in the wall by the drive), and climbing to the top of the
work shed under the apple tree.

The tin roof of the work shed was their clubhouse.
They would lie on its heated corrugated surface and inhale the sweet odor of fallen apples while they ab-
stractedly considered the myriad small holes that pocked
the trunk and branches of the tree. The apple tree wasn't
good for climbing; it wasn't tall and it had countless
thornlike twigs along its branches. Nor did they have
much to discuss, since life was safe and unchanging: in
the distance their father would be pushing the lawn
mower, and occasionally their mother, slender and dark-
haired, would emerge to say something to him.

The greatest source of excitement was snakes. The
large black milk snakes were impressive in a boring sort of
way, but more promising was the rumor of copperheads
and rattlers. These were almost mythological creatures, to
be numbered with trolls and goblins as likely inhabitants
of the hills; but their father insisted that the snakes existed and had to be guarded against, and consequently
they never went for a walk without arming themselves
with sticks, though what to do with these if they encountered a snake was another question.

When in later years the boys discussed these matters, they had to confess that they had never actually seen a poisonous snake.

But there could be no question about the raccoon.

It was Paul who had discovered the animal; it had been writhing on the ground in the garage, a surprisingly large and hunchbacked creature foaming at the mouth. Paul had backed away respectfully and had run to get his dad.

But when his father entered the garage with one of the snake sticks, he couldn't find the raccoon. He searched thoroughly, getting down on his hands and knees to peer under the car, but the large creature seemed to have disappeared.

"I did see it, Dad. It was right there, I didn't make it up!"

"I believe you, son. You sure it was foaming at the mouth?"

"Yes—and making a strange sound."

"Hm. Well, he must have run away when you weren't watching. Maybe he won't come back."

Paul didn't see how the raccoon could have run away, there hadn't been enough time; but he didn't know what else to say. He felt vaguely embarrassed, as if he had invented the whole thing.

A half hour later he found the Hubbard's dog whining and pointing down the trail that led to the orchard on the farther side of the hill—and again he got his father.

His father spoke quietly to the dog, trying to calm it down; but the animal wouldn't be appeased.

"Something's sure bothering him," his father said.

"Could it be the raccoon?"

"Let's go have a look."

Paul followed his father down the trail, and he was glad his dad was there.

The dog wouldn't go with them.

"Do you see anything, Pauli?"

"No—not yet."

They started to climb the hill—and then his father stopped.

"There he is!" He was speaking now in a hushed voice.

"Where?"

"There—in the top of that pine."

Paul looked, and there was the raccoon way up the tree clinging to the side of the trunk.

"Do you think he's sick, Dad?"

"Yes, I'm afraid he is."

"What are we going to do?"

"We'll have to get him down—we can't leave him loose like that."

"How we gonna do that?"

"I'll have to shoot him."

Paul was stunned: he had never seen his father shoot, they didn't even own a gun. He looked at his father but didn't say anything.

He followed his father back down the hill.

When they came into the cottage his father said, "You'd better keep the kids inside, Catherine. There's a sick raccoon out there."

"Did you find it?"

"Yes—it's up a tree on the other side of the ravine."

"What if he runs away?"

"That poor beast isn't running anywhere."

"Well, what should we do?"

"You stay inside—I'm going to go get Bill Hubbard's rifle."

Matthew, who had been reading, was now watching his father closely.

"I want to come."

"That's not fair!" Paul said. "I wanna go too."

"You boys stay with your mother," their father said. Then he went out the door.

He came back about twenty minutes later carrying a rifle, heavy and wood-stocked. Matthew stared at the gun, and his brown intelligent eyes lit up with excitement.

"Let me hold it, Dad."

Their father looked at Matthew and smiled.

"Not right now, Matthew—it's loaded."

"I want to go too," Matthew insisted. Their mother took Matthew by the shoulders.

"It's dangerous," she said. "You do what your father says."

"That's all right," their father said, "the boys can come. But they've got to keep their distance. Do you hear?" he asked, looking at Matthew.

Matthew nodded his head.

"Do you want to come?" he asked their mother.

"No, I'll stay here," their mother said. "The poor thing."

They went out the door. Paul wasn't certain his father could hit the raccoon high in the tree. It was a hard shot. What if he wounded the raccoon and the raccoon climbed down and ran toward them?

They turned into the trail toward the orchard and now they were walking more slowly. Paul could hear the late-summer crickets singing in the grass. He thought of the raccoon lying on its back in the garage, and even though the sun was hot he shivered.

"All right," their father said to them in a low voice, "I want you boys to wait here."

"Why can't we go with you?" Matthew asked.

"Matthew, that was our agreement! Now I want you to stay here." He turned and proceeded up the path.

When he was fifty feet up the trail he stopped and checked his rifle; then he leaned against a tree and, bracing, took aim.

As soon as their father's back was turned, Matthew started following him up the path. Paul watched his brother nervously, but after a moment he followed too.

Then Paul heard a shot. The report rebounded off the hills and reechoed. Paul looked up, but he couldn't make out what had happened. Their father was motioning for them to stay where they were; then he proceeded up the hill.

Matthew kept coming; but he stopped when he reached where their father had been, and then Paul came up too.

"He must have winged it," Matthew said. Paul looked, and the raccoon was no longer in the tree. Then they heard their father call.

The raccoon lay curled at the foot of the pine. Paul looked at the raccoon, and he could see the flecks of foam by the side of its mouth. It was a sizable beast—but not as large as when it lay writhing in the garage.

Their father had killed it with a single shot.

"Nice shooting," was all Matthew said.

4

Again Paul accompanied Nicole Swann to the movies. They held hands, and after a time he put his arm around her until the heat of their bodies rose to his head and intoxicated his brain pan.

When after the movie they walked together in the spring air, he felt dazed and elated. People were out strolling in the night, enjoying the new heat, and his sense of the city became inextricably mixed with the odor of her hair and with the excitement of standing near her.

"Let's go into the park," he said.

"Isn't it dangerous?"

"Naw, it'll be fine. We won't go far."

He was under the necessity of being alone with her.

They crossed the street, and the night, tangled in the tops of the trees, was broken only by the occasional glow of a lamp light.

"I love the darkness," she said.

They had stopped against a tree just outside the swaying circumference of the light, and at first he could barely see her.

"My whole family is afraid of the dark—isn't that stupid?"

"The dark?" He wasn't paying proper attention, he was wondering whether he might kiss her.

"Yes, it's so—exciting!" And she gave a laugh. "I always give things colors—flavors and things like that. Don't you? What color would you give Dostoyevsky?"

"Dostoyevsky?"

"Yes—if you had to give him a color."

"What color would *you* give him?"

"Black!" she said. "Don't you think Dostoyevsky is just—*blackness*? That's what I wanted to talk to you about! Don't you find Kirillov's suicide just fascinating? I mean, I'm not sure I understand it and all—but the whole thing about suicide. Don't you find that fascinating?"

He could see her better now—could see she was strangely worked up.

"Philosophically," she added. "You know, as a *problem*."

Paul tried to think about suicide, but it was nothing he wanted to have any truck with.

"I love to be frightened!" she said. "It makes me feel— alive!"

Being frightened didn't make Paul feel alive. It's a game, he thought. But he realized he didn't understand the rules.

But just then she leaned forward and kissed him.

They kissed for a long time, leaning against the oak in the darkness, and while they kissed he touched her, kept touching her, touched her all over as if her body were a lesson he was trying to learn; but he could not undress her there in the park, and he did not understand her bra. He did not understand how it worked. And so he kept fondling her through her clothes.

She kept collapsing against him, unable to remain standing, trying, it seemed, to climb onto his lap—until, exhausted, they both had to stop.

That Monday in school Brigit Bloom said to him, "I hear you're very fast!" And she smiled meanly.

He had taken Brigit to a party during the time when he

wasn't speaking to Nicole, and when he danced with her in the hall with the lights turned down, he could feel her press against him—but it was Nicole he wanted.

He remembered walking with Brigit in the autumn night under the leaves. When she turned, one of her breasts came to rest in his hand. But though her eyes grew bright, they continued talking as if nothing had happened, her breast still cupped in his hand like that. Later she asked him to come upstairs. He felt the animal excitement of their bodies, and of the heat of the autumn night, but he did not go up. He did not even kiss her.

Brigit's eyes went soft and gooey when she spoke to him, and she had large firm breasts and a small waist and nice shiny brown hair, and she was one of the best students in their class—but it was Nicole he wanted.

Richards had dubbed Claude Farrino "Whitey," ostensibly because of his name, though in fact because of the inordinate soft whiteness of his flesh, a sort of melting muscleless pudge that jiggled from his frame like fatigued rubber.

To the unoriginal eye Farrino might pass as a young man devoid of promise: obliging to the point of invisibility, small and white, he floated unnoticed from class to class like a species of jellyfish. It required the cunning of a Richards to recognize the potential in Whitey. For Farrino had one distinguishing characteristic: he was a kind of idiot savant in physics and math. He could find the square root of any number in his head. He could add, subtract, multiply, divide vast numbers in the wink of an eye. He could perform prodigious feats of homework.

Whitey was a sad sack of a fellow given to melancholy self-depreciation, but he would light up when Philip addressed him, and he could even evince a kind of wry, tentative wit.

One afternoon when Richards was rushing to some appointment, he inquired if Farrino would do him the courtesy of performing his physics homework for him.

"Why, sure, Phil," Whitey said, blinking at his patron out of dark, adoring, long-lashed eyes. "No problem!"

"Oh, Whitey, you beautiful bowl of suet," Richards exclaimed, pinching Farrino on his dropsical cheek, "you unspeakable creamsicle! But leave one or two mistakes, Whitey, or that flatulent bag of eggnog will know we've been up to tricks."

Whitey giggled and blushed and peered at Richards through glowing eyes.

"One or two, Phil, one or two!" and he laughed as if this were highly amusing.

After that it became the custom for Whitey to do Richards' physics.

"Oh, Whitey, you éclair, you custard, you cream puff," Philip would say, poking Farrino in his doughy midriff, "don't forget to leave one or two mistakes, you perfect little tapioca, you rollicking bowl of flan!"

And Farrino would laugh at their joke.

Philip pretended to consult with Whitey on all manner of topics.

"Come, Whitey," he'd say, "let's take counsel about Suzanne Pratt's tits. Don't you think they're an affront to the scholastic community? Don't you think they should be whipped and scourged about the corridors? Or do you think they should be worshipped, and sacrifices should be offered to them, and hecatombs of billets-doux and turtle-doves? I'm of two opinions, Whitey, so please don't spare me your thoughts."

Whitey would laugh and blush and his flesh would jiggle like one of Santa's elves, but after some coaxing he would offer his opinions, shy and oblique but not without a certain shrewdness.

"Aren't Suzanne Pratt's breasts too *profane* to be worshipped, Phil?"

"Whitey, you dog! You Don Juan! Wherefore art these talents hid? I didn't know you had an eye for the ladies, you little disguiser, you Tartuffe. But how dare you speak of Miss Pratt's mammary perfections with such familiarity? Are you not a curd, are you not a dollop of English cream?"

Once during physics as Paul's turn approached, Whitey opened his notebook so that Paul (who to the best of his knowledge had never previously addressed a word to Farrino) could read his answers. Paul availed himself of this assistance (for as usual he had not done his homework), whereupon Whitey looked at him and smiled.

After that Paul went out of his way to talk to Farrino from time to time, though the interviews were often lugubrious.

"So how are you doing, Whitey?"

"Oh, I'm not doing so well, Paul."

"Why aren't you doing so well, Whitey?"

"Oh, I don't like being me, Paul."

"That doesn't sound so good, Whitey. Who would you rather be?"

"Oh, I'd rather be anyone, Paul. I'd rather be you."

"Me?"

"Yes. Or Phil. I'd rather be Phil. Don't you think Phil is marvelous?"

"Sure, Philip is a wonderful guy, Claude—no question about it. But so are you! Think of how good you are at math."

"Oh, I don't care about math, Paul."

"No? What do you care about?"

"Basketball! I'd like to be good at basketball."

"Basketball? Why basketball, Whitey? I'm not particularly good at basketball."

"But Phil is. Phil is a whiz at basketball."

"Not such a whiz, Whitey. He's just a bit taller than you."

"No, Phil is a whiz at basketball. If I could be anything, I'd like to be a whiz at basketball—like Phil. I'd like to be like Phil."

"That's a useless way to think, Whitey."

"Is it? And what about Suzanne Pratt? Have you given any thought to Suzanne Pratt?"

"What's to think about?"

"This, Paul—that she's in love with Phil."

"Suzanne Pratt? With Richards? What gave you that idea?"

"I can see! I can see by the way she looks at him!"

"No, Whitey, I assure you—you're mistaken. Suzanne Pratt is not in love with Richards. She takes no interest in him."

"Oh no, Paul—*you're* mistaken! Basketball and Suzanne Pratt—that's what I'd like to be!"

. . .

"You're in a slump," Scotty said. It was batting practice and Paul was standing in the batter's cage in the lower field with the sun low behind him in the west. "You're getting out in front of the ball. You're trying too hard and swinging in front of the ball. Try to stay inside yourself, Werth. When you're in a slump you've got to stay inside yourself."

Paul didn't need Scotty to tell him he was in a slump. He knew his timing was off but he couldn't see what was wrong: he wasn't losing the ball, he had it in sight out in front of him in his area, he wasn't being fooled by its movement, but when he swung, nothing happened. Instead of a deep, satisfying *thwack!* there was only a swoosh of air and he'd come around hard on nothing.

The late-afternoon sun played off the face of the gym building in the distance and touched the young leaves on the hill behind the upper field where the track team was practicing; he could hear the lilt of voices on the clean air and the occasional distant *crack!* of the starting gun as they ran heats.

"Now you're trying to pull the ball," Scotty called. "You're waiting too long on the swing."

Wolf wound up on the mound. Paul planted his feet and waited, attempting to concentrate, attempting to find his spot; then the ball had been released and he could see it coming and then, swinging, he felt the reverberating jolt of misconnection. The ball slammed into the turf halfway out on the infield.

"Damn!"

"Okay, Werth," Scotty called wearily, "that's it for today."

"What's wrong with you, anyway?" Scotty asked when they were in the locker room. "You getting enough sleep?"

"Yessir," he lied.

"Too bad," Boom-Boom said. "You're in a slump, that's all. It happens to everyone."

But what was a slump? He hadn't been in a slump the previous year when he had been the only sophomore on the team. So what had gone wrong?

Paul suffered from insomnia. He would lie in bed in an agony of wakefulness, his body aching as if someone had beaten him, his mind polluted by a kind of lunatic racket in the back of his head. Sometimes this sound would mimic the rhythm of a poem he had been reading, the words transmogrified into idiot gibberish; sometimes the scrap of a song would whirl about his cranium, the lyrics repeated again and again as if a record had been caught in a groove.

He did not know which was worse, this sleeplessness or the anxiety that provoked it. Certain thoughts had to be avoided, the death of his father of course, but anything could panic him: the thought of an exam, or of the SATs, or of Harvard, or of Nicole Swann—or just some chance remark a teacher had uttered.

Finally he would slip into a troubled sleep, only to be awoken by the clamor of his alarm. He would drag himself from bed, splash water on his face, now streaked and swollen with sleeplessness, and stagger to school, where he would stumble from class to class in a stupor of fatigue, only in imperfect communication with the outside world, which hummed and buzzed about him like some giant hive set alarmingly astir.

Paul went to Nicole's apartment and met her parents, two dumpy, puffy-visaged, middle-aged persons with guttural accents. Paul could not conceive how two young women like Nicole and her beautiful older sister, Peach, could be their daughters.

"Hello, Paul," the mother said, and looked at him out of calculating mistrustful eyes, as if he had come with ulterior purpose to appropriate the silver. She pronounced "Paul" with a flat, matter-of-fact distaste, as if she had known him a long time and had long drawn her conclusions regarding his moral character.

Some species of electric identification and hostility circuited between Nicole and her mother, as if each read in the other the mistrust she felt in herself.

Nicole led him into her room, but she was soon called out, and Paul could detect a subdued commotion that transpired beyond the door, a clamor of discordant intention stifled to near-suffocation.

Left to himself, Paul cruised the room for hidden signs of femaleness—panties, a bra, tissues, hidden love notes; but he found nothing but a notebook which, upon surreptitious perusal, revealed only a half-filled page of desultory notes on *The Return of the Native* and a flurry of abstract doodles.

The room—the entire apartment—was bright, clean, low-ceilinged and decorated with bouncy Miami colors like flavors of sherbet. He touched Nicole's bed, with its spongy white coverlet, and his heart gave a trip.

When Nicole returned she was scowling.

"My mom wants us to go out. She doesn't want us in the apartment alone."

Paul shrugged. "Sure."

Just then a little bald-headed, shirttailed man entered the room swiftly.

"Hello, boy, how'r'ya?"

It was Nicole's father.

"Fine, thank you, sir."

They shook hands.

"Nice to meet you, Paul. Nicole tells me you're a great scholar."

"Daddy!"

"Oh, isn't that right? Aren't you the right one?"

"I wouldn't say I was . . ."

"I told Daddy you were very smart."

"Yeah, smart. Can ya tell me the first nineteen Presidents of the United States?"

"The first nineteen . . ."

"Oh, Daddy—not right now!"

"Got ya, huh?" And he uttered a bark of amusement. "Let's see. Washington Adams Jefferson Madison Monroe Adams Jackson Van Buren—I betchya forgot about him, huh?—Van Buren Harrison Tyler—not bad, heh? Can you go on from there? Let's see, let's see!"

"Daddy!"

"Not bad for an old man, right? Well, it's nice meeting you Paul, it's nice meeting you."

"Oh, Daddy's just *awful*," Nicole said with affection. "If you come for dinner he'll grill you something terrible!"

"I see," Paul said weakly—though he noted the suggestion about dinner. He'd have to bone up on his Presidents.

"I just have to finish what I'm doing," Nicole said. "Then we'll get out of here."

She disappeared into the bathroom, leaving the door open.

"Do you share the room with Peach?" he asked.

"No—why do you ask?"

"Because I see a picture of Bob Tucker."

"Oh, that. It was Peach's room last year. I haven't cleared out all her junk."

"Is she liking Vassar?"

"Don't ask me." Her voice sounded annoyed. "I don't know what Peach likes."

Shorter, darker, and "cuter" than Nicole, Nicole's older sister Peach had graduated from Highgate the previous year; she was still going with Bob Tucker, the former captain of the Highgate basketball team, now away at Yale.

Paul ventured to the edge of the bathroom door; Nicole was putting her lipstick on before the mirror.

He tried to decipher the significance of his standing there watching her perform this operation, her mouth opened in a pout, the sharpened end of the pink lipstick distorting her lip upward as she applied the pigment. There was something darkly attractive about her languorous body and the dark, lazy pull of her mind.

"What's that?" he said. He was now hanging in the door.

"That? Oh, that's an electric toothbrush."

"A what?"

"Toothbrush. It's electric. See?" And she pushed a button so the stout, weird instrument began to buzz. Paul laughed.

"What do you need *that* for?"

"For your gums." And she pulled back her lips to reveal large, handsome teeth, streaked slightly with the lipstick, and, above, the firm pinkness of her gums.

They went to the movies, where she again let him hold her hand, and he began to hope that things were improving between them. Maybe he *would* go to dinner at her house!

Afterward they had Cokes at a coffee shop. She sat across from him while he studied the thickness of her eyebrows, the pout of her lower lip, the brooding, veiled darkness of her eyes.

"Can we go back to your place?"

When she looked at him it was as if she were debating something with herself.

"Okay."

"Good!" And he laughed. "I'm sick of doorways and oak trees."

But she didn't return his smile.

He touched the top of her thigh as she opened the door to her apartment. It was dark inside and rank with the odor of cooked vegetable. Then she turned on the light.

"They'll be back soon," she said. "You shouldn't be here, my mom won't like it. She's a real pain."

"Do you want me to leave?"

But she only touched him on the arm, drawing him farther into the apartment.

"They won't be back before eleven-thirty."

In her room she plunked herself down on her bed, brooding, watching him from under her brows, and he felt anger mix like some turgid current with the desire in his blood.

"Well, what are we going to do now?"

She looked at him, and he could see her relent, and he *knew* she liked him. He didn't understand the game.

"You look very cute like that," she said.

"Do I?"

"Yes. Does that make you angry?"

"It sounds a little condescending."

"Well, I don't mean it that way. Can I get you something to eat?"

"I'm not hungry. Jesus, Nicole," he said in exasperation, "what's this all about? Why can't we ever be alone?"

"We're alone now."

"No we're not. Your parents will be here any minute. Isn't there anyplace where we could ever be—*alone?*"

She moved uneasily under the weight of his anger, as if guilty before him.

"I dunno," she said uncertainly. "I suppose if it was warmer we could go to my country house."

"Your country house? Is it far?"

"No, we could take the train."

"Why can't we go now?"

"It's locked up," she said.

"Isn't there some way we could get in?"

She looked at him a long time.

"Would we be alone there?" he asked.

"Yes—all alone."

"Well—wouldn't it be fun?"

She smiled slightly. "Yes, it would be."

"So—how can we get in?"

He looked at her, and he saw the excitement in her own eyes. For he knew—and he knew that she knew—that they weren't just talking about going to her country house. What they were talking about was *going all the way*. If he could get her to go to her country house, she was agreeing to sleep with him; and she seemed to be agreeing.

"I don't think we can get the keys," she said.

"Isn't there any other way to get in?"

There was a long pause, and he realized too late that he had made a tactical error, for he had left her open to saying no and ending the entire negotiation.

"Well, I suppose you could climb in through the back window."

"The back window?"

"Yes. My mom's a fanatic about keeping a back window open at the top so there's air in the house in case the pilot light blows out. It sounds crazy, but that's my mom. She doesn't like me to use my electric toothbrush because she thinks I might electrocute myself."

"How high is the back window?"

"I dunno. Pretty high."

"Well, I can get into it."

"How do you know?"

"I can climb into any window ever made." And for the moment he believed this to be the case. "If the window's open," he said, "I'll get in."

She looked at him slightly breathless, her dark eyes wide, and he knew that if they were now in her country house he would attain his desire.

After he had left the apartment he stood outside in the

night air. The street was empty, only an occasional car passed with an empty hiss of tires on the black pavement. Looking up, he could see the balconies and extinguished lights of the buildings. It was a long way home.

He started to walk, and suddenly he felt a lurch of excitement. She had all but agreed to go! He would get her to go with him to her country house!

"Akillaus," Philip Richards said, "let us go walk by the wine-dark sea," so the two young men went to the river and walked by the railroad ties where the freight cars waited on the siding beside the dirty water.

"Where is there an end to it, the wailing?" Richards intoned, sweeping with his hand the stained urban landscape. Wearing his sombrero and his blue business suit, with his blond hair slicked back and his arms outstretched, he resembled a young stockbroker struck suddenly by mental derangement.

"Do you know what is our one and only duty?" Richards continued. "It's every young man's duty to get himself laid as frequently as possible. Tell me frankly, how many times a week do you beat the meat? No, I'm being serious—it's nothing to be ashamed of. In my opinion masturbation is the only healthy exercise for a young man. Sometimes I jerk off twice a day."

Paul smiled and grimaced and didn't bother to answer.

"Oh, I shall arise and go now," Philip intoned, "and go to—Philadelphia! By the way, is there such a place as Philadelphia? Ah, Akillaus, you of the swift feet, how shall we ever accomplish the things we were destined to accomplish when there is such a place as Philadelphia? Think what it does to the soul."

"I thought it burned with a hard, gemlike flame," Paul said.

"Don't joke, *bambino*. Don't joke about sacred matters."

Paul looked across the waters to the western cliffs and suddenly he remembered how his father had taken him and his brother there to hike. A ferry had crossed the river at that time, and they had carried canteens and hunting knives and sandwiches prepared by their mother. The day had been brisk and the leaves brilliant with autumn. They had gone, Matthew, he, and his father, to spend the day together, and now, ten years later, his father was dead.

"What shall we accomplish?" Philip was saying. "You will write poetry, and I—I will write advertising. No, not really. Together we will write—what? The Great American Novel! Like William Burroughs or Nathanael West!"

"I think we'd better write our great American novels separately."

Richards looked at him and frowned.

"Separately?"

"Well," Paul relented, hearing the note of reproach in his friend's voice, "can we write the Great American Novel *together*?"

After that the two young men walked in silence. The wind came up, bringing with it the chemical stench of coke and the bilgy odor of rotting marine life.

"Why so saturnine?" Philip inquired. "Does the great god Pan worry your midnight lucubrations?"

"My what?"

"Don't worry—it's not what you suppose! Your midnight toils, your midnight scrivenings. Are you still hankering after that dim bulb, that dark siren of pseudoliterary posturing?"

"What are you talking about?"

"You know perfectly well what I'm talking about, that pretentious bitch goddess, Nicole Swann. Has it ever occurred to you that that young woman isn't who you think she is?"

"No, it hasn't," Paul said. "I'm in love with her."

"Love, phoo! Don't be in love with anyone, it's a bad investment. It turns the soul into soggy white bread."

Paul Werth took tea with Miss English. She had invited him, somewhat shyly, and, somewhat shyly, he had accepted; and so he found himself sitting in her doily-appointed apartment with heavy bookcases lining the wall and potted plants decking the windowsill. Brownish late-afternoon shadows accumulated in the corners, investing the room with a heavy funereal silence, into which Paul, balanced at the edge of an overstuffed chair, teacup on his knee, was terrified he would momentarily slip and drown.

Miss English was a tall, slender, aquiline woman, plain and rather grim, with colorless gray hair swept back from the sides of her head and gray pellucid, arrogant eyes. She had taught the course in Ancient Civilization for twenty years and in that time she was not known to have altered a single text she offered or a single attitude she professed. Her information was invariably uttered with the inalterable concision of truth.

Ancient Civilization was one of the rare classes where Paul felt at ease, and this was all the more remarkable because Miss English was a notorious bitch.

"You mean you actually *like* Miss English?" Jeb had said to him in disbelief.

"Well, I don't know that I like her," Paul had allowed. "But I think she's a good teacher."

Paul knew that Miss English liked him, just as he knew that Mrs. Wagner didn't. He knew Miss English liked him by the set of her head when she listened to him, by the way she called on him when the rest of the class seemed stymied, by the intangible attention of her gray eyes when she observed him as he spoke—or even as he walked into class.

And he liked Miss English. He liked that she was tough and condescending and arrogant and set high standards for herself and her class, and he could even see through her old maid plainness that she was not unpretty. He liked her spinsterish reserve, as if it guarded a warmth, perhaps even a vulnerability, that she had long since learned to conceal.

"I've been reading Trollope," Miss English announced in her cool, steady, refined manner. "I can't say I would recommend him as highly as Dickens, but he has his own substantial appeal. What are you reading, Paul?"

"Hemingway," Paul said somewhat shyly.

"Ah, Hemingway! I've never taken to Hemingway the way his supporters do, but I suppose I can see his attraction—for a young man. What is your favorite?"

"Well, I like all of it, really. It's the way he writes. I like the way he puts words on paper. I guess I think of him more as a poet than a novelist."

"Yes, I can see that. I'll have to take another look. I haven't read Hemingway in years. My taste runs more to the large, solid Victorian novels where you can become lost for weeks. But, yes, as a poet, I can see that. Do you write, Paul?"

He felt himself blushing.

"I try a little."

"You should! You should be writing. Your papers are very original. You have a very original mind."

He felt himself sweating with embarrassment. He looked around for aid, but the room offered no escape from its implacable gentility.

"You know, I knew your mother and father years ago," she suddenly offered. "We worked together in a summer camp when we were very young. Your father was so handsome!" And she gave a little chirp of laughter. "I was shocked by his death, Paul. Such a young man! Such a terrible loss!"

Paul did not want to talk about his father's death, and, coloring, he merely lowered his eyes and muttered "thank you."

"I hope you've recovered by now, Paul. I mean, insofar as one can recover."

"Yes, thanks."

"It was such a disappointment to me," she continued, "that I didn't have your older brother in my class. I looked into changing things around, but nothing was to be done. He's off at Harvard, isn't he?"

"Yes, he's a sophomore."

"Is he enjoying it?"

"I suppose so. I don't really know."

"And is that where you want to go, Paul?"

He felt himself coloring again. "I don't know," he said. "It still seems a long ways away."

"Well, it's not so long. You should be giving thought to these matters. I want you to know that I'm here to help you in any way I can."

He muttered how kind that was—he hardly knew what to say.

"You should continue your Hemingway, but I'd like to give you something else to read as well. Have you ever read Emerson?"

"Emerson? You mean like 'Self-Reliance' and all that?"

"Yes, precisely. He's a marvelous writer, someone a young man can get his teeth into."

"I see."

"I have a book I'd like to lend you, if you are interested."

"Oh, I'm sure we have Emerson at home."

"No, I'd like to lend you my copy."

She got up, setting her teacup down decisively, and as she ferried across the room, he noticed that one of her hips was higher than another—and again he felt embarrassed.

She returned with the book, placing it on his knees, from which he had hurriedly removed his cup.

"There," she said. "I'll want to know your opinion."

Paul stood at the plate with the afternoon sun leveling at his eyes. He removed his cap and wiped the perspiration from his forehead and replaced the cap on his head. He could smell his uniform as it clung to his underarms.

He felt heavy and leaden and fatigued, as if moving in a dream.

"C'mon, Paul," Doyle called from the sidelines. "Let's get hot!"

Paul surveyed the infield and saw they were playing him short, and his stomach tightened with anger and disgust. Then the redheaded Woodtown pitcher went into his windup while Paul waited tensely.

"Strike one!"

Okay, Paul thought, okay, fine. I can hit that stuff.

From the third-base line Keith Firman signaled him to hit away.

Again the pitcher went into his windup. Paul swung, but he already knew he was under the ball and a fraction too late. He heard the foul clatter into the backstop.

"Strike two!"

"Come on, Werth!" Scotty, low and intense, called from the sidelines.

Paul could feel himself getting flustered and he struggled to keep his concentration.

The next ball was low—Paul saw it coming and held off. Perhaps he hadn't lost his eye. Then there was another ball and the count was two and two.

Paul stepped out of the batter's box and took a deep breath. Then he stepped back to the plate.

The next pitch was a strike on the outside corner that caught Paul looking.

Paul sat down heavily on the bench. The odor of grass came up to him from the field and its sweetness was bitter in his nostrils. It seemed to him the other guys avoided looking at him, as if he brought bad luck.

In the locker room Bower was solicitous and condescending.

"Are you taking your eye off the ball? The main thing is not to take your eye off the ball."

Paul hated to be patronized by this jerk, with his straight back, bulging muscles, and rounded, close-cropped skull, but Bower wasn't in a slump.

Paul threw his dirty towel into the hamper and passed the forward lockers where the seniors were dressing: Doyle glanced at him briefly; Hillman, naked and belching, gave him a baleful stare. Then Paul emerged into the clear April air.

As he came out he could see the crane towering in the evening twilight at the top of the hill.

Mrs. Richards' face lit up when she saw Paul.

"Why, Paul, it's so good to see you!"

She was a tall, languorous woman, negligently beautiful, and she had decided, on little evidence though much to his pleasure, that Paul was a beneficial influence on her son. She was now dressed (to Paul's embarrassment) in nothing but a silk bathrobe held partially closed across her breast with one hand, and as she advanced to kiss him, she smelled slightly of cold cream.

"Hail, proud warrior," Philip drawled, issuing from his room and greeting Paul from across the large foyer. They were congregated in Mrs. Richards' well-appointed apartment, where Philip resided in the city, a spacious suite of rooms decorated in French Empire and smelling vaguely of roses.

"Now, I have to go out early," Mrs. Richards said, addressing her son with faux asperity, "but I want you to be certain to feed Paul properly, Philip. Do you understand? Matilda has left food for you in the kitchen—all you have to do is heat it up. And I don't want you staying out too late. Is that clear, young man?"

"Yes, Mummsie." And Philip, placing his hands on her, nuzzled into her neck, tickling her on the side of her body. Paul looked away.

"Oh, naughty boy," Mrs. Richards laughed, kissing the top of her son's head. "What am I going to do with you? What are we going to do with this naughty boy?" she asked Paul, turning to him as if they were two adults consulting about a much loved infant. Paul colored and shrugged and averted his gaze.

"He's such a naughty boy," she pursued, still laughing throatily. "I depend on your judgment, Paul, to keep him out of harm's way."

"I wouldn't do anything to upset my mummsie," Philip said, still holding her and caressing her with his eyes.

"Oh, you terrible man!" she said, laughing as she pushed him away. "Let me go or I'll be late."

The two boys went into Philip's room and shut the door.

The room offered a remarkable assemblage: boxing gloves, hockey sticks, a signed photograph of President Kennedy, a signed photograph of Tab Hunter, a Greek grammar, comic books, part of an electric train, silk ties, aftershave lotion, an atlas of the world, a collection of

Playboy magazines, a water pistol, an empty fish tank, a doorstop made from a horseshoe, a deck of girlie cards, photographs of Philip at all ages standing or sitting or lying, photographs of Philip at all ages with his mother, a diploma from a baseball camp, a straw hat, a large cat's-eye marble, a crushed box of Trojans. Cigarettes were strewn about the room.

Philip threw himself onto his bed and looked at Paul with lazy, ironic good humor.

"So, *caro mio—la madre.*"

"She's terrific."

"She's okay," he allowed with feigned indifference, and smiled.

"Wait a minute," Philip said, "I have to make a telephone call." And jumping up from where he sat, he strode across the room.

Among the clutter he unearthed a telephone, and he stood with his back to Paul staring out the window while he put through his call.

"Berger? Is everything set? Okay. No. No. Just do it my way. Okay, fine. Whatever you say. Okay, fine." And he hung up the phone.

"That little prick. I don't know why I have anything to do with him."

"Why *do* you have anything to do with him?"

"He amuses me, *caro mio.* He amuses me. The best reason for doing anything on this terraqueous globe. He satisfies the only serious question in life—how to stay amused. Besides," Richards continued, turning now and addressing Paul directly, "do you know how much that little prick and I make out of these party deals? We rent these halls and throw these parties and charge five dollars admission, and we often make five hundred dollars a night. Not bad, eh? And of course I have Berger do all the donkey work. By the way, do you want to come in on it with us?"

"No, I don't think so, Philip. Thanks anyway."

"Well, suit yourself. But I couldn't do without Berger. Should we go see what Mummsie has for us to eat?"

They ate potpies and salad with croutons and cherry tomatoes, and creamed spinach which Matilda had prepared, and they drank ice water out of crystal goblets with ice cubes that came directly from a machine in the refrigerator, and all this seemed exotic and highly enjoyable to Paul, who was delighted to be there with Philip. For dessert they had small individual apple tarts with fresh whipped cream.

"Let's go back into my room," Philip said. "I have to have a cigarette. The mummsie has a fit if I smoke in her august presence, as if it were some kind of secret that I smoke. Here, have one."

"I can't because of baseball," Paul said regretfully.

"That's right—Mickey Mantle here. Werth, fleetest of foot, who taketh the hurdles of life with pride. Have a cigarette anyway—it will do you good."

"So," Richards said when the door was closed, "we going to go to this Kinski party or not?"

"I dunno," Paul said. "I don't know Laura Kinski and that crowd."

"That doesn't matter. She's just giving the party, for chrissake. Besides, Kinski's a great kid, you'll like her."

"I don't think she's my type."

"Well, who can tell? Besides, no one is asking you to marry her. All you have to do is say hello."

The boys decided they'd try the party, though they wouldn't stay long if Paul wasn't comfortable.

"Now let's see, let's see," Richards said. "Whom should I take to this gig? Do you know that little sophomore, that Stephanie White chick—you know, the stacked one? What about if I called her?"

"Do you know her?"

"No, I've never spoken to her in my life."

"Well, why do we have to 'take' anyone?"

"You just say that because you're not going with what's her face. I think I'll call this Stephanie chick. That is her name, isn't it?"

"Philip, I've never spoken to the girl. I don't know what her name is."

"Well, I'll call her Stephanie. She won't mind, right?" And Richards produced a crumpled piece of paper from his pocket and began dialing the telephone.

"Jesus, Philip . . ." But Richards motioned him to be quiet.

"Hello, Stephanie—is this Stephanie? Oh, *Susan*, yeah. Well, listen, Susan, I wondered what you were doing tonight. Who? Oh, Philip Richards in the senior class at Highgate—you know. Yeah, that's me—the handsome one!" And he turned and winked at Paul, who had colored to the roots of his hair and was trying not to laugh. "Well, listen, Susan. My friend and I were wondering what you were doing tonight, because, you see, there's going to be a *senior party* and we were kind of wondering if you would like to attend. Yeah, of course with us! Yeah, I know it's a little late to be calling but—actually I just got your name, Susan, because a special friend of yours—no, never mind who—was telling me what a swell girl you are, so my friend and I were thinking it might be kind of cool to hang out together, if you see what I mean. Yeah? Really? Well, that's too bad, Susan, because I think you're passing up something really special that could lead to a really special friendship, but you've gotta please yourself in these matters. As the Italians say—what? Yeah, well, no matter. Another time Susan. *Ciao!*"

"The bitch!" he said after he hung up. "I mean, the stupid bitch is only a *sophomore*, for chrissake! I don't know what the younger generation is coming to!" And he winged his straw hat across the room.

Philip walked restlessly to his bed and, throwing himself onto it, he began to fuss with something in the drawer of his bedside table. He drew out a crumpled Camels cigarette box, from which he extracted a smallish cigarette pinched closed at either end. This he lit with a shaking match and, inhaling deeply, he retained the smoke in his lungs for what seemed a long time. Then he looked up at Paul and smiled.

"You want to try a joint?"

Paul looked at his friend and smiled uneasily; he had never seen a joint before.

"Where'd you get that?"

Richards shrugged. "Pursy gave it to me."

"Pursy? See, I told you Hillman and his jocks were behind that stuff."

"Other people in the world besides Hillman have dope, Paul. Besides, so what? That's Hillman's problem. Here, have a drag."

Richards pinched the reefer between two fingers and put it to his mouth; then he inhaled deeply, his nostrils splaying. Again he held the smoke in his lungs before exhaling.

"Phew, that's good! Here, take a puff."

Paul took the reefer and held it to his lips. He inhaled deeply and retained the smoke the way Philip had, but the smoke only cut his insides.

He gave the cigarette back to Richards.

"Go ahead, take some more."

"No, thanks."

"What's wrong—you don't like pot?"

"I've never tried it before, Philip. I've never even seen the stuff before."

"*Povero bambino!*"

"You think it's such a great idea—smoking that stuff right now?"

"What's the big deal?"

"There's no big deal."

"You're always making a big deal. Listen, Paul, you've got to loosen up a bit. You're always so fucking uptight."

"I'm not uptight. I just don't think it's a particularly great time to start smoking pot, with Bates up in arms, and Craig Lewis acting like a goddamn vigilante, and Hillman . . ." Paul shook his head in distaste.

"Don't worry so much about Hillman. I have nothing to do with Hillman. Jesus, Paul, you don't think I have anything to do with Hillman, do you?"

"Of course not."

"So what's the big deal if I have a reefer in my own room once in a while? Come on, Paul—don't be a drag!"

．　．　．

Laura Kinski lived in an elegant building with three doormen and a fancy wrought-iron entrance with brass lanterns by the side of the door. Paul and Philip had to wait while the doormen rang up on the intercom before they were allowed to proceed down the long hall to the elevator.

Paul could hear the music from Laura's apartment as they exited the elevator on the fifteenth floor.

Laura answered the door. Paul had never stood this close to her before and he was struck by how good-looking she was; she was even more beautiful up close than from a distance.

"Hi, Laura," Richards said, slipping into his friendly routine. "Bobby Bower said we should drop around."

"Sure, come on in." Her voice was friendly.

"And this is Paul Werth."

Paul was aware of her dark almond-shaped eyes looking at him.

"Hi, Paul."

He followed her into the apartment. He had heard all sorts of things about Laura, that she was a snob, that she was a bitch, that she was *fast*—but in fact she seemed nice.

He recognized most of the people in the room: some kids from other schools, but mostly the jock crowd, Hillman and Doyle and Pursy.

"You guys want a drink or something?" Laura Kinski asked. "There's Coke and stuff in the other room."

"Hey, this is groovy," Richards said.

"I'm glad you like it!" And Laura lifted her eyebrows in amusement.

"Yeah—it's cool. Cool apartment, Laura—just what I'd expect. *Très chic!*"

"*Chic?*" And she laughed at him good-humoredly while he laughed back.

"Well, you two guys take care now," she said, and she smiled at Paul before trailing off into the crowd."

"She doesn't seem so bad," Paul said.

"I told you—Laura's groovy. Well, I'm going to check out the scenery, *bambino.* You'll be all right on your own?"

"Sure, Philip—don't worry about me."

"Okay," Richards said. "See ya latah alligatah."

And he patted Paul on the shoulder. In his blue business suit with his blond hair slicked back, he appeared like the resident attorney taking inventory of the furniture.

Paul circled the apartment, an immense place with heavy curtains hanging to the floors and polished mahogany tables with silver candelabra. A large crystal chandelier glittered from the ceiling.

Kids danced or smoked in the large rooms, from which there issued music in a steady boom boom boom.

"So, h . . . how are ya?" It was Robbie Doyle smiling and stuttering at him with pseudo-friendliness, his slightly heavy underjaw protruding and his blond hair bristling about his face like a boar's.

"Hi, Robbie!" Paul could detect the pseudo-friendliness in his own voice.

"So, w . . . w . . . whaddaya you doing here, Paul? I thought maybe you'd be st . . . studying or something."

"Studying?"

"Yeah—you know, cracking the books."

"No, Robbie—I'm not studying."

"Well, you gonna shake this slump?"

"I dunno—I hope so."

"You just gotta relax."

"It's not that." Paul hated discussing his slump. "I dunno what it is. But I'm relaxed just fine."

Doyle shrugged, his smile fading.

"Whatever you s . . . say. We should have a gr . . . great season, with Bower and Boom-Boom and me."

"Yeah, maybe we'll win the championship again." And he remembered how Nicole had promised to come and see him play.

"Yeah, maybe—if you shake that slump! W . . . well, see ya later." And Doyle turned and walked away.

Paul saw Ned Hillman across the room joshing with Pursy; and suddenly, for no apparent reason, recalling the rumors linking Hillman with Laura Kinski, he scowled.

He stood by the buffet sipping a Coke and considering what to do. He wished Nicole was there. He decided he would complete the circuit of the rooms and then leave.

In the hallway he encountered Brigit Bloom, whose face lit up when she saw him.

"Hi, Paul, what are *you* doing here?"

"Hi, Brigit. I came with Richards. Nicole was busy," he added for no apparent reason, and he felt himself blush.

"Oh?" And she looked at him significantly. "Too bad for Nicole. By the way, what did you get on the math quiz?"

"The math quiz? Jesus, Brigit, I dunno." Mention of the math quiz caused his stomach to tighten.

"Oh, I'm sure you did great," Brigit said. "You do great even when you don't try!"

This wasn't the case, but it pleased Brigit to think so. It puzzled him why Brigit should be forever concerned about quizzes, which she always aced. He could see she was waiting for him to ask her to dance.

"I was just going," he said.

"Oh?" And her face fell. He liked Brigit, he liked her a lot, but he didn't want to dance with her.

"Hello, Paul," Jeb said as Paul was leaving the room.

"Hiya, Jeb! What's up?"

"Oh, nothing much." Jeb was dressed in black loafers and dark, pressed slacks and he peered at Paul out of his pale, serious face. "Do you believe there is any chance of our picking up women?"

Paul smiled at this choice of words. Jeb had a way of lowering his voice when he spoke, selecting his words with care and pretension.

"Why not? Aren't we eligible bachelors?"

"Yeah—eligible to stand and watch."

"Get out on the floor and wiggle your tail, Jeb. That's what the girls like."

"You think so?"

"Sure! Get out there and dance up a storm."

Paul was just about to leave when someone else spoke to him. He turned, and it was Laura Kinski.

"Don't go," Laura said. "I haven't had a chance to talk to you."

She came up to him, and he noted that she was almost as tall as he. She was smiling.

"I wanted to ask you about Mr. Lemming's class. Aren't you in one of the sections?"

"Yeah, Tuesday's."

"Yeah, that's what I thought. Too bad you're not in mine!"

"Oh?"

"Yes—everyone says you're so smart."

"Who says that?"

"Oh, everyone!" And she laughed. "Why—isn't it true?"

He liked the way she laughed.

"It surprises me that you even know who I am," he said.

"Of course I know who you are. It surprises me that you know who *I* am."

"Oh, *everyone* knows who you are."

She gave an ironic snort, and Paul blushed; he hadn't thought how it might sound.

"I mean, I didn't know any senior girls knew any junior guys."

Again she merely laughed.

"Where's your friend Richards?"

"I dunno—he seems to have disappeared."

"Oh? The old French leave, eh?"

"So it would seem."

Paul looked about the room, and he saw Berger across the way. He hadn't noticed him before, and the sight caused him to grimace with distaste.

"What's wrong?" she asked, amused. "Don't you like our friend Berger?"

"How do you know that creep?"

She laughed good-humoredly.

"Oh, Berger's all right. He's just a creepy little hanger-on. You shouldn't make your feelings so transparent."

"Listen!" she said, and she rested her hand lightly on his

forearm. "Can you tell me what to write about *The Return of the Native*? I mean, the book is so clunky!"

He had never been touched like that, and it seemed to him the height of sophistication.

"I don't know why Lemming makes such a fuss about the novel," she continued. "It's not nearly so good as *Tess*."

Paul had never read *Tess*, but he agreed about *The Return of the Native*. This was all very surprising: he was talking with Laura Kinski, one of the most popular and notorious girls in the school—and liking it.

"Hey, I just had an idea," she said, "maybe you could come over sometime and help me with my paper. I mean, I'm really stuck about what to write, and there's nobody to talk to in my section. It would be a big help."

"Well, I dunno . . ."

"Yes, do come! It'll be fun!" She smiled at him in a straightforward, disarming manner, and again he was struck by how good-looking she was.

Paul ran into Jeb on the elevator.

"So, did you dance?"

"No—my efforts were inefficacious."

"Inefficacious?"

"Yes—not tending to success or achievement. It was on the PSATs."

"Well, better luck next time."

"I don't think there'll be a next time. I think it's celibacy for me."

"Oh, no, Jeb. Richards says it's our responsibility to get laid."

"Richards! Some talker!"

And the two boys laughed.

"Where did Philip disappear to, anyway?"

"I dunno," Jeb said. "He's probably off somewhere con-cocting some scheme. Hey, listen," he added, "why don't you come home with me. My parents are out—and it'll save you that long journey home."

"Sure," Paul said, "that's a great idea."

They had come outside and were standing in front of the building in the night air, and there was Berger at the farther corner.

"Hey, Berger," Jeb called, "what's up? You waiting to pick up some dame?"

"Yeah, sure—fat chance." And Berger offered his ner-vous deprecatory laugh.

"Have you seen Philip?" Paul inquired. "He's disap-peared."

"He went home," Berger said. "I saw him leave a while ago."

"We're going to my place," Jeb called. "You wanna come?"

"No can do," Berger said, to Paul's relief. "But you guys have fun."

Jeb and Paul sat in Jeb's kitchen eating English muffins and discussing the Meaning of Life. Jeb's parents were out and his brother away at Yale, so the boys had the place to themselves.

"Listen," Jeb said after a while, "do you want something to drink?"

"What do you mean?"

"You know—something alcoholic, like whiskey or something."

"Sure—why not."

Jeb led the way across the apartment to the living room, where he opened a paneled highboy and produced a quart bottle of Dewar's; he then took two large cut-glass tumblers and filled them with strong-smelling whiskey.

"To your good health!"

Paul took a gulp and almost choked. He knew if he drank this stuff he would be ill.

Jeb watched with amusement as he sipped his own whiskey. Then the boys settled into two large overstuffed chairs.

"Who needs Laura Kinski's party, anyway?" Jeb said after a while. "Who needs dancing and singing? Don't we have everything we need right here?"

"You bet we do!"

"And who needs girls?" Jeb continued. "Is there anyone here who can answer that question? I ask you, who needs girls?"

"That's right," Paul agreed. "Or oxygen or sunlight."

The two boys laughed wryly.

"By the way," Paul said, "did you get to speak to Laura Kinski?"

"Laura Kinski? Are you kidding? You think Laura Kinski would speak to the likes of me?"

"Why not?" Paul said. "Just because she's beautiful? Just because she's a senior? Just because she dates football players? Why shouldn't she speak to you?"

"Indeed why not? That's what I'd like to know! Why should any of that stand in my way? In fact, I'd like to propose a toast to Laura Kinski!"

And rising unsteadily to their feet, the two boys lifted their glasses and drank to the beautiful Laura Kinski.

After they sat down they were both silent for some time.

"Actually," Paul said after a while, speaking as if to himself, "she turns out to be very nice."

"Who does?"

"Laura Kinski."

"Yeah, well, she turns out to be very pretty. She's not for the likes of us, kiddo. Would you, however, excuse me for a minute? I have to retire to the other room—to be sick."

And rising with dignity, Jeb walked unsteadily from the room.

Later Paul lay in the darkened bedroom watching the lights cross the ceiling. Jeb slept in the adjacent bed. Paul was ill at ease in a strange house and the whiskey had only excited him. He lay long into the night thinking.

Paul's father used to insist on "meal hours," a semi-sacred occasion when the entire family assembled. This entailed their all being dressed and washed for breakfast by seven-thirty, an agenda that suited no one's temperament—including their father's.

Their father was a moody man, sometimes overflowing with jokes and snatches of song, but also given to terrible spasms of anger which visited him with the swiftness and unpredictability of a summer storm: a glass would be overturned, a facetious word uttered, and suddenly he would throw his napkin down, pound the table with his fist, and demand in a resounding voice, "Can't a man have peace even in his own home?"

Often he would spring up and rage from the room.

These paroxysms were terrifying when the boys were young, but little by little they became less awesome, certainly for Matthew, who instead of averting his eyes, began to taunt his father, smirking and wagging his head and staring directly at him.

At first Paul was terrified by Matthew's audacity. His father was a towering figure in his imagination, and he was certain his brother would be struck down by lightning. But slowly Paul began to understand, first with amazement, then with growing compassion, that it was his father who ran away.

"Go to your room!" their father would shout, brandishing his finger like a prophet. But his brother replied with equal force, "Go to *your* room!" And their father, in an apoplexy of anger and frustration, would—go to his room.

This was comic, and Paul couldn't help laughing—but sadly, with rue in his heart. Soon his father would return as if nothing had happened, for his anger never lasted more than a few minutes, and he couldn't stay away from his family, whom he adored.

Paul was now old enough to understand that his father was hounded by something in his life, some disappointment that he hid in the world behind his suave exterior, but which he vented, sadly and unfairly, in the safety of his home; but Matthew seemed to understand none of this.

"He's all bark and no bite," Matthew explained with contempt.

This appeared to be true.

Paul recalled the time their father had threatened to whip them with a belt. They were very young, and the family was staying in the mountains by a rushing river. Every summer someone drowned in that river, and the boys were forbidden to go near it alone.

On the first morning Matthew and Paul awoke early. The air was cold and luminous and lay in a thin golden blanket over the sides of rocks and trees like some ethereal, exhilarating snow. Restless and excited, the boys decided to climb the mountain behind the cabin. They had not been expressly forbidden to do this, but they both suspected that their parents would take a dim view of their doing it alone; so they climbed with haste in order to be back before their parents awoke.

But the mountain stretched higher and higher: they never did reach the top. Finally they had to turn around. They knew they would be in trouble by the time they got down.

At the bottom they couldn't find their parents; they circled the cabin, but no one was there. Finally they found their mother wandering in a kind of daze.

"Matthew! Pauli! Where have you been?"

She hugged them to her, while their adventure tumbled out of their mouths.

"But you shouldn't have gone without telling us! Do you know you have been away for over two hours? We had no idea where you were! We thought you had drowned in the river!"

"We wouldn't have gone to the river," Matthew said. "You told us not to go there."

"But we didn't know where you were! We never thought you climbed the mountain! Your father has been frantic."

Matthew frowned. "We didn't do anything bad. You never told us not to climb the mountain."

"Matthew, Matthew—I never told you not to put your head in the oven!"

Their mother went to fetch their father where he was searching for them by the banks of the river.

"We're in for it now," Paul said. They were sitting where their mother had left them.

"We didn't do anything," Matthew insisted, though Paul knew he didn't entirely believe this. Their intentions had been innocent, but two hours was too long.

When their father arrived he looked pale and frightened; the first thing he did was to run to the boys and hug them against his sides.

"I thought you had drowned. I thought you two were gone forever."

"We climbed the mountain, Daddy." Paul could feel his father's hand on his head and smell his familiar odor. He wasn't truly afraid.

Matthew said nothing.

"You foolish boys! You foolish little boys! Don't you know that your mother and I were scared sick?"

"You never told us not to climb the mountain," Matthew said. "We didn't go near any river."

Their father bent down and looked at Matthew, and now his face had set.

"You're foolish, foolish boys! I thought you knew better. You scared your mother sick. You especially, Matthew. You're the oldest, I count on you. You've got to be taught a lesson."

"Don't be too hard, Ed."

"No, they've got to learn a lesson, they've got to grow up!"

And with that he removed his belt from around his waist.

Now, their parents did not believe in corporal punishment. The children had never been spanked, certainly not with a belt. Spanking was a form of ignorant nineteenth-century chastisement that existed in some lurid, vague mythology passed down from their grandmother's distant childhood in Texas. When their father wanted to impress upon them the benighted nature of his own upbringing, he hinted that sometimes he had been punished with a belt.

Their father led them toward the shed, his belt in hand; by the time they arrived he had worked himself into a rage.

"I'm going to teach you a lesson you'll never forget!" he said. "I'm going to give you something for your own good!"

Matthew's face had set, his skin pale and his eyes large and angry; but Paul, though scared, did not believe that their father would hit them. It was an act—he saw that—though for him the act was sufficient punishment.

Paul saw that their father had been scared and was angry because he had been scared, but mostly he was thankful because they were safe and not drowned as he had feared. He had backed himself into a corner with his threats, which he would never be able to carry out, and this made him rant and carry on, which was just a bluff.

He also saw that his brother believed every word their father said: he believed their father was about to whip him.

Their father swung his belt, which cracked against the side of the bench where they had been seated.

"Have you no consideration for others? Don't you know what you did to your mother? I expect more from you, Matthew. You're the oldest." And he struck the bench (not so hard this time) close to where Matthew was sitting. Paul, watching from where he sat, observed that his father took care not to let the belt touch his brother, though Matthew was rigid with fear and outrage.

"You too, Pauli, I expect more of you too!" and he slapped with his belt, much less resolutely, in Paul's general vicinity.

"That's enough," his father abruptly concluded, and Paul could hear the relief in his voice. "I'm not going to spank you any more! But if it ever happens again . . . !" And he raised the belt as if to bring it down resoundingly. "Both of you are docked! Neither of you may leave the cabin until your mother or I am up!"

They came out into the sunlight and Paul could smell the wood chips by the cutting block. He knew that their father was already eager to forget the whole incident. He too was eager to forget. But when he turned to Matthew, his brother was shaking with anger.

"He hit me with the belt!"

"No he didn't—he hit the side of the bench."

"Yes he did!" Matthew insisted. "I'll never forgive him! He hit me with that damn belt!"

5

There was no further talk from Nicole Swann about going to her country house. When Paul saw her in the Quad she seemed distant—cold perhaps, perhaps embarrassed, he couldn't tell which.

"What gives?" he said. "Are you trying to avoid me?"

He had caught her at the end of the day when she was alone.

"I'm sorry, Paul. I've just had so much studying to do. I don't understand the math. We have this incredible test coming and I just feel sick."

Nicole struggled to be a mediocre student. She was a great worrier about grades, a great appreciator of academic success—which she imagined he enjoyed.

"Well, I thought maybe you were trying to avoid me."

"Don't be angry at me."

She looked at him with large, hurt, pleading eyes, like a beautiful Labrador, and his heart moved with a wrench.

"I'm not angry," he said. "I just thought maybe we could see each other."

"I'd like that! I'd really like that a lot! But can't we just wait until this exam is over? I mean, right now I don't seem to be able to concentrate on *anything*."

"Sure," he said, his heart sinking, for he didn't see why the exam should stand in the way of their going to a movie on Saturday night.

"When will it be over?"

"Next Thursday—if I live that long."

"Well, then what do you say about next Saturday—not this one, but the one after?"

"Sure—that'd be great!"

That Saturday he took her to the movies, but though she again allowed him to hold her hand, she seemed self-conscious and restrained.

"Are your parents home?" he asked after they were again walking through the darkened city. She looked at him briefly, and her eyes were dull and blasé and her lip was slightly turned up.

"No."

She said it with indifference, drawing out the *o*: No-wo.

Still, she could have said they were there.

"Should we go to your place?"

"Don't you want a Coke or something?"

"No—I'd rather go to your place."

"Whatever you want."

They didn't speak as they walked back to her building; he was trying to assess what her silence meant.

The apartment was dark when they entered. She switched on the light and came to a halt in the center of the foyer with her back to him.

He came up behind her and instinctively put his hand where her waist met the flare of her hip.

He felt her shiver.

He kissed the side of her neck before she pulled away. "Don't."

"Why not? Don't you like it?"

"Yes, I like it. That's why I say don't. Don't start. We should never have come here."

"Why not?"

"Because I can't see you anymore, Paul."

He frowned heavily, his hand on her; he knew that if he stroked her she wouldn't stop him.

"Why can't you see me?"

"Because I don't like you that way. Don't be angry at me, Paul. I like you very much, only . . . not that way."

"Is there someone else?"

"I can't talk about that."

"Are you trying to tell me you don't like what we do together? That time in the park, for example."

"I like it too much."

"Then why can't we do it again?"

This time she turned to him.

"Don't you understand, Paul? I'm asking you to leave."

She was looking at him now and he winced.

"You're making a mistake," he said.

"Yes, very likely."

"If I leave now, there'll be no coming back."

She looked at him, her eyes determined.

"You're asking me to leave?"

"Yes, please."

He turned abruptly and departed.

Downstairs he stopped in anger and confusion. And as he stared into the shadows of the park across the street, he swore that no matter what the cost, he would never speak to Nicole Swann again.

Paul Werth's slump hadn't gotten better. Now he stood at the plate in the seventh inning and prayed to get on base.

The count was full but Paul was afraid to swing. He was afraid to strike out and have to turn around and walk back to the dugout without getting on base again.

Then the pitch came and he didn't even watch it properly. He braced himself for the strike. "Ball four," the umpire called.

Paul felt a wave of elation. He threw his bat to the sideline and ran to first base; it was the first time he had been on base in three games.

The pitcher started his windup—and then fired over to first. But Paul was ahead of him, his hand safe on the bag as the first baseman dusted him.

Paul stood up and laughed. Oh, what fun!

He watched the pitcher go into his routine: his leg went up too high. Paul knew it would be easy to steal, he knew he could beat the catcher's throw.

Again the pitcher had the ball. He looked at Paul and Paul leaned toward first; then the pitcher went into his windup, and then his leg came up, and then Paul was gone. He didn't wait to see what else would happen, his head was down and he was digging for second base.

He dove headfirst and came in under the second baseman and he was lying across second when he felt the slap across his legs. Safe by a mile!

Paul stood up and dusted himself off, and he could see the Highgate crowd jumping up and down and his teammates shouting from the sidelines. He had made it! He was in scoring position.

Then Boom-Boom flied out.

Now there were two outs and Bower was up. The pitcher went into his windup and he wasn't watching

Paul. Then the ball was released, and Bower took the first pitch for a strike.

Paul knew he could steal. The pitcher was acting as if there was no one on base. Again he wound up, again his leg went up, again he released—and this time it was a ball.

Paul tagged up and then moved farther away from the base. He had gotten so excited that he couldn't think properly.

The pitcher wound up, his leg went up—and Paul was off. He streaked toward third, his head down. But he was aware of the plate; the ball arrived faster than he anticipated. Then the catcher was up, his mask off, his arm cocked to throw. With a burst Paul tore for the base, he dove straight in for the baseman, colliding, and he felt his hand hit the base just before the baseman whacked him with his glove.

"Out!" he heard the third-base umpire yell.

He wasn't out, he was safe by a hair.

Paul stood up and dusted himself off. He felt dazed.

The umpire was standing on the infield side of the base; he couldn't see that Paul's hand had just beaten the throw.

Paul looked around, and he saw his teammates taking the field, heads down. Keith Firman was looking at him reproachfully. He had made the third out. Stealing third, he had made the third out.

"What were you doing trying to steal third base with two outs?" Scotty asked him in the dugout. "The third out should never be at third base, son—don't you know that? That's one of the cardinal rules of baseball."

He spoke in sadness rather than anger, shaking his head—and of course he was right. There was no excuse for what Paul had done. It made no difference that he *had* been safe.

From playing bad ball he was now playing stupid ball.

"Hey, Whitey," Berger called between classes, "what'd you get for number seven on the physics homework?"

Berger had a habit of guffawing and covering his mouth with his hand and looking out from under his brow with dark, roguish eyes, but he made his voice go tough when he spoke to Whitey.

"Seven?" Whitey said, blinking and smiling and looking hesitantly at Berger.

"Yeah, seven—that's what I said."

"Well, I don't know—I'm really not sure that I . . ."

"Don't give me that shit, Whitey. Just give me the answer."

"Not so fast," Richards intervened from across the corridor, "what do you want to know?"

Berger immediately began to shrug and smile.

"Gee, boss, I just wanted the answer to number seven. It's no big deal, I just wanted to see what Whitey got."

"Oh, yeah? You afraid maybe he got it wrong? Is that it?"

"I just wanted to see how he did it. It's no big deal."

"Yeah, I bet. Listen, hotshot—you want to see the answer, you pay for the answer."

"Sure, that's no problem. Whaddaya want, Whitey—a nickel? Here, catch!" And fishing a nickel from his pocket, he flipped it at Farrino. Whitey made no effort to catch the coin, which landed on the floor and bounced under the radiator.

"Come on, Berger," Richards said, "get real. Whitey's not going to sell you his brains for a nickel. It's a dollar an answer, jockstrap. Let's see the color of your money."

"Gee, Philip," Berger whined, "that's real cool. I mean, making me pay a dollar like that—that's just great."

"Yeah? Well, I'm giving you a discount, shithead. You keep complaining and the price goes up—isn't that right, Whitey?"

Whitey smiled and blushed and tried not to look at Berger.

"Okay, okay," Berger said, disgruntled. "Here's your dollar!" And without looking at Whitey he gave Farrino a crumpled dollar bill.

"Not like that, *paesano*—smooth out the dollar bill."

"Aw, c'mon, Philip!"

"Smooth the dollar bill!"

Later when they were standing alone in the Quad, Richards said to Paul, "Do you know what I've been thinking? If we can get an insect like Berger to pay a dollar for Whitey's answers, we can probably get others to pay as well. What do you think?"

"I dunno," Paul said. "It sounds a little nuts to me."

"No, really—what do you think we could charge? Two bucks a set? Five bucks?"

Paul laughed. "I have no idea, Philip."

It took Paul some time to realize that Richards had set this scam into motion: he was selling Whitey's answers to the math and physics homework for one dollar an answer or five dollars the set. Whitey refused to take any of the money, though Richards set aside a third for him—"in escrow," as he scrupulously explained.

"What if you get caught?" Paul asked Philip, but Richards only laughed.

"Why should I get caught, *bambino?* Who's interested in hurting a nice guy like me? Besides, I'm not stupid, I exercise some caution, I don't sell my goods to just anyone!" And he smiled complacently.

Laura Kinski showed Paul around her apartment. Cavernous and empty, it possessed a peculiar odor that he could not identify but which was compounded of coffee and dust and empty space, like some immense familial urn. Her father, she informed him, was a psychiatrist.

Laura herself smelled of perfume, which impregnated everything about her, her sweater her coat her hair, as if she radiated a kind of nimbus of perfume. Paul had little experience with perfume.

Slender and elegant, Laura was tall with small, shapely breasts. Her wrists were slender and her fingers tapered, moving nervously with delicate energy as if she were playing the harpsichord. She had a long neck, and when Paul watched the smooth ripple where her Adam's apple should be, he wanted to touch it. There seemed always to be an ironic, amused edge to Laura's voice, and he couldn't be certain she wasn't laughing at him.

Laura had straight, dark hair cut off at an angle just below her ears. She had large, almond-shaped eyes, a fine, straight, rather prominent nose, and a small, puckered mouth. Her skin was white and flawless and Paul realized to his considerable unease that he had been thinking about licking it, the way he might lick an ice-cream cone.

Her room was surprisingly small for such a large apartment. Bookcases and records lined the walls. A large and rather jolly drawing showing two topless women doing the cancan adorned the space above her bed, and from outside the window came the sound of pigeons.

Laura threw herself onto her bed, where she propped herself on one elbow and studied him at her leisure.

"Well, how do you like it?" she asked. "The apartment, I mean."

"It's large!"

She laughed easily. "Is it? I'm used to it, I guess."

"Where are your parents?"

She scowled slightly. "How should I know. Daddy's in his office, I suppose, seeing some weirdo. God only knows where Mommy is. Half this place could burn down before they'd notice."

"Whose room is that other one?"

"That's Feifer's, my brother."

"Feifer?"

"Yeah. Weird, isn't it? It's some sort of family name. Feifer's real smart but a goofball. He goes to McBurney. Feifer got into some kind of trouble once and my uncle went and spoke to the cops and my parents never even knew."

"What are all those pigeons up to?"

The cooing had persisted in a low, continuous tumult outside.

"Those aren't pigeons," she said, swinging her feet off the bed. "Those are *damned* pigeons. They eat all the food. Here, take a look." And she raised the shade to reveal a bird feeder.

The pigeons scattered grudgingly into the air.

"Do you like birds?" she asked.

"I don't know. I've never thought about it."

"A surprising number of birds pass through—finches, orioles, grosbeaks, even tanagers—but mostly I just get pigeons."

"You mean *damned* pigeons."

"Yes, precisely!" And they both laughed.

"What are we going to do about Hardy?" he asked.

"Oh, to hell with Hardy! I'd rather read Colette!"

"I've never read a word of Colette."

"That's because you're a boy!" And again she laughed. He liked that she laughed so easily.

"I read all the Colette I can get my hands on," she said. "Only I can't read it in French—the vocabulary is too hard."

"Is your French that good?"

"Oh, my French is awful! But I don't care! Someday I'm going to live in France and learn French like a native. I'll take a French lover and learn from him! Don't you think the French are cool?"

"I dunno," he said. It was easy to see her charm.

"The French aren't all uptight the way Americans are. Don't you think Americans are uptight?"

"I dunno," he repeated. "Very likely. But then I'm an American."

He examined the objects on the top of her bureau:

powder, vials of perfume, a lipstick, carmine in color (he opened and closed it, rather daringly), an old showbill from *West Side Story*, a polished good-luck stone, a volume of *Les fleurs du mal* in French, a stuffed-animal bunny. He proceeded to examine her collection of records.

"What's all this music? I don't know anything about jazz."

She looked at him, sizing him up.

"Oh yeah? Well, it's high time you got with it, kiddo!" And she snapped her fingers at him as if in time to music.

"Here, listen to this."

Bending down, she selected a record.

"Listen!"

They were silent while the record spun and then the music began to play.

"Wow!" he said after a while, "What is that?"

"You like it?"

"Yeah—really!"

"It's Coltrane. You ever heard of him?"

"Yeah, I guess so, but I've never heard him before. Play something else."

She played Miles Davis, and then Dave Brubeck, and it seemed the perfect music for her, sophisticated and syncopated.

After that Paul would go to Laura's apartment after school or on weekends and she would play jazz records and they would lie parallel to each other on her bed and listen to Ella Fitzgerald and Charlie Parker and Benny Goodman and Chet Baker and Duke Ellington.

Sometimes they would eat hamburgers at the corner counter or at Prexy's, where she ordered him pound cake with a dollop of ice cream and hot chocolate sauce; or they went to galleries to look at Atget or Cartier-Bresson, or attended the Lutheran church where the choir sang Bach cantatas. Once they ventured uptown to hear Ray Charles in the old Olympia Theater, run down but still elegant as an old Southern belle.

Under her influence he took to listening to Miles Davis and Thelonious Monk while he sat at home in his chair by the window reading instead of doing homework.

She did not mind his long silences, she remained unfazed by his superior airs—a kind of sophisticated older sister, he thought, eager to share her knowledge and enthusiasms. In exchange he told her about the books he was reading; and though he wasn't always certain she read what he recommended, when she did comment on something it was always smart.

But days could pass without Paul's seeing Laura in school; often when he wished to speak with her he couldn't find her.

"Where have you been?" he'd asked. "I haven't seen you around in ages."

"Oh, I've had appointments! My calendar is booked."

"What are you talking about?"

"I play hooky, kiddo—don't you?"

He laughed. "No, Laura—I don't have the guts. Who signs your absent slips?"

"I sign them. I sign my mother's name."

"So what's on your heavy schedule? What did you do yesterday?"

"I went to *La Dolce Vita*. Have you seen it? It's fantastic!"

"I'd love to see it."

"Well, you should play hooky too! Haven't I explained to you my First Theorem of Hooky?"

"No, what's your theorem of hooky?"

"Oh, it's very simple. Ordinarily one sleeps through physics on Monday, through English on Tuesday, through math on Wednesday, and through history on Thursday. But the First Theorem revolutionizes all that. I sleep through nothing on Monday, Tuesday, Wednesday, Thursday—but Friday I take off. You see? That way I don't sleep through any of my classes—and I get a day off, so everyone gains."

In April, Laura took Paul downtown to the Village: it was spring now and the warmth of the sun caught the buds along the branches while the sounds of motors came heightened in the thin air. Laura was dressed in black, with a black turtleneck sweater; and with her eyes made up and with her black leather jacket slung over her arm, she looked like a young Anouk Aimée out for a stroll.

"I don't want to live in this city when I grow up," she announced. "I want to travel all over the world and see all the different countries and never be trapped like my parents."

"You could join the Merchant Marines."

"Yes, I'd like that! Why do men have all the luck? No one thinks it's crazy if you say you want to join the Merchant Marines, but if I said it, it would be a big joke—or worse."

"Well, that's the way it is."

"Well, it isn't fair! I'll be a short-order cook on a ship

and I'll be the only woman on board!" And she laughed with delight.

"Have you been to Europe?"

"Oh, oodles of times with my parents—but that doesn't count. All they do is go to expensive hotels and sit by the pool or go shopping and out to dinner at fancy restaurants where everyone speaks English. I don't call that Europe."

"I've never been at all."

"We'll go together—okay? Is it a date?"

He laughed at her enthusiasm.

"Sure, why not?"

"Good! It's a date, then. When we're—let's see, when we're twenty. Okay? You'd better watch out, because I'll hold you to it, kiddo!"

"Okay," he said, "it's a date."

He was happy with her. He saw men eye her as they passed. And he couldn't get over the fact that he and Laura Kinski had become friends.

"Tell me about your mother."

"Oh, my mother! You wouldn't be interested in her. My mother has her hair done in the afternoon and she has her first martini when she comes home at five. Then she comes into my room and starts screaming at me. Then she opens my closet and throws all my clothes on the floor. Then she goes into her room and slams the door."

"Why does she throw your clothes on the floor?"

"Because I'm a thankless little bitch who doesn't know all the sacrifices she's made, that's why. Ooh, I hate her! I'm never going to get married!"

"I thought all girls wanted to get married."

一
132

"God, that's a stupid thing to say! Boys do say the stupidest things!" And she slapped at his arm to indicate her displeasure.

They sat in a great patch of sunlight and watched the crowd of students and winos and hustlers that bobbed about them. Kids passed on bicycles and roller skates; across the way men sat playing chess.

"I think beatniks are so *cool!*" she said. "They're the only cool people in America. If I ever do live here I'm going to live in the Village and be part of the scene and stay up till three every night!"

"I thought you told me you can't stay awake past eleven."

"Well, I can't. But it would be different if I lived in the Village. Boredom puts me to sleep. Sometimes I swear boredom is killing me. But if I lived in the Village I'd never get bored. I'd only know artists and poets and they'd write me poetry and paint pictures of me lying naked on my couch!" And she laughed naughtily.

"Are you serious?"

"Sure—why not? I don't care about any of that!" And she tossed her head.

"You're a wild girl, Laura!"

"Yes—that's what I want to be," she said defiantly. "I don't want to be like everyone else!"

They wandered through the side streets and looked at the little shops and restaurants and she pointed out the small houses and brownstones she favored while they discussed what it would be like to live there as if cohabitation were a real possibility.

"I can't stand prejudice," she said. "I think it's so sad! I mean, people who don't like Negroes or homosexuals or anyone who's a little different. What I want to know is, what's so great about the same? I've been living with the same for eighteen years and in my opinion it stinks!"

She took him to a bar where she thought they might negotiate a drink. They sat in the darkest booth and they agreed that she would do the ordering since she was older by a year and looked older than he.

"You look like a baby." She laughed, and she put her hand on his.

"I tell you what," she continued, "you go to the bathroom so the bartender doesn't see you, and I'll order for us both."

He did as he was told, and when he returned there were two glasses of white wine on the table.

He felt pleased being there with Laura Kinski. She puzzled him, he couldn't square what he knew of her with her reputation, but he liked her.

Much later he was telling her about his ambition to become a writer. He had never confessed this to anyone before, but with his head fuzzy with two glasses of wine, he was ready for any foolishness. Laura watched him with her chin resting in one hand and her elbow on the table, her sleeve drawn back to reveal her slender forearm.

"My dad hoped I would be a writer," he explained.

Her face darkened and she reached out to him spontaneously.

"I'm so sorry about your dad. That must have been terrible."

He swallowed. He hadn't anticipated mentioning his father, and he feared he had done so to gain her sympathy. The reference to his father sobered him.

"You don't like to talk about it, do you?"

"No, not really."

"But maybe you'll talk to me about it sometime. Not now, but sometime when you feel like it. I'd really like that."

"Yeah, Laura—maybe."

"Well, I think it's neat that you want to be a writer," she said, and her eyes rested on him in a new fashion.

"What do *you* want to do?"

"Oh, what's there for a girl to do? I guess I want to be a *femme fatale.*"

He laughed.

"Oh, you're that already!"

"Well, what's wrong with being a *femme fatale?*" A note of petulance had crept into her voice. "I can't stand this double standard! Aren't girls flesh and blood too?"

"Actually you're not a *femme fatale,*" he said. "Maybe I thought you were at first, but that's not who you are."

She looked at him, and then suddenly she covered her face and he thought she was crying.

"What's wrong?" he asked in consternation.

"Oh, I don't know. It's all so meaningless. It's all so stupid."

"What is? What's so meaningless and stupid?"

"Oh—everything. Life. It doesn't have any meaning."

He was astounded by this. He had never seen this side of Laura before.

"But why do you say that?" he asked in genuine concern, deeply shaken.

"Because it's true."

"No it's not. Don't say that! It's not true!" He wanted to dissuade her but he didn't know how.

She dried her eyes and smiled. "You're very sweet," she said, "but of course it's true. Only Thelonious isn't meaningless."

When it was time to call the starters before the next game, Paul's name wasn't called. Paul had known this would come, but it cut him anyway.

He went and sat on the bench along the sideline and hung his head between his legs.

So this was failure! He felt publicly humiliated. He wanted to get up and leave but he knew he couldn't; he would have to stick it out where he was.

"Hey, Werth," Firman called, "can you look after the water? I've gotta go inside and get something."

Paul looked at Keith but he didn't say anything. The taste in his mouth was bitter.

"I heard you got high at Kinski's party," someone said after physics class. Paul turned in annoyance.

"Where'd you get that?"

"Well, jeez, Werth! Don't get on your high horse. It's just the word, that's all."

And it was. Soon Paul heard it elsewhere as well: there had been drugs at Kinski's. Richards had been pushing drugs.

To Paul it was preposterous. He had been with Philip and there had been no drugs.

He discussed the rumor with Laura, who didn't seem eager to be drawn into the conversation. "I wouldn't allow drugs at my place," was all she would say. "I already have enough trouble with Feifer."

"But they say Philip was pushing drugs."

"So what?"

"I mean, that's preposterous. I was with Philip."

"What makes you so keen on Richards?"

"Come on, Laura. He's my friend!"

She merely shrugged.

"I wouldn't be so keen on him if I were you."

But it wasn't a question of being keen. Paul flattered himself he could take Philip's measure. It was a question of intuition. Richards was too smart to push drugs: an occasional reefer in his own room, sure; but selling drugs was stupid. Hillman, yes maybe. Hillman was wild and might pull any idiot stunt. But Philip was too smart.

"Weren't you at that party?" Craig Lewis asked him.

"Yes," Paul said. "I was at the party." They were standing in the corridor by the lockers, and the rumor had already transmogrified into another school brouhaha.

"Did you see any drugs?"

"No—I didn't see any drugs."

"Nowhere? Not any?"

"No, Craig—nowhere, not any. I'm sorry to disappoint you."

Lewis stuck out his lower lip and shrugged; he intended to pursue the matter until he discovered a culprit.

Paul put the topic out of his mind, but later Jeb said to him, "I'm worried about Berger and this drug business."

"Berger? Do you think he's involved?"

"I don't know. That's what Craig suggested. He said he was going to clean out the whole nest of vipers."

"That's really cool," Paul said in disgust. To his mind they were all equally unsavory.

"I don't like to see anyone get in trouble," Jeb said. "I know you don't like Berger, but we've known him a long time."

"It has nothing to do with me one way or the other. I'm sure the football squad is at the bottom of this."

"Perhaps—but Berger would make a much easier target."

Paul considered that for a moment, not without some grudging respect for Jeb's insight.

"You mean the faculty wouldn't want to touch the football team."

"Something like that. Not if they had a victim as easy as Berger to throw to the wolves."

"Well—let them throw him. He serves himself up with an apple in his mouth."

"But what about Philip?"

Paul frowned. "What *about* Philip?"

"I dunno," Jeb said, and he looked at Paul carefully. "The two of them are awfully tight."

"Don't be stupid," Paul said with annoyance. "Philip's too smart to get himself wrapped up with drugs. Don't you remember what he said—that only a dumb son of a bitch would sell drugs?"

"Yeah—that's right," Jeb said. "That's a relief, because I have a feeling that Craig or someone is gunning for Berger."

. . .

"Can I talk to you?" Paul asked Richards.

They were in the Quad and Richards was discussing something with Berger.

"Sure! Anytime, *bambino!*" Philip exclaimed, spreading his arms and smiling.

Paul glanced at Berger, who smirked and guffawed with his hand before his mouth and offered a kind of officious bow.

"Here, Berger," Philip said, "get lost. Werth and I want to have a word."

Paul watched Berger sidle away with hands in his pocket and he experienced a moment of foreboding.

"What do you see in that clown?"

"Berger? He amuses me. Everyone can't be as serious as you, Werth. The whole goddamn globe would sink. So tell me, *bambino.* What's on your mind?"

"Remember Laura Kinski's party?"

"Of course. How could I forget Laura Kinski's party?"

"Where did you disappear to that night, anyway? I kind of thought we were going to stick together."

"Oh, I'm sorry, *caro!* Did I leave you in the lurch? The truth is I felt lousy and went home early. Are you pissed with me?"

"No—of course not. But have you heard this stuff about drugs?"

"Yeah, I've heard. So what? What's that have to do with us?"

Paul looked at his friend, and Philip's eyes were blue and perfectly clear.

"They say you were selling drugs."

"Me? Who says that? They're full of crap! You don't believe that, do you?"

"Of course not."

"Pushing drugs is for suckers. I mean, Christ, just because a guy has a joint once in a while . . . Besides, you were the only one who saw me smoking that night."

"It has nothing to do with that," Paul said.

"I mean, you wouldn't rat on me about *that*, would you?"

"Don't be stupid."

"So what's the big deal? Let people say what they want."

"I've been telling people it's all nonsense."

"Is that right? Whom have you been telling that to, Werth? What's going on?"

"That's what I'm trying to tell you. Craig Lewis tells me the Bates committee has evidence—thinks it has evidence—that you were selling drugs at Laura's."

"They're full of shit. All I had was one joint at my place, and the only person who knows about that is you. So who's been telling what to whom?" Richards' eyes glittered strangely. "What have you been telling Lewis, anyway?"

"I didn't tell him anything. I told him you weren't selling drugs."

"Did you tell him about the reefer?"

"Of course not, Philip. What do you take me for?"

Richards scrutinized Werth closely. Then, throwing out his arms in a gesture of embrace, he smiled.

"So what's all the fuss? Tell Bates and his committee to shove it!"

Paul knew that Philip was telling the truth, but the entire transaction unsettled him anyway. He didn't like the fact that he had come to warn Philip, yet Philip had somehow turned the tables until Richards was all but accusing *him*. That was preposterous! Yet why did he feel guilty, as if he had done something wrong? He hadn't betrayed Philip—and he never would!

Nonetheless, Paul wasn't surprised when he was summoned to testify before the Bates committee; somehow he had been expecting it. The notice was delivered that Thursday asking him to appear on Monday. He crumpled the paper and shoved it into his pocket.

He didn't want his mother to know anything about this.

Paul didn't tell anyone about the notice—except Laura. She had already testified before the committee and he wanted to hear how it had gone; but he also knew she would be sympathetic.

"Poor you!" she said, reaching out and touching him impulsively.

"It's no big deal. I have nothing to hide. Besides, Miss English is on that committee—and she loves me."

"It'll be over before you know it. Still, it's a pain. Bates is a pain."

"That's for sure. Did I ever tell you he once made me cut my hair?"

"No—you're kidding!"

"Nope—he said it was too long."

"What a creep!"

"And Mrs. Wagner is on the committee and she can't stand me."

"So now they're on your case! Well, that's what you get for hanging out with me!"

"Don't be silly. It has nothing to do with you."

"Listen, there's some stupid party tonight—do you want to go? I mean, maybe it would take your mind off things. We don't have to stay very long."

"Sure," he said. "That'll be great."

It was the first time he had danced with Laura, and she was light in his arms and graceful. While they danced she placed her hand on the back of his neck.

He could hear the noise from the jock crowd in the farther room, and once or twice Pursy came to the door and peered at them dancing, but Paul paid no attention.

"Do you want to leave?" she asked.

"Why?"

"Because of that noise. Because of those fools. They're probably getting drunk."

"They're the ones Bates should be talking to. I thought they were your friends." He tried to sound facetious, but there was an edge to his voice.

"Why do you say that?" He felt her go stiff in his arms.

"I don't know. It's just what people say."

"People are idiots!" was all she said.

Later when he went to get her a Coke he passed couples dancing in the living room, and, pausing in the half-light, he saw Nicole Swann. She was standing close to her partner while the slow, syrupy music pulsed in the background. Paul turned away abruptly before she saw him.

"Maybe we should leave," he said to Laura.

He watched as she drank her Coke, her head back, her long neck working in graceful swallowing rhythms; and he suddenly realized how much he liked her. How bizarre! She was really his best friend.

"Has anyone seen Nicole Swann?"

It was Keith Firman, chunky and slightly shorter than Paul, his round, nice-looking face frowning in preoccupation.

"I saw her a while ago," Laura said, studying Keith with amusement.

"She asked me to take her home at twelve." Firman was talking to himself while he scowled about the room. "She doesn't want to stay too late."

Paul could feel the hostility radiate from Firman.

"I saw her dancing in the other room," Paul said.

"Where?"

"In the other room." Paul shrugged and turned away.

"What's eating *him*?" Laura laughed, but Paul wasn't listening.

How could Nicole prefer someone else? It was preposterous! And he recalled the feel of her through her dress when he had put his hand on her in her foyer.

"Don't."

"Why not? Don't you like it?"

"Yes, I like it. . . . We should never have come here. . . . I can't see you anymore, Paul."

"Why can't you see me?"

"Because I don't like you that way. Don't be angry at me . . ."

"Is there someone else?"

"Don't you understand, Paul? I'm asking you to leave."

"You're making a mistake."

"Yes, very likely."

"If I leave now, there'll be no coming back."

"Well, do you?"

"What?" It was Laura Kinski, and she had been talking to him.

"Do you want to leave now?"

"Yes, sure."

"Good. What are you thinking about so hard?"

"Me? Nothing."

Again she touched him, letting her hand rest lightly on his forearm.

"It's okay," she said.

"What?"

"Nothing."

They came out into the night and he could feel the spring in the high wind. Suddenly he wanted to be alone with Laura.

"Where should we go?"

"Follow me!"

They hurried along the darkened streets, shadowed now with leaves, and as she pressed against him, he smelled the perfume of her sweater. It was pitch dark when they climbed the small stone wall into the Kaiser estate.

It was cold in the park and the earth felt damp underfoot. He walked with care, following one of the paths that led to the gazebo. Laura trailed close behind, and he could hear her laughter, low and excited.

She sat next to him in the gazebo. When he reached for her she came to him instantly. He kissed her, undoing her clothing, until his hands had found her beautiful young woman's breasts.

"Oh, Paul!"

He kept kissing her in the darkness as if he would never stop, and his only regret was that his eyes could not find her too.

Finally she pulled away, gently.

She leaned her head against his shoulder while she rearranged her blouse and sweater.

"Do you care for me?"

He was startled by the sound of her voice; it took him a moment to come back to himself.

"Of course I care for you. You know how much I care for you."

"No, I don't."

It was only a whisper.

"What?" His voice was louder than he intended—almost harsh. His eyes had adjusted now and he could make out her form against the surrounding darkness.

"Nothing."

He moved uneasily. Why did life have to be like this, complex and confused and unsatisfactory?

He was still thinking of Nicole Swann.

"We'd better go," he said after a while. "These people could show up at any time."

Lucius Bates, Harriet English, and Eva Wagner faced the room like three derby hats set on a ledge. Paul Werth took his place before them, and through the large windows behind their backs he could see the world outside edging slowly toward summer like a great ocean liner pointing toward sea.

After some perfunctory greeting Lucius Bates cleared his throat and called the meeting to order.

"As you know, Mr. Werth, this committee is conducting inquiries into the question of drug usage by students at Highgate. Our investigation has come to center on what happened on the night of Laura Kinski's party. We understand that you were present at the party and may be in a position to help us. Needless to say, we can't force you to divulge anything, but anything you do say will be held in the strictest confidence."

Mr. Bates paused to look at Paul. Bates was a thin, dry man with refined features and a cultivated, ironic voice, and everything about him suggested prissy condescension and censorial superiority.

Paul hated being called before this committee. He had nothing to do with drugs. He hated the thought that word of this interview might get back to his mother. He also hated the suggestion that he might rat on one of his classmates. Now he spoke softly but evenly.

"I have nothing to say."

Mr. Bates smiled faintly, as if a student had offered a particularly fatuous response in class.

"You were at the party, weren't you?"

"Yes."

The three adults were scrutinizing Paul carefully. Mr. Bates and Miss English both appeared dry and parsimonious and seemed to Paul to smell of gray chalk and dust; Mrs. Wagner emitted her hearty, habitual Rabelaisian energy, a kind of amused, indifferent bonhomie barely contained within the wool tailoring of her tweed suit.

"How long were you at the party?" Mrs. Wagner inquired.

"Till twelve, maybe."

"Did you see any droogs?"

"No, I didn't. Not personally."

"Not personally?"

"I didn't see any drugs."

Miss English leaned forward and interrupted; she had been regarding Paul with subdued concern.

"You understand, Paul, that no one here is accusing you of anything. No one here believes you had anything to do with drugs."

Mrs. Wagner looked at her colleague with amusement.

"No," she said, "nor that you did *not*. To date this committee believes nutink."

Mr. Bates drew himself up as if to intervene in an unseemly dispute.

"Let me see if I can set the record straight," he said dryly. "Paul, your position in this school is well known to us. Both my colleagues have you in their classroom, I had the good fortune to have your brother in my advanced tutorial, and I presume I will have the pleasure of having you when you are a senior. Nonetheless, certain allegations have reached us, not, to be sure, concerning you directly, but concerning students with whom you are said to consort; and it is our duty to investigate these allegations."

Bates had been gaining emphasis as he spoke; now he

was leaning forward across the desk examining Paul sternly.

"Respectfully, sir—I don't know what you are talking about."

The room emitted a kind of sigh of silence, drawing back into itself, and Paul became aware of the rippling distortion of the light coming through the windowpanes, and, outside, the great blank explosion of sun bathing all in its brassy, equitable glow.

He had begun to perspire in the heat.

"Paul," Miss English said, and her voice was full of accommodation, "I regret that this conversation has gotten off on the wrong foot. Let me repeat that no one is accusing you of anything. Nor would it be proper at this point to mention other names. But the fact remains that your name has cropped up in conjunction with a number of students—and with one young man in particular—who have incurred some serious accusations concerning drugs. It is our responsibility to look into this. May I ask you please, for your own sake as well as ours, to treat this matter with the care it deserves?"

Paul could see that Miss English was regarding him kindly, but it galled him that these three with their know-it-all airs should be questioning him so haughtily.

"If you mean Philip Richards," he blurted out, "you are barking up the wrong tree."

The three adults grew very quiet.

Paul saw that Mr. Bates was peering at him attentively over his glasses and that Mrs. Wagner had drawn herself up and was knitting her brows furiously like a painted Indian on a barber pole.

"What do you mean by that?" Mr. Bates asked in a measured, judicious tone. "Is there something you know of which this committee should be informed?"

Paul regretted he had spoken, though their attitude still infuriated him.

"I don't know anything," he said, "except that Richards had nothing to do with drugs."

"How do you know that?"

"I just know it. I know he had nothing to do with drugs at Laura Kinski's party."

"Can you tell us why you are so certain?"

"Because I was with him."

"You were with him that evening?"

"Yes."

"You were with him *all* evening?"

"Yes . . . yes, I was." Paul realized he had gone too far but he didn't know how to stop himself. He was scowling, and he could feel the slick of perspiration under his arms.

Mr. Bates settled back quietly in his chair.

"Let's see if I've got this right. You're telling me you spent the entire evening with Philip Richards."

"Yes, I am."

"And that at no time did Richards use or sell drugs."

"That's right," Paul said, and the blood pounded in his ears.

"And that's your statement before this committee?"

"Yes, it is." But he had run out of steam. Already his stomach was beginning to churn. Mrs. Wagner was looking at him sardonically.

Again there was a long silence, and Paul was vividly aware of the reek of his own perspiration. Blond, pleasant light fluttered from the window.

"Do you have anything else to add to your statement?" Mr. Bates inquired, and Paul thought he sounded tired.

"No."

"Then we have no further questions at this time."

Paul pushed his chair back; Mr. Bates seemed to be watching him closely.

"We may have other questions for you at another time," he added.

Paul merely nodded. He was sickened by the stench of his own body. Quitting the room, he felt he was going to stumble; and as the door closed behind him, he thought he heard animated conversation. But he didn't stay to listen. Trembling, he hurried away.

6

Paul's father had his second heart attack in the kitchen while he was looking out at the gray of the early dawn. The pain caused him to double over. He grasped the corner of the sink, where he crouched under the bite of the attack, watching in a kind of dull fixation the *drip drip* of the faucet, which he had been intending to fix.

Later Paul's mother would say, bitterly, that it was a New Year's present.

It was January then in Paul's sophomore year, and bitterly cold. The emergency team took his father to St. Luke's, the closest hospital; Paul watched in incomprehension as they strapped him into the gurney and wheeled him down the front path and into the ambulance.

The doctors assured them that the attack had been

mild. There was no cause for Matthew to hurry home from Cambridge. Paul returned to school, the routine of the previous hospital sojourn commenced again.

Two weeks later his father died of a massive cardiac infarction.

As a child, Paul would wake in the night frozen by some undefined menace. He would hoist himself out of bed, his feet touching the coldness of the floor, and grope his way through the blackness of the house toward his parents' room. Finally he would see his parents, two sleeping mounds of safety, and, with a lightening of the heart, he would slip in almost unnoticed beside his father.

For a short time when he was seven or eight he experienced an understanding of death so clairvoyant that it resembled immersion in icy water. The experience stunned him, depriving him of his sense of self. He tried to talk about this with his father.

"What is death, Daddy?"

"Death? Why, I don't think you have to worry about that right now, Pauli."

He was sitting on his father's lap, his father's strong arms about him.

"But, Daddy—just to stop living! What does that mean?"

"You don't have to worry about it," his father repeated. "I promise you. You won't die for years and years. You can put it out of your mind."

Even then he knew his father was wrong, he couldn't just put death out of his mind, but it comforted him nonetheless to sit on his father's lap and listen to his low, reassuring voice.

Then his intuition of death began to fade. One day it was less intense, then it was just a phrase, finally it was no more than a formula. Death became what it was to remain for many years—just a word.

Susan Koch had entered Paul's class in fifth grade. The teacher, Mrs. White, assembled the students prior to Susan's arrival and lectured them about their behavior. Susan was not to be stared at. Susan was not to be teased. Susan was a normal child, only she suffered from a disability. Susan had to be in a wheelchair. Susan had muscular dystrophy.

It was a privilege, Mrs. White told them, to have Susan in their class. Susan wasn't on trial, *they* were. They had been chosen because it was believed that they were *mature* enough for Susan. Mrs. White was proud that they had been chosen, and she wanted to ensure that they lived up to this honor.

Susan didn't arrive the next week and she didn't arrive the week after that and nobody said anything more about her or about the honor of having her in class. Then, one Wednesday, Danny said to Paul, "The new girl is in the principal's office."

"What new girl?"

"The girl Mrs. White told us about. The one in the wheelchair."

"Oh, *that* girl. How do you know she's in the principal's office?"

" 'Cause I saw her. I saw her being wheeled in. She looks kinda weird."

Paul shrugged, and that was the extent of their conversation about the new girl. Paul expected she would show up in her wheelchair, but she didn't. Not that afternoon.

But the next morning when they were at their desks for math, Mrs. White said, "Children, we have a new member of the class joining us today. It's Susan Koch, the girl I told you about the other week. I'm very proud and pleased that Susan is joining us and I know you are all going to be very nice to her. Now I'd like to ask Paul if he would go down to Mr. Dudd's office and accompany Susan to the class."

Paul rose from his chair. He sensed the other children's eyes on him and felt a flush of pleasure that he had been selected to accompany Susan to the classroom. He was also thrilled to miss some of math. He sauntered out of the room with his head up.

He didn't know why Mrs. White had chosen him to accompany Susan, but he could guess. He had a difficult relationship with Mrs. White, who was new that year and was young and pretty, with fresh, even features and (he hardly knew how to think this) a "full figure." Mrs. White and he had started as friends but had ended in a kind of standoff of mutual misunderstanding and distrust.

Mrs. White was forever telling Paul not to stare out the window during class. Then Paul fell behind in arithmetic. Then Paul punched Dicky Stooks in the belly and knocked him onto the ground. Dicky Stooks, who had red hair and freckles and was the most obnoxious kid in the class, had it coming, not only because he cut in front of Paul in line but because he was a creepy, disgusting kid and Paul had knocked him down in every grade since prekindergarten. It was only a wonder that so much time had elapsed this year before he knocked him down again.

But Mrs. White didn't see it that way. When she had come into the class, all the kids were sitting politely in their chairs except for Dicky Stooks, who was writhing on the floor. Mrs. White's face went white and she rushed to Dicky, who was crying like a baby.

"Who did this?" she demanded. "Who did this to Dicky."

For a moment no one moved. Then Paul stood up. He was proud of himself for standing up, for, like George Washington, he could not tell a lie, and he was also proud for having laid Dicky low with a single blow, a well-considered punch to the solar plexus, which, in his experience, was the quickest way to take out an opponent. He wondered whether Mrs. White would consider him manly.

But apparently that wasn't the effect on Mrs. White. Furious, she sent Paul to the principal's office—a distinction he rarely achieved.

However, Mrs. White soon discovered that it wasn't all fun and games being on the outs with Paul, since a significant section of the class looked to him for leadership. In an act of appeasement she asked Paul to fetch her coffee for her from the kitchen, a token gesture which Paul repaid by spitting in the cup when he was alone in the corridor. Since then there had been an uneasy standoff between them.

Now, as he approached the principal's office, Paul ran his finger along the wall, stopping at the water cooler for a drink and at the door to the fourth-grade classroom to peer in. He took as long as he could in order to miss as much of math as possible.

When he turned in to Mr. Dudd's office on the second floor at the head of the stairs, he could see that the door was closed. While he waited patiently by the secretary's desk he tried to hear as much as he could through the closed door, though all he could discern was the subdued murmur of voices. Then the door opened and Mr. Dudd exited with Susan Koch.

Mr. Dudd was beaming broadly and Susan Koch was beaming too and was drooling out of the corner of her mouth. She was seated in an aluminum wheelchair which she propelled by means of a lever on the side of its arm that she depressed with her scrawny, emaciated hands— hands which were bent double with thumbs protruding into the air like gnarled roots. Paul took this in at a glance. Then he looked away.

"Paul," Mr. Dudd boomed, "I want you to meet Susan Koch. Susan, Paul will direct you to your new classroom."

Paul looked at Susan and smiled, and he could see that Susan was smiling at him out of a large, crooked, drooling mouth and that everything about her was crooked and that she had large, brown, pretty eyes that shone at him shyly and eagerly.

"Come on, Susan," he said, and he made his voice sound cheery, "I'll take you to class."

He spoke to her as they proceeded down the hall.

"It's great that you're here, Susan. We're all happy you're in our class."

She beamed and drooled and spoke to him in a slurred voice while she bent double in her chair.

"I'm happy to be heah!" She smiled and laughed and gesticulated excitedly with her broken-looking hands, and he smiled and led the way and noticed the thick yellow wax encrusted in her ear.

That was Susan's first day in school. She was a fey bright-eyed child, quick to laugh or participate in a joke, and she was so thin that one could see up the sleeve of her dress all the way to her chest, which was covered by a flannel undershirt.

Paul made a point of talking to Susan every day. He was gallant and flirtatious and fetched her things at her request and kidded with her in a series of running jokes which they improvised from day to day. He felt he had a special relationship to her since he had conducted her from the principal's office, as if he had invented her, and he took her under his wing and extended his protection to her and monitored how the other children treated her; and for this he was casually proud of himself, the way he might have felt had he rescued some small, drowning, useless, bedraggled creature from a rainstorm.

When the class had to pair up to do a report on a poem, Paul volunteered to work with Susan. They chose Edgar Allan Poe's "Annabel Lee," a stupid, treacly, singsong affair in Paul's estimation but Susan's "favorite poem," so he wheeled her to the library, where they spent an hour or two researching the life of Poe and taking notes in a soiled green notebook which Susan supplied. Then outside the school in the afternoon light with the shadow of clouds darkening and lightening the steps where they sat, they committed the verses to memory.

'Twas many and many a year ago,
    In a kingdom by the sea,
That a maiden there lived whom you may know
    By the name of Annabel Lee.

Susan recited the verses over and over in her high-pitched, tremulous voice with its slurred pronunciation, her thin, dark hair flying in all directions and her nose running and her bright, dark eyes flashing at Paul hungrily as if the words of the poem were in some special manner appropriate to the two of them, and he laughed and kidded with her and tried to avoid the hunger in her eyes and the sight of the food that was smeared at the corner of her mouth.

After that she would refer jokingly to their "kingdom by the sea," and would recite passages of the poem at him, jabbing him with her eyes, and joking and laughing until she all but fell forward in her chair onto her face.

Susan sat in the back of the class in her wheelchair, from which she couldn't rise without assistance, and she drooled and beat time with her pencil against the side of her chair and hummed a tuneless song of her own devising until even Mrs. White had to request, with mounting asperity, that she desist while class was in session.

Klak klak went Susan Koch's spoon against the side of her plate as Paul passed her table in the dining room on the lower floor where the sun came pouring through the window. Susan Koch smiled and laughed as he passed, and she smacked the side of her plate with her spoon.

"Baby, baby, stick your head in gravy!" she sang as she rattled her chair and looked about her mischievously, her large, clever eyes rolling in her head and her ruined hair pointing out in all directions like charred, broken straw.

"Susan!" Miss Twine, the assistant teacher, whispered in a concerned, constrained manner, "don't be so loud."

Susan paid no attention.

"Wipe it off with applesauce," she sang, walloping her glass with her fork and laughing hysterically, so that Paul could see the mashed potato that adhered to her gums and to her large, crooked teeth.

"Why don't you sit with me, doody-head?" she called, spluttering and laughing and enjoying herself uproariously.

"Susan!" Miss Twine repeated sharply. "You mustn't make a spectacle of yourself! You're disrupting the other children."

Paul only smiled and continued on his way.

"How's your girlfriend?" Eddy Dier sneered at him one day, but Paul only laughed and reported the incident to Susan as a good joke.

"Eddy Dier says you're my girlfriend!"

"Oh—well, aren't I?"

And she laughed and smirked at him out of her large eyes—the only pretty feature she possessed—and he laughed too and smirked, and thus the routine was established between them.

In his report card that season the teacher wrote how gratified she was that Paul was getting along so well with the new student, Susan Koch, and what a credit it was to the school, and his mother read this passage to Paul with special pride.

Susan devised a game called "pins and needles" in

which, birdlike, she poked at Paul with the beak of her pencil, uttering small, shrill, chirping noises. At first she was careful not to hit him, but she would practice with staccato vehemence against the top of her desk until it was riddled with sharp graphite marks like a wall hit by a machine-gun enfilade.

"I'd like to *hit* that girl," she'd say, pointing to the pretty Peggy Birch across the room, whereupon she'd lower her head and say "hit hit hit" as she rat-a-tatted the point of her pencil with alarming vigor off the Formica surface of the desktop; and then she'd lift her head and laugh.

"Poor Peggy," he'd say. "That's not very nice."

"Oh, I'm *not* very nice," Susan would answer, leering and laughing while her great, liquid, brown eyes snapped with frenetic excitement.

Then one day she hit him in his hand with the point of the pencil.

"Ouch!" He drew back with a jerk while she watched him in great excited curiosity, a smile frozen on her puckered, crooked face.

"Did it hurt?"

"What do you think?"

"Oh, goodie, goodie!" And she burst out laughing.

"Will you marry me?" she asked him. She was invariably decked out in a pretty dress with a round lace collar and lace on the sleeves, and from these her matchstick arms protruded, and her matchstick neck with its sinuous blue veins, and as the day wore on she would soil the dress with ink and food and saliva, so that as he joked with her Paul would have to avert his eyes from the encrusted spots and stains.

Now he said, "I thought I was supposed to ask *you!*"

"Well, why don't you?"

This set Susan off in a series of hiccups and guffaws that had her rocking back and forth in her chair, her thin, bent frame wheezing and shaking under the influence of such risqué humor.

"Oh, Paaaul," she whined, and a thin thread of saliva escaped like spider silk from her mouth, "you're not going to marry meee!"

There was a satiric edge to her humor, for she observed the world sharply from her constrained, uncomfortable kingdom in her wheelchair, and there was nothing amiss about her sharp little brain.

"Georgie Porgie," she sneered at him one day after watching him maneuver in the class. "Kissed the girls and made them cry!" And she uttered her high-pitched, sardonic laughter.

Cassandra had been a funny little oddball of a girl, always tagging along, always laughing, a tomboy with her dungarees rolled up above her socks and her dark hair falling over her forehead and her funny, slightly Oriental eyes watching him intently (her mother, she said, was part Indian). There seemed no time when he hadn't known Cassandra—no time when she wasn't running along at his elbow.

Was he talking now about third grade, when they studied the Indians and made their own Indian costumes? She had decorated hers with macaroni which she dyed blue so that it hung like wampum on the tassels on her small, flat chest, and he had thought her as pretty as Pocahontas, whom they read about in class.

Each morning he went to school with his brother, and each morning they ran the entire way, their bodies invisible as they whooped down the hills, jumping the rocks (he knew every one by heart), leaping the bushes, taking the small fence at the bottom of the long hill in a single bound, and then racing across the slope of the lawn to the school.

Running was a form of being. When he was running he was indistinguishable from movement, a flash of becoming, a portion of the wind. There was no body then, no resistance, as when on skates he sped over ice until the landscape was only a blur. He loved to run. Sometimes at home he would run from room to room just for the joy of running.

Sometimes, when Matthew and he went the back way through the high school grounds (taking the high fence in two bounds, one to mid links, then to the top, vaulting the smooth bar and dropping without pause to the ground so that you continued with almost unbroken stride in the race that was against yourself), sometimes he would pause at the crest of the hill overlooking the playing fields, from where he could view in the distance the pile of red-brick buildings where he would be incarcerated for the day; and, standing for an instant in that stasis (a moment caught between time; a fissure in Being like a crack in ice where you stand and gaze down to observe a leaf, a twig, a bubble caught in delicate perfect suspension like a planet seen from outer space), sometimes he would think, *What if I didn't go? What if I stood here forever? Stood like a tree forever?*

Then with a whoop his brother would be off, and, pursuing, clattering down the steepness of the hill, he left behind the small gash in time, left it behind to close after him like water.

But sometimes in midstream—rushing down the stairs, running into a room, swinging on a swing—he would be stopped by the wonder of it until he was all but lost, and he feared that unless he shook himself, unless he roused himself from his reverie, all would disappear, nothing would remain—not even the world.

Cassandra lived in a tall brown house on the further side of the parkway about halfway toward the river. He was thinking now of a time before they had cleared the neighborhood and built the high-rises. Cassandra's house was at the end of a half-paved road lined with unkempt bushes; it was surrounded by bushes and by a raggle-taggle lawn that descended in the rear to the tangle of forest and brake.

When Paul played at Cassandra's they would run outside to the backyard. There were little paths of paving stones that ran through the garden, and as you descended the paths toward the forest, the house would disappear. Along the sides of the paths were old trellises where ivy clung like seaweed, and the profusion of greenery was knee high and as wild as some overgrown herbarium, with thick sprouts that resembled untamed eyebrows bristling from around stones, and furry, tendril-like growths like the hairs that Paul sometimes observed protruding from the nostrils of grown-ups.

She was a laughing, chirping, dervishing little girl who shared with him a predilection for running, jumping, hopping, laughing, playing, *being*, rather than any reflexive scrutiny of existence. That would come in due order. But for the moment they were points of light, birds or quick-witted cats, rather than empty, reverberating spaces.

What they liked to do was draw. Both had decided they wanted to be artists, like Cassandra's mother, and so they spent hours filling pieces of paper with birds and trees and the small figures of children, while they related to each other elaborate stories which their pictures were meant to illustrate.

The art teacher was a man named Mr. Dannon, and Paul thought him the most wonderful man in the world. He was short and dark with prominent cheekbones that he clenched when he was thinking, and muscular, heavily veined forearms which Paul watched closely with great admiration, and his nose was prominent and slightly bulbous, and his thick, glossy hair went back in a wave from his forehead, and he had beautiful round, dark eyes and a soft, throaty voice. The only class Paul loved was art class, and he would stay late to help Mr. Dannon clean up after class, scraping the tables and washing the brushes in the cold water from the faucet until the paint ran like blood; and he came early to set out the art equipment, paper and jars of paint and heady-smelling white glue as thick as tapioca pudding.

At Easter, Cassandra took him to the botanical gardens and they roamed together through the new heat, looking at the fresh grass and first-budding flowers, pink and turquoise and lemon. They held hands and raced downhill, and the wind caught in their windbreakers, causing them to luff like sails. Everything smelled new-made, as clean as the odor of metal, and the birds, plump and new-invented after the winter, hopped gamely about and sang from the trees like magical birds in a picture book.

They entered the hothouse and the air was muggy and rubbed against them like a cat, and the atmosphere was heavy-scented with the odor of orchids and oranges and other exotic blooms. The hothouse was a great glass bubble atop a hill, and if you looked out from the glass walls you seemed to be floating, for the world seemed insignificant and far away, unreal compared to the jungle profusion of the interior. Soon they quit the central pebbled walk for a sinuous side path shaded by dark green leaves the size of elephant ears and webbed with veins of lighter green. Vines hung like snakes from the tufted trees and banana-shaped leaves curled and fluttered above them, muffling the light.

Shadows moved beneath them, breathed lazily, rippled like water over their shoes. Cassandra bent to inhale a cluster of vibrant pink flowers, their cups bobbing beneath her like flames; and when, smiling, she turned to him, thick yellow granules like particles of yellow egg adhered to the tip of her nose. Leaves as large as themselves hung around them like shields, baffling and attenuating sound into a continuous incomprehensible murmur, and the sun, a diffused brightness, moved against the sides of the trees in bland, lazy patches or fluttered like down among the leaves.

Paul could taste the green of the leaves, the powdery yellow of the sunshine. At any moment a beast might spring from behind the trees.

"Look at that pond," he exclaimed in excitement. "How strange! They've put carrots in it."

"Those aren't carrots, silly," she laughed. "Those are goldfish!"

And sure enough they were, great carp, gold-plated and as long as footballs, skimming lazily past the surface to show their large, froglike eyes and then, with a whisk of the tail, their white unhealthy-looking bellies almost breaking the water, disappearing into the depths of the pool.

Outside again, they sat in the high April wind and ate the chocolate-covered marshmallow bunnies that Cassandra's mother had provided.

She took him with her parents to a square dance, and the two danced and whirled and clapped their hands and do-si-doed and sashayed up and down the floor until they were red in the face and breathless. They went outside and stood in the dark and held hands and drank cool cider out of small waxed Dixie cups and ate raisin cookies.

"I don't want you ever to go away," he said.

"I won't go away. I'll stay with you forever!"

He leaned over and kissed her, half on her soft, round cheek and half on the side of her mouth, tasting of apple cider.

In the car going home the two of them sat very still together in the back seat in the dark, and he could feel her small, wiry body pressed against him, so that he felt very quiet and happy.

The next day he heard his mother talking to Cassandra's mother on the telephone and he knew they were talking about the square dance and how "cute" they had been. He heard his mother laugh good-naturedly, amused at what she was hearing, and he turned away in disgust.

It was April then, and the weather was chilly but the sun warm. In class it poured in through the window and burned on his knees where he sat pretending to listen to the teacher, and when he went outside he could stand in the lee of the building and soak up the warmth like the young shoots of the forsythia. Everything smelled of wind and cleanness, with occasionally the sweet odor of honeysuckle.

After school Cassandra and he hid from her mother under a large bush where they could climb on hands and knees and not be seen.

"Sh!" they cautioned one another. They sat close together and savored the moist odor of earth and new-budding leaves.

"Cassandra," they heard her mother calling, and her voice sounded far away. "Cassandra, where are you? It's time to go home."

"I don't want to leave!" she whispered to him, and he could smell her odor, a little like curdled milk.

When he next visited Cassandra she led him into the garden behind her house where everything smelled of the earth and of the new greenness of the ivy. They sat protected by bushes cross-legged in a patch of sun.

"I'm never going to leave you," she said matter-of-factly. "It will always be like this."

She had rich, glossy brown hair cut in bangs across her forehead and short at her ears, and the sun glowed in her hair like honey. Her cheeks were fat though she was thin and wiry, not breakable like a doll but sturdy and well knit, her skin tawny, copper-suffused, burnished as if perpetually in the sun, and her eyes were large and round when she was excited but squinted slightly when her face was at rest. Her wrists and ankles were small and he could see the bones in her shoulders and in the collar of her neck. She wore brown corduroy overalls with brown buttons and a long-sleeved cotton shirt striped in yellow and red. Looking at her in the warmth of the sunlight beneath the bush, he felt strangely moved, and he said, "I want to see you undressed."

She looked at him with her large, serious eyes.

"Okay," she said. She didn't smile at all.

He watched her undo the brown buttons of her corduroys. She removed her shoes and socks and she put her socks into her shoes and then removed her overalls. She took the striped cotton shirt off over her head. Then she lay back on the earth in the sunlight and closed her eyes.

"You take my panties off."

He looked at her lying beneath him, and she didn't look any different from a boy, her small chest perfectly flat, the small brownish nipples hardly distinguishable from the even tint of her skin, only there was a smallness to her that touched him, the thin bones visible beneath the smooth, even-colored skin, the beat of the heart evident in the blue vein beside her neck.

When he reached forward his hand was shaking. He pulled her panties down smoothly to her knees while she helped him, lifting her hips slightly from the ground, her body at ease, her eyes still closed.

He stared at her, the small delta nestled between her

legs, the lips of her vagina pressed together, the bud of her visible between her lips. But he didn't touch her—not yet. He looked in a kind of awestruck, desperate longing, uncertain what to do.

Her skin was perfect, her body as delicately incised as a shell; only, when he looked closer, there was a fine down to the skin, less visible than the hair on her arms, and there was an odor to her, salty and familiar, as if he had known it before. Bending, he grazed her with his tongue.

She sighed, adjusting herself in the sun. Her eyes were still closed.

Taking a smooth stick, he probed gently the lips of her vagina, parting them; and suddenly there brimmed a liquid, clear and plentiful.

He sighed too. Stretching, he pressed himself full-length against her.

Afterward whenever he visited they would disappear into the garden and undress. She would squat and pee for him, her small buttocks almost touching the ground, the stream of her water a strong, steady hiss into the earth. Then she would curl into a fetal position and he would curl around her, cupping her warm body against his like a good-luck charm in the palm of his hand.

And then Cassandra became ill. He watched his mother speaking with Cassandra's mother on the phone, and he could tell by the way his mother frowned that something was wrong.

"Is something wrong with Cassandra?" he asked when she had hung up.

"Why do you ask that?"

"I dunno—it's just the way you look."

"Well, Cassandra's come down with something. It's nothing you have to worry about—she'll be all right in a little while, I'm sure. But she won't be in school for a few weeks."

"A few weeks?"

"Yes, that's what the doctor says. Now you're not to worry yourself, Paul. Cassandra is going to be as good as new."

But he knew that something was wrong.

Cassandra wasn't in school that Monday, and she wasn't in school the next day or the next.

On Thursday, Paul walked by himself to Cassandra's house. He had never done this before, and though there was no definitive prohibition against his doing so, he knew his mother wouldn't approve. He had always previously been accompanied by some adult.

He was slightly nervous when it came to crossing above the highway, but he waited patiently for the light to change as he had done many times with his mother, and then when the light turned green he looked both ways, stepped off the curb with care, and crossed in the wake of a woman with a grocery cart. After that everything was easy.

When he rang the front doorbell, he could feel the beat of his heart as he waited for Mrs. Thatcher to answer.

"Why, Paul! What are you doing here?"

"Hello, Mrs. Thatcher. I came to see Cassandra."

"Well, that's very nice, Paul, but I'm afraid Cassandra can't come to the door. She's not very well, you know."

"What's wrong with her?"

"Well, she has a disease in her blood, Paul. She needs

lots of rest. I'll tell her you visited—she'll be very grateful. But how in goodness did you get here?"

"I walked."

"Does your mother know you are here?"

"Yes."

"And she said you could walk by yourself?"

"Yes."

"Well, thank you for coming, Paul. Be careful crossing the streets."

Paul waited by the tall bushes until Mrs. Thatcher had closed the door and the house was again quiet; then he circled to the back of the house.

Cassandra's room was on the second floor. It was easy to let himself in the back door and go up the back stairs; he had done this many times.

The door to Cassandra's room was half open and he could see Cassandra lying in the middle of her bed staring at the ceiling. When she saw Paul she rose onto her elbows and looked at him with surprise.

Paul gestured for her to be quiet.

Cassandra's eyes grew round with amusement and approval as she saw Paul.

"Did you come up the back stairs?"

"Yes—ssh! Your mom told me to go away."

"I'm not supposed to see anyone," she said gravely. "I'm sick."

"Yeah, that's what your mom told me. What's wrong with you, anyway?"

"I don't know—something with my blood."

"Is it serious?"

"I think it must be."

He stared at her, and he felt a kind of gallant yearning,

as if he would like to save her from burning houses or wild beasts.

She returned his stare.

"What do you do all day?"

"Nothing. I stare at the ceiling. Do you want to get in bed with me?"

She pushed back the bedcovers while he removed his shoes and pants. Then he got into bed.

It was warm under the sheets and he snuggled against her. She had taken off her nightgown.

She curled into a fetal position, her back to him, and he curled around her, holding her body against his; and thus after a while she drifted to sleep, nestled in their warmth, moving farther and farther away, until there remained only her breathing.

And so it happened that he would come to her after school, crossing the highway, circling the house, mounting the stairs so no one would know he was there, and entering her room, where she lay waiting. Then they would curl next to each other like two small animals, and she would drift to sleep in his arms.

"I might have to go away," she said.

"Where do you have to go?"

"They say I might have to go to the hospital."

"To the hospital!" He held her closer. He wished there was something he could do to make her stay.

He didn't understand what was happening.

"I don't want to go," she said.

"Just say you won't," he said after a while. It didn't sound like reasonable advice, but he didn't know what else to suggest.

"Will you come see me in the hospital?"

"Yes," he promised.

He would study her as she slept: the small whorl of her ear, the descending scale of her backbone, the armature of her rib cage, graceful as a mandolin.

He watched the tick of her vein in her wrists, the fingers curled half open. Her eyebrows curved from nose to temple, and when he touched them they were smooth as fur. He could see the slight hairs of her mustache at the corner of her mouth.

She had a clean, tangy odor and he pressed his nose against her, breathing her. Her legs tucked against him, the tops of her feet smooth, the soles slightly rough, and her buttocks, bony and small, nudged him as she slept.

She was a deep sleeper, her breath coming in steady, even sighs, then ceasing, then starting again in a different rhythm; and sometimes, as she drifted farther and farther from him, he would become afraid lest some reckoning be demanded for their illicit meetings and he would lose her forever.

But no one discovered his visits. And so, later, when he tried to remember, he could never swear that he had not invented the entire thing, made it up out of whole cloth from some bizarre chapter of his imagination: years would elapse before he found again, as in some fairy tale, some room in the top of some tower, this private hidden space that exists between men and women.

And then she began to look ill: he could see the change in her skin, which appeared greenish, and she didn't smell right either, as if she was taking too many vitamin pills.

Then she was taken away. His mother told him one morning before he left for school.

"Pauli, I have something I have to tell you."

"Yes, Mom."

"Perhaps you'd better sit down for a moment."

He sat down, but he knew exactly what it was she was going to say.

"It's about Cassandra."

"Yes—what about Cassandra?"

"You remember I told you that she's very ill?"

"Yes—I remember."

"Well, I'm afraid they've had to take her to the hospital. I'm sorry, Pauli."

"Why are you sorry, Mama?"

"Because I'm afraid she's very ill. I'm not certain when she'll be coming home."

That day in school their teacher gathered the children to tell them about Cassandra: she had been taken to the hospital with leukemia. Paul had never heard the word *leukemia* before, but it didn't add anything to what he already knew. Cassandra was leaving him.

He couldn't concentrate on anything. He couldn't even write her a card. He was the only member of the class not to send her a folded piece of foolscap with a crayoned picture on the outside and a greeting scribbled within.

When his mother asked him whether he wanted to visit her he said no. He didn't want to see her in a hospital bed.

But he did go to visit her—once.

It was after a month and now she was very ill. He could smell her sickness when he came into the hospital room. She looked very small in the bed, shrunken, yellow, and something had happened to her beautiful hair.

He stood by the side of her bed and for a while they didn't say anything. His mother stood to one side.

"You didn't come to see me," she said without reproach. It was merely a statement of fact.

"No."

He felt angry.

"I'm going away," she said after a while.

He didn't say anything, he stood with his head down, stubbornly staring at the floor.

"Look at me," she said.

He raised his eyes, and he saw her small face, gallant and unafraid.

"I want to see you," she said. "I want to memorize the way you look. I won't forget you."

So they remained silently looking at each other.

"I won't forget you either," he said.

And he didn't.

The relationship between Paul and Susan Koch deteriorated. She adopted a querulous chiding tone that got on his nerves and subverted his sense of moral commendability in paying her court. Increasingly he avoided her.

Susan became a problem in class. She started fighting with the other children, made noise during instruction, had temper tantrums if Mrs. White wasn't paying her attention. She was good at her studies and kept up with her work, but she'd ask odd and disconcerting questions in class.

"If the Indians didn't like the whites," she asked during social studies class, "why didn't they just go away?"

"What do you mean, Susan?"

"I mean go away—the way a dog runs away." And she

started to laugh, rocking back and forth in her chair and holding her hand in front of her mouth as if she had said something clever.

About the *Hindenburg* blimp she said, "If it burst it would make rain come out of the sky."

"What do you mean?" Mrs. White asked with a frown.

"Just like a cloud!" Susan said, beginning to laugh. "Boom!"

This made some of the other students laugh—though not *with* Susan—which only set her off more.

"Don't play the clown," Mrs. White said with asperity, which sobered Susan up precipitously. Now she was threatening to cry.

Once in Paul's presence Eddy Dier called Susan disgusting, and in a last burst of gallantry Paul shoved Eddy Dier in the shoulder. But the event did not end as Paul anticipated.

Though a soft, sluggish-looking boy, Dier had been taking boxing lessons, and he now put up his dukes in classic boxer's style. Paul had no more idea how to box than how to twirl on his toes, and he read in Dier's eyes a feral intensity that inspired restraint. Shrugging, he walked away.

He thought no one had observed this act of questionable prudence, but it hadn't escaped the sharp notice of Susan Koch.

"I guess Eddy Dier knows how to box, huh?" she asked him slyly.

"Aw, Eddy Dier is a fatso."

The next day in passing her in the classroom he casually called her Suzy.

"Don't call me Suzy!" she snapped, throwing up her chin with regal dignity. "Only my *friends* call me Suzy."

"Well, excuse *me*!" he said, strangely cut by her words. "I didn't know you were such a fancy pants!"

"Sticks and stones will break my bones," she sang, "but only my friends can call me Suzy."

And putting her wheelchair forward, she began peering over Eddy Dier's shoulder.

After that he avoided Susan—and she hung around Dier. He knew she did this to annoy him, but he didn't care. He had had enough of her.

So the year ended, and he didn't speak to Susan anymore. Once, maybe twice, they fell into their old bantering manner, as if nothing had changed—but this never lasted for more than a day.

The next year they were sixth graders and he hardly noticed whether Susan Koch was in his class; she was just another irrelevant presence past which he had sped. He didn't even notice at what point she disappeared entirely. Was it the end of sixth grade? Or was it later? He didn't know. No one would guess that once he had led her proudly to class in her shining wheelchair. No one would suspect that once they had bantered about marriage.

Paul's father lay on his back in the hospital with his eyes closed while his breath came in stertorous wheezes. Paul approached cautiously, and he noted stubble the color of metal filings on his father's chin, and the rise and fall of his father's chest, rhythmic and shuddering as a beached whale.

Paul watched beside the bed; and he remembered the loping powerful gait of the man, bearlike in its unlikely speed, which he had known as a boy, when his father, cradling him on one hip, would hit a baseball with one hand; then the two of them would be off, the boy riding the lopsided up-and-down gallop like a young Bedouin on a runaway camel.

For a time Paul sat by his father while the hospital room darkened, and as he waited he tried to think of nothing, neither fear nor hope nor love nor disappointment, for it seemed to him that the darkening light was itself a dimension of thought deeper and clearer and more profound than anything he could attain.

"Paul?"

The sound startled him.

"Yes, Dad—here I am."

Paul stood up, and now he was looking down at his father as he lay disoriented on the hospital bed, the corner of his mouth crusted with a slight whitish precipitation like a dried salt at the bottom of a petri dish. *But you, my father, there on that sad height, Curse, bless me now with your fierce tears, I pray!*

"Is that you?"

"Hi, Dad—I'm here."

His father reached out his hand, and the boy took it while the man lay quietly in his bed and breathed.

"Where am I?" he asked after a while.

Paul felt his stomach shift with apprehension.

"You're in the hospital, Dad."

"Which hospital?"

"St. Luke's."

"Why am I in St. Luke's? I thought I was in Abraham."

"No, Dad—that was the other time."

"The other time? What do you mean?"

"Dad—you've had another heart attack—don't you remember? Abraham was the first time."

His father lay on his back breathing heavily and trying to absorb this information while Paul, alarmed before the spectacle of this disarray, wondered whether he should call a nurse.

"Where's your mother?" his father asked after a while.

"She'll be here later, Dad. She had errands to do."

"I guess I'm a little confused, Pauli."

"That's okay, Dad. You've been asleep."

"When did I have this other heart attack?"

"Some weeks ago."

"Was it severe?"

"No, Dad—they say it was mild. You've been okay until now."

His father lay thinking about that, absorbing what seemed to be news. Slowly he closed his eyes and put his hand over his face, and Paul could see the pain cross his features like wind across the surface of water.

"Damn!" his father said.

Then there was quiet between them.

"Is your mother all right?"

"Yes, Dad—we're all all right."

"Where's Matthew?"

"He'll come if you want, Dad. He's been up in Cambridge. You've really been all right."

"What a stupid thing to do," his father said slowly, and it was as if he was ashamed.

"Don't say that, Daddy. It's not your fault."

His father looked at him and smiled wryly.

"Kidneys," he said, tapping his forehead with his finger. It was a saying they had between them.

The boy squeezed his father's hand, holding it as tightly as he dared. Then they were silent again.

"Why aren't you in Cambridge?" his father inquired after a time.

"W . . . what do you mean?"

"Why aren't you at school? Why aren't you studying?"

"I'm not at Cambridge, Daddy."

"What do you mean? You should be at Cambridge studying."

"Daddy, Daddy!"

"What's wrong, Pauli?"

"I'm not at Cambridge, Daddy. I'm still at Highgate. I'm in my sophomore year."

"Sophomore year?"

"Daddy, what's wrong?"

His father paused, attempting to sort things out.

"I seem to be confused. I'll be better in a minute."

Then he lay and breathed through his mouth while the darkness thickened in the room.

"You know, Pauli," his father said after a while, "your mother loves you very much."

"I know that, Daddy."

"I know you think sometimes that she favors Matthew, but that's not true. She's very proud of Matthew, of course—we all are. And she worries about him because— well, you know why she worries about him."

"Yes, Daddy." He didn't want to have this conversation. He wondered again whether he should call a nurse.

"She can't always show what she feels," his father continued.

"You don't have to say this, Daddy."

"I want you to know."

"I do know."

"She'll need you, Pauli. She needs your love."

"I know that, Daddy."

"You know I love you, don't you?"

"Daddy!" Again he squeezed his father's hand.

"Okay," his father said. "Okay. I'm depending on you, Pauli."

"What do you mean, Daddy? What do you mean by that?"

His father looked at him and smiled slightly. Then he motioned with his finger for Paul to draw near.

Paul bent near to his father and he saw the handsome familiar features beneath him and the stubble on his father's chin and he smelled the unwanted odor of hospital sickness. His father motioned him nearer, and when he put his ear to his father's lips his father whispered something that he couldn't make out.

Paul drew away and swallowed dryly. He didn't want to be hearing secrets from his father, who was apparently not quite right in his judgment; but he also burned to know what his father had said.

"I couldn't hear you, Daddy."

Again he put his ear to his father's lips, and again his father muttered something, he couldn't make out what. It was like hearing voices through a wall.

"I can't understand, Daddy. I'm sorry."

His father frowned and waved him away and shook his head, and a mysterious half smile crossed his face.

"That's all right," his father said. "That's all right." Then, as he turned to Paul and squeezed his hand, his expression again darkened. "I'm depending on you, Paul. Don't forget—I'm depending on you."

7

After his appearance before the Bates committee, Paul spent more time by the river. It was May now and he would ride the trains.

He would wait in one of the empty freight cars while they were coupled together; then after the jolt there would come a pause as the locomotive changed direction—the last moment to quit the ride. Then he'd feel the grinding, slow-motion, speed-accumulating shuffle as the unthinkable tons of weight lurched forward under the bulldog strength of the engine.

When the train was lumbering at full tilt Paul would climb the ladder up the side and would stand at the center of the car feeling the wind beat against his face. He knew it was dangerous to do this but he didn't care and he would edge his way forward with the train rattling and lurching beneath him until he reached the end of the car; then, hesitating for an instant, he would leap to the next car, crouching low to maintain his balance.

Though at first this gave him a high, he could soon accomplish the feat without forethought, and the theoretical danger was outweighed by the blandness of the actuality.

Then he would sit with the full-bodied stench of the

river in his nostrils as they raced northward, the wind blowing in his face and tangling his hair. The instinct to keep going was powerful.

But he never did. Two miles down the siding the train slowed to switch to the main track, the cars lumbering and screeching as metal ground against metal, the whistle issuing a long, plaintive warning howl, and it was here that he would descend and drop safely onto the gravel on the riverside and stand watching as with abrupt immense grace, the vehicle shunted from track to track, each car following in place like logs in a mill, before, turning with a sigh, he started his walk home.

"Thanks for telling me about *The Bear*," Laura Kinski said. They were standing under one of the chestnut trees that lined the road outside the school, the new leaves fluttering like fans above them.

"Do you like it?"

"I love it!"

"Yeah, I love Faulkner—it's like eating vanilla ice cream."

"Vanilla ice cream?" She laughed. "More like raw steak or something."

When she laughed her throat moved and he could see the soft hair, invisible except at this range, along the side of her face. He hadn't seen her since the Kaiser estate, but he didn't want to become further involved. He didn't want to be involved with anyone.

"So have you heard from Vassar?" he now asked, out of politeness more than true curiosity.

∼∼∼∼∼∼∼∼∼∼∼∼∼∼∼∼∼∼∼∼∼∼∼∼

"No, not yet, but it should be soon."

"You think you'll get in?"

"That's what my advisor says—but who knows? It's no big deal."

"Listen," he said suddenly, "have you been hanging around outside my house?"

She colored deeply.

"No, why should I be doing that?"

Paul's intuition told him that it was she. He saw he was hurting her by mentioning the occurrence, but he persisted.

"No reason. It's not important. My mother saw someone—that's all."

"You mean like hanging around outside?"

"Yeah—once or twice. It's no big deal."

"What did she look like?"

"Dark and slender, my mother said. Good-looking."

"Well, it wasn't me!"

And she turned away haughtily.

Philip said to him, "I'm worried about Whitey."

Paul took Richards' words as a sort of peace offering—though he couldn't define why there should be tension between them. Since his meeting with the Bates committee he had felt some kind of constraint: he was angry at himself and angry at Philip—and just plain angry. He wouldn't have unsaid anything he had said, but he was annoyed that he had had to say it in the first place.

"So how did it go with old Lucius?" Richards had asked him after the meeting.

"Don't worry—everything was cool."

"Oh yeah? Simpatico?"

"Sure, Philip—I covered your ass."

Richards merely lifted his eyebrows in mock surprise.

"You *are* clean, aren't you?" Paul asked.

"Clean? Clean as a baby's fart. *Mens sana in corpore sano*—that's me." And Richards had winked.

"What's wrong with Whitey?" Paul now asked.

"Yeah, what's wrong," Berger interrupted. He was lounging to one side with his hands in his pockets. "Is he sprouting a triple chin or something?"

It always troubled Paul that Berger, with his even features and clever, insinuating brown eyes, was good-looking, as if that constituted some violation of nature, for a ratty creep like Berger should be immediately revealed by his face, whereas Berger was short but well knit and his eyes were large, humorous, often pleading, like some perpetual younger brother asking indulgence.

"Berger, you know what your problem is?" Richards said. "You're a cynic."

Berger instantly began to guffaw, covering his mouth with his hand.

"No, I'm being serious," Philip said. "You're a goddamn cynic, that's what your problem is. You ought to be reported to Lucius Bates or someone. There ought to be a committee formed to investigate you."

"So tell me about Farrino," Paul interrupted.

Richards looked at him, and his face changed expression.

"I'm serious about Claude," he said, lowering his voice and putting his hand confidentially on Paul's shoulder.

Paul could see Mrs. Wagner marching toward them, her lip downed with hair and her sharp, intrusive eyes surveying them; and suddenly he felt uncomfortable with Philip's arm draped about him.

"There goes Brunhilde," Philip said, divining Paul's scruples.

And Paul, ashamed, made himself listen to what Philip had to say—though at the moment he couldn't have cared less about Claude Farrino.

"Tell me about Whitey."

"He's depressed," Philip said, leading Paul toward the window where they wouldn't be interrupted.

"Like a soufflé?"

"Like a Quaalude—only many times over."

"I don't know about Quaalude," Paul said with some asperity.

"Well, they send you toward Nirvana land—the big fat farm in the sky."

"What are you talking about?"

"Depressed, baby—*capisce?* He's dragging his ass around like Dumpy. He won't speak to me."

"He won't speak to you?"

"Yeah—that's what I'm trying to say."

Paul sighed and looked out the window. He didn't care about Whitey, and that did him no credit, and it was a tribute to Philip that he *did* care. For all Philip's folderol, there was something about him that Paul admired.

"What do you think we should do?"

"I dunno. That's what I want to talk to you about."

"Can't we go over to his house or something?" Paul gritted his teeth at the thought.

"That won't do the trick—I've tried that. He says nobody loves him."

"Well," Paul said, "he's got a point."

"Not love that little tart Tatin? Not love that India-rubber ball?"

Paul couldn't help smiling.

"So what do you suggest?"

"Well, I've been thinking it over, and I think I see an angle."

"You always see an angle, Philip."

Richards looked at him and offered his Cheshire cat smile.

"Here's how I see it," Philip said. "I think we should run Whitey for Student Council president."

Paul started to laugh.

"Student Council president! Philip—are you mad! Why not just run him for President of the United States?"

Richards looked at Paul with amused irony.

"Not so fast," he said. "I've got a plan."

"Yeah, I'm sure."

"Think of the number of people who've used Whitey's homework. Think of the number who owe him."

"Yeah—so what?"

"Ah, here's the beauty part. We can use that. We can call in Whitey's cards, don't you see? We can get them to vote for him."

Paul looked at his friend in wonder.

"How's that, Philip? Explain that to me."

"Well, some of them will do it for the fun of it, some because I ask them to, and some because—we'll blackmail them."

"You're too much!"

"No, listen, I'm being serious. We'll blackmail the suckers. Didn't they pay illicitly for Whitey's answers? Well, the least they can do is to vote for him for president."

"You can't be serious, Philip."

"Listen, *paesano*—something's gotta be done. Even if it doesn't work it will give Whitey a kick. And think what it could do for *us!* Think what it would mean to have access to all that privileged information about Highgate! Besides—the whole thing should be a gas!"

"I've been invited to Amherst this weekend," Laura said to him in the corridor. "Megan is going too and we thought we'd go together. Do you want to come?"

"To Amherst? No, I don't think so."

The wind was blowing in the trees, the branches rocking back and forth as if someone were shaking them violently. Light spiked through the leaves, a harbinger of things to come. Students hurried by on their way to classes.

"You'd have a good time, I know you would. And New England is so beautiful in spring."

He looked at her briefly.

"Naw, I'm not much interested in New England in the spring."

"Oh, you'd love it! There's nothing better than getting away! You feel so—free!"

"Really, I can't this weekend. I've got baseball practice."

"Oh!" She looked down and frowned. She was wearing a light silk shirt open at the throat with the collar turned up, and he could make out the delicate lines of her collar-bones and the small firmness of her breasts.

"Do you want me to go?" she asked. He was taken by surprise.

"What do you mean?"

"I mean that if you don't want me to go, I won't."

"Why shouldn't I want you to go?"

She was trying to say something but he refused to acknowledge it.

"Oh, I don't know." She looked at him seriously. "But if you don't want me to go, just say so."

"Why is it any of my affair?" he said. "I mean, didn't you just say you loved to get away?"

"Yes!" She raised her chin defiantly.

"Then of course you should go. You'll have a great time."

"Yes, I will."

"Tell me about it when you get back."

Signs now appeared throughout Highgate proclaiming "Claude Farrino for President!" with a picture of Whitey smiling, his thick black hair plastered across his forehead and his cheeks bulging like a chipmunk's with nuts. Richards, masterminding the campaign, moved along the corridors with a "Whitey" pin on his lapel, buttonholing people as he jotted notes and counted votes.

Whitey was hardly to be seen.

"He's suffering from some kind of a glandular thing," Philip explained to Paul. "He can hardly get out of bed."

"Glandular thing? Is it serious?"

"Naw naw naw."

"Don't you think you should call this whole campaign off?"

"Call it off? What for?"

"I don't know. It just gives me the willies."

"Buck up, *bambino*," was all Philip would say.

"Your friend Richards is a creep," Craig Lewis said to Paul.

"Why's that?"

"This thing about Claude Farrino, this campaign, is scandalous."

Craig was his usual bundle of earnest, focused energy, outraged by the delinquencies of the world. He was himself much favored to be elected Student Council president.

"You afraid of the competition?" Paul smiled.

"That's not the point!" Lewis was immune to Paul's irony. "This thing is just making a fool of Claude. It's outrageous."

Paul secretly agreed with this and so he said nothing.

"You know, Paul, you're a goddamn tergiversator," Craig said. Paul didn't know what that word meant but he suspected it was nothing good. "You started out as one of *us*, but now you've gone over to *them*. Tell me, what's the attraction of this Richards guy, anyway? Don't you know he got kicked out of his former school? Doesn't that tell you something?"

"What should it tell me, Craig? That he isn't a pussy-cat? I'd get kicked out of those schools too."

"No, you wouldn't, Paul. That's where you're wrong. You've got to *try* to get kicked out of one of those schools. You've got to *do* something."

. . .

Paul was shocked when Whitey appeared in school: he had gained weight, his locks hung about his forehead, his flesh had assumed an even more fungoid shade of white. Paul observed him slinking about the corridors like a criminal; when students greeted him he would smile uneasily and shrink further into himself.

"What gives with Whitey?" Jeb asked Paul.

"Damned if I know. Philip says he has something wrong with his glands."

"I suspect he's always had something wrong with his glands. It looks now as if he has something wrong with his head."

"What's wrong, Whitey?" Paul asked Farrino when he encountered him in the elbow of the corridor to the library building. He was alone and seemed to be hiding. "Don't you want to be Student Council president?"

Whitey laid his hand on Paul, and it was damp and shaking. There were brownish rings under his eyes and he gave an impression of general ill health and mental implosion, like a building collapsing into itself.

"Paul, do you think we can stop this whole thing?"

"What whole thing?"

"This campaign thing. This crazy farce. I don't know how I let Phil talk me into it in the first place."

"Why is it a farce?" Paul said. "*I'm* going to vote for you."

"It's a farce," Whitey insisted, his voice shooting up and his face cringing in flabby horror. "It's a farce, I tell you!"

"Claude, for godsakes, nothing so terrible has happened."

"Oh, please please please! Talk to him, talk to him. He'll listen to you!"

"Whitey, you've gotta get a hold of yourself. Who is it you want me to talk to?"

"To him, to him. Talk to Phil!"

"Why don't you talk to him?"

"No, no!" He seemed actually to cower. "He'll be angry at me. I don't want him to be angry at me!"

"He won't be angry at you, Whitey. Why should he be angry at you?"

"Because I've disappointed him."

"You haven't disappointed him, Whitey. You haven't disappointed anyone."

"Yes I have, yes I have. I've disappointed *everyone*."

Later that day Paul found Philip standing in the Quad consulting odd-sized pieces of paper which he had stuffed into the pockets of his blue business suit. Apparently he was counting votes.

"Who are you, Everett Dirksen?" Paul said.

Richards lifted a hand to silence him until he had finished counting, his face clouded in concentration.

"You know, we might just pull this thing off."

"Pull what thing off, Philip—the slaughter of the innocent?"

Philip looked at him quizzically. "What's eating you, *bambino?*"

"Nothing's eating me—but your little creation, Whitey, is all in a dither. I think he's feeling a little exposed here, Philip. I think he's feeling a little hung out to dry."

"Who cares about Farrino?" Richards said, his face hardening. "He'll just have to hang tough for a few days."

"Yeah? How can an éclair hang tough?"

"You know, *bambino*," Richards said, "no disrespect intended, but sometimes you can be a pain in the ass."

Of course Whitey lost. It was a landslide for Craig Lewis, Mr. Responsibility, the vigilante with the golden slide rule.

"What do you expect from a place like this?" Richards said in disgust. "All these suckers can say is gobble gobble gobble. Still, it was a brilliant conception, *bambini*. If we could have controlled the Student Council president's office we could have controlled the world!" And he threw his myriad slips of paper into the air like pieces of confetti.

Whitey seemed relieved. He was back in school with his hair slicked back into place and his intelligent eyes blinking again in wonder.

"Better luck next time, my little chickadee," Richards said, putting his arm about his protégé and chucking him under his double chin. Farrino blushed and looked apologetic and confused.

"So how was the trip to Amherst?" Paul asked Laura. Whether he had been avoiding her, or she him, he couldn't say, but almost a week had elapsed since they had spoken. Now she had greeted him in the corridor with a large smile—rather too large, he thought. Standing close to her, he inhaled the familiar scent of her perfume and noted again despite himself how attractive she was.

"Oh, it was great fun! You should have come." And she tossed her hair and laughed.

"I haven't seen you around school."

"Oh, we didn't get back until Wednesday. Playing hooky again!"

"So what did you do?"

"I really don't know. We went to a baseball game, of all things. I don't know what you guys see in that sport. Most of the time it's just a bunch of guys standing around in a field. Then somebody hits a ball and then they all run, and then they all stand around some more. But it's a good excuse to sit in the sun. Here, did I get a tan?"

"You look great."

"Do I? Well, we drove around New England with the top down, so I might have gotten a windburn."

"Who drove around New England? Where'd you get the car?"

"Oh, we met this guy—this middle-aged guy named Charles or something—and he drove us around in his MG."

"Middle-aged guy?"

"Yeah, he must have been thirty-five or something. So at any rate we stayed a little longer because Megan's got this crush on this guy at Amherst. Anyway, why should we hurry home?"

"Beats me."

"And besides, this guy Charles—the one I told you about—well, he was driving back on Wednesday and he offered to take us along."

"I see."

"I told you, he had this neat little sports car, and it seemed like a better idea than taking the train. Only Megan couldn't fit in. So I ended up going alone."

"I see. You mean you and this Charles."

"Yes. It was neat! Only we didn't get off until late in the afternoon, and though he drove really fast it got dark and began to rain, so we had to stop."

"What do you mean?"

"I mean we stopped in a motel for the night."

Paul didn't respond for a moment; he studied the tips of his shoes.

"Didn't your parents mind?"

She scoffed. "My parents! How would they know? They thought I came back on the train with Megan."

"But actually you spent the night in a motel with some middle-aged guy you'd never seen before."

She looked at him challengingly.

"What's wrong with that?"

"I didn't say there was anything wrong with it. It's a matter of taste, I suppose."

"Oh, yeah, taste! I forgot about taste. I forgot you're the great connoisseur of taste!"

"I didn't say I was a connoisseur." But his lip curled.

"You think I slept with him, is that it? Well, first of all, what business is that of yours? But for your information it just so happens that I *didn't* sleep with him, okay?"

"You expect me to believe that?"

"Yes, I do expect you to believe that, because it happens to be the truth. Charles was forty years old, for chrissake! He was a *gentleman!* We had *separate* rooms, Paul. You know—like *one* . . . *two?*"

He snorted.

"You don't believe me? Who do you think I am?"

"Everyone knows who you are."

Her eyes tightened as if he had slapped her.

"What do you mean by that?"

"Nothing."

"Yes, you do. You mean something. You mean something nasty."

"I mean I don't believe that this guy, this middle-aged creep who's never met you before, would pick you up at a *college weekend,* and offer to drive you home in his goddamn MG in the middle of a rainstorm, and then just blithely rent two motel rooms for the night. I mean I just find that a little hard to believe, okay?"

They stood staring at each other, the air charged between them.

"So you believe I slept with him. You probably believe I sleep with all kinds of guys, right? Jesus, Paul, I mean, really! . . . What would you say if I told you I was a virgin?"

He looked at her coldly.

"I wouldn't believe you."

"Oh, really? Why not?"

"Come on, Laura. Everyone knows about you and Hillman."

Again it was as if he had struck her.

"I see."

Then she came back.

"Well, I'm glad my private life is a matter of such public interest. What did they do, pass around my medical records? Jesus, what a bunch of creeps! You too, Paul. You're a nasty little creep, did you know that? I mean, I thought maybe you might have stuck up for me. I *asked* you whether you wanted me to go!"

"It's not *my* business whether you go. It's not my business whether you go to bed with some middle-aged creep you pick up on the road."

Again they were silent, and she seemed to be struggling hard. Then she raised her head.

"You're right, Paul. It's *not* your business. I was wrong. I've been wrong about a lot of things. I'm good at being wrong. But let's just forget it. Let's shake hands and call it quits." And she held out her hand.

"What do you mean?"

"I mean you're a nice kid, Paul."

"Don't patronize me."

She snorted.

"Okay, you're a nasty son of a bitch, do you like that better? Good luck, Paul." And she tossed her hair and walked away.

And so he had blown it with Laura Kinski. It was another emptiness in his life. A loneliness. An ache. For though he was angry and hurt, he found as time passed that he missed her. He had to admit to his amazement and surprise that of all the girls he knew he had *liked* Laura the best. He had really liked her.

Paul knew something was wrong as soon as he heard Jeb's voice on the phone.

"Have you heard about Whitey?" Jeb sounded frightened.

"No—what is it this time?"

"It's not funny, Paul. It's something terrible."

Paul felt his stomach go tight but he still kept up the front.

"What so terrible could happen to Whitey?"

"He's dead, Paul. He committed suicide."

Paul's mouth went completely dry. He could feel himself begin to shake.

"Are you sure?"

"One hundred percent."

"How do you know?"

"Craig Lewis called me. He's been calling to get the word out."

"Craig Lewis?"

"Yeah."

Then it had to be true.

Paul rested the telephone against his shoulder and put his head in his hands. He tried to think but all he brought up was an image of Claude Farrino looking pudgy and innocent and very much alive.

"But why?" he said after a moment.

"I dunno." Jeb's voice sounded frightened and hollow. "Philip said he was suffering from some medical problem—something about his glands."

"Do you think that could be it?"

"I dunno."

Again the boys were silent.

"Does Philip know?" Paul asked.

"Yes. Claude's mother called him."

"I see."

"Well, I've gotta go, Paul. I've gotta make some more calls."

"Okay," Paul said, and he hung up the phone.

He stood shaking, his head against the wall. He had no idea why Claude Farrino's death should affect him so powerfully. He had hardly known Claude, had barely spoken to him. Now he was dead.

And now a thousand questions swarmed into Paul's mind. How had Whitey done it? When? Who had discovered him? Had he left a note? Had he told anyone his plans? Had he confided in Philip? Could someone have stopped him? Could he, Paul, have done something?

He wanted to speak to someone but he didn't know whom. He might have spoken to his father but that was of course impossible. His brother wouldn't understand. He thought of Philip—Philip had jumped into his mind instantly; but somehow there was something distasteful about the idea of calling Philip.

It was Laura Kinski he really wanted to speak to; Laura Kinski, with whom he was no longer speaking.

And he wondered why Craig hadn't called him. He tried to put this petty thought out of his mind, but it nagged at him anyway. There had been a time when Craig would have called him. Tergiversator—a turncoat. By now he had looked it up, but it wasn't right. He had changed, that was all. Had grown away from what he had been. Had no desire to go back.

But Whitey was dead. What did it mean? How had he ever found the courage to do it? Paul thought of falling into an unconsciousness from which there could be no reprieve, and his mind reeled with panic.

.   .   .

That Friday a new rumor swept the school: The Bates committee was about to expel someone because of drugs. It was unclear how the rumor started, but it ran through the corridors exciting speculation, anxiety, fear.

"They say it's Pursy," Jeb said to Paul. They were standing in the corridor, and Paul's nerves, taut to begin with, were stretched to snapping.

"That wouldn't surprise me."

"There must be something wrong with the conjunction of the stars—first Whitey and now this."

"Yeah, it's lousy."

"So what's the story?" Jack Wheeler said, coming up to them. "What's all this shit about drugs?"

"They say Pursy's getting expelled."

"Pursy—nah, never. He's too suave. I figure it's gotta be some dip like Berger."

"It's Pursy," Paul said with irritation. "I've always said it was Pursy."

The other two boys looked at him.

"Well, excuse me," Wheeler said, "I didn't know you were an expert."

"I'm not," Paul corrected, sorry he had said anything. "I don't really give a damn who it is."

"Well, I suppose it doesn't make a lot of difference," Jeb said. "Compared to Whitey, I mean."

"Yeah," Jack Wheeler agreed, frowning. "What a crapper."

Paul looked for Philip but he didn't see him in school. They had spoken only once since Farrino's death.

"What are we going to do about Whitey?" Paul had said.

"What do you mean, what are we going to do? There's nothing to do."

"Well, it feels like we should do something."

"There's nothing to do, Paul. Whitey's dead. The Big Sleep—dig it?"

Now he looked for Philip to ask him about Pursy, but he wasn't there.

He saw Laura Kinski at the other end of a busy corridor but she turned away. He wasn't sure she had seen him.

"God, I'm upset about Claude Farrino," Brigit Bloom said between classes. She looked pale and tired but pretty, with her nice figure and large bright eyes.

"Yeah, me too."

"You were friendly with him, weren't you?"

"Not really. Richards took him under his wing."

"What was that crazy stunt, running him for president?"

"I dunno," Paul said, feeling uncomfortable. "It was some crazy idea Richards had. It doesn't make much difference now, does it?"

"I don't know. It just seems a little crazy."

Paul stuck his hands in his pockets and didn't answer.

"Are you going to Marsha's party?" she asked him.

"I don't know—are you?"

"I don't know. It seems sort of wrong going right now, after Claude and everything, but I could use something to get my mind off things."

"Yeah, I know what you mean."

"Listen," she said, "why don't you talk to Nicole anymore?"

He moved uneasily. "Is that what she says—that I don't talk to her?"

"Yeah—but I've noticed for myself. You don't have to be enemies."

"I'm not enemies."

"Well, she's going to Marsha's."

He looked at her, trying to understand what she was saying.

"Oh, yeah? Did she ask you to tell me?"

"No, of course not. I'm just saying it in passing."

He didn't say anything for a moment.

"Did you hear this thing about drugs?" he said.

"No—what thing about drugs?"

"That somebody's getting expelled. Because of drugs, I mean."

"Oh, who cares about that?" she said, wrinkling her nose. "Who cares about drugs?"

Paul went to Marsha's party only because he was too distracted to do anything else. He worried constantly about the Bates committee; he brooded about Whitey.

It was hot at the party and crowded, and Nicole was in the front hall acting bizarre; she was talking too loud, and when he entered she stopped talking and stared at him.

Paul left the hall, but a minute later she followed into the other room and came up to where he was standing.

"I've got to talk to you," she said. Paul looked at her but she had already turned away.

"Who was this Farrino guy, anyway?" he heard someone from another school ask. "I heard he was some kind of a math nerd or something."

"Yeah, he musta had some kind of a problem."

"Yeah, I bet. That's tough, though. I mean, that must be real tough on everybody."

"Yeah, like it stinks."

"Yeah, I'm surprised the guy had the guts to do it. He musta really been fucked up."

Paul didn't want to overhear any more and he walked away.

After a while he stood by himself drinking beer. He wanted to leave but he didn't know where to go. He didn't want to be alone.

"I have to talk to you!" Nicole whispered again; he hadn't seen her approach. "It's important," she added, leaning toward him.

"What are you talking about, Nicole?"

"Let's get out of here, I've got to talk to you now."

"Are you drunk or something?"

"Yes—maybe. But that's not the point."

Paul looked at her, and he didn't have the resolve to say no.

"Let's go, then," he said, and he took her by the elbow.

Outside in the night air she leaned against him and he could smell the alcohol.

When he walked with his eyes down he saw only the sidewalk and the cars parked bumper to bumper and the windows of the first floors with their gratings and their air conditioners protruding like strange muzzled snouts; but when he lifted his eyes he saw that he was caught in a vast machine that hummed and whirred beyond reckoning or design.

"So what's so important?"

"Important?"

"Yeah—you said you had something important to tell me."

"Yes—I'll tell you when we get home."

He feared she didn't have anything to tell him, that it was all part of some ruse, some unfathomable game, and that he had broken his promise not to speak to her for no purpose, only because she had beckoned.

They rode up in the elevator, and she clung to his arm as she had never done before.

The familiar odor of the apartment assailed him and his stomach tightened in excitement and alarm. She switched on the hall light.

"Where are your parents?"

"They're away for the weekend—they left me here alone."

He followed her to the kitchen, where she reached down a large plastic bottle of Pepsi and poured two tumblers partway full; then she opened a cabinet and, taking a bottle of dark rum, filled both glasses to the top.

"There!"

Paul sipped the drink, and it tasted like Pepsi with an undercoating of shellac. He watched Nicole's throat pump as she drank.

"Well," she said, "now we're alone! Isn't that what you always wanted?"

Later, on the love seat, she said, "I've thought of an argument to prove that there is no such thing as free will."

Her cheeks were flushed and her eyes wide and she spoke with strange animation.

"Is that what you had to tell me?"

"Yes—yes, it is. Remember our talk about Raskolnikov? Remember all that?" She reached and touched his hand.

He tried to keep his mind straight.

"Now listen to this," she said. "How does this go? . . . Let's imagine a man falling . . . No, that's not it. Let's imagine a man in a box. Yes, let's imagine a man lying perfectly still in a box. He's buried under the ground and he has no way to escape . . . Now, let me see, I thought this all out—it made perfect sense. I'm a little confused right now, but it made perfect sense when I thought of it. I wanted to tell you."

"Nicole, Nicole . . ."

"No, this is it, this is different, just listen. Imagine a person, a man or a girl, who keeps acting in a way she knows to be against her own . . . No, let's see! Don't you think that proves . . . ?"

He leaned over and kissed her. He wasn't sure why he did this, it was an act of unhappiness more than otherwise, perhaps the only way he could think to stop her ramblings; and the sweetness of her lips filled him with sadness, for he knew he no longer loved her.

"Let's get smashed," she said. "I mean let's get blotto!" And she uttered a strange laugh, as if the guttural sound had caught in the back of her throat.

As she drank greedily from the lip of the bottle, he observed the brown liquid spilling down the side of her face.

"Oh, God," she said, "blotto!" And handing him the rum, she threw herself backward onto the couch and lay sprawled among the pillows, her arms thrown back helter-skelter and her face flushed and her legs open at a thirty-degree angle.

He accepted the bottle and drank from the mouth where she had drunk, the alcohol hot and gagging in his throat; and as his eyes watered, he watched her watching him, her eyelids half closed and her feet lolling at the ends of her legs.

"Blotto!"

Later he was lying next to her on the couch and she was naked from the waist up, her blouse and bra crumpled and thrown to the ground, one leg in her tight black slacks lifted to the back of the couch, the other extended beside him. Her breasts were smooth and the areolas brownish, the nipples small and erect, the color of a slightly bruised peach.

He couldn't remember removing her blouse.

"Blotto!" she kept repeating. "Goddamn completely smashed—tha's what you've done to me. Tha's what I am!" And she giggled in amusement, her eyes closed, her features contorting in a strange comic mask.

He reached for her, but she slapped his hands away good-humoredly, continuing to laugh, as if they were engaged in some outlandish children's game.

"Mushn't mushn't—musht be a good boy now, Mama won't approve!" And she laughed more heartily as if this was a joke.

He attempted to clear his head but he felt sick and disoriented, and though he tried to convince himself that this was one of the great moments of his life, lying next to Nicole, naked and blottoed, with no one else in the apartment, in fact he felt nothing but sadness and a strange distanced curiosity.

"Bottle, bottle, who hash the bottle," sang Nicole, half lifting herself, her breasts jiggling; and, lying close to her, he inhaled the odor of her body, warm and intimate, and felt his stomach sicken with desire.

Nicole sat up, and, leaning backward, she tried to drain the last liquid from the bottle, the rum splattering onto her face; and as she shook the bottle she laughed.

"Oh boy oh boy oh naughty boy oh boy . . ."

Suddenly she slipped and, falling, landed with a thump on the floor. She sat in amazement beneath him, looking at him as if for that instant she had regained sobriety; then with a rush she threw herself backward onto the carpet, and, stretching her legs wide, she began to laugh.

He came down onto her immediately. She locked her legs around him, digging into him; and even then he was astounded by the outlandishness of their frenzy as, bucking, he dry-humped her there on the floor.

8

On the way to the funeral parlor Paul had sat in the back seat with Matthew while his mother sat in the front with his uncle, who drove. It was a clear, bright day and Paul watched the familiar streets and houses pass outside the window. He tried to avoid the thought that he could never speak to his father again.

"I keep wishing I had come home," Matthew said. "If only someone had told me to come home."

His brother kept rocking forward in his pain, bending from his waist toward his knees, his face screwed up in a manner that Paul recalled from their childhood.

"It's not your fault," their mother said. "There's no way you could have known. I won't have you blaming yourself."

"Your father wanted you to stay in Cambridge and continue your studies," their uncle said from behind the driver's wheel.

Paul turned and looked out the window, and he saw that the sky was a shell beneath which they were trapped like creatures in an aquarium. Beyond that there was nothing.

"Pauli," Matthew said, turning to him, his eyes large and dark, "did Daddy say anything at all, did he say anything to you?"

"He said he loved us," Paul said, and he saw tears fill his brother's eye, though he knew, strangely, that he himself wasn't going to cry. "He said he didn't want to die."

"Oh, God!" Matthew said, and again he began to rock.

They drove into the funeral parlor and Paul could hear the hiss of the tires as they rounded to a stop in one of the spaces marked for parking. Paul could see the back of his uncle's neck and he hated the fact that it was his uncle and not his father. They got out of the car.

Paul stood by the side of the car in the thin sunlight that glittered like the finest gold, and this day was like any other except that now Paul understood that it was all without meaning. He was afraid he wouldn't be able to remember this, and he tried to hold it in his mind.

His mother had taken Matthew's hand.

The funeral parlor was a squat, rectangular red-brick building with a wide green awning and two large brass-fitted doors, behind which the business of death was transacted daily. Paul had never been in such an establishment before, and he was struck by a sense of unreality.

The lobby was hushed and windowless, the flowers

bright, the proprietor obsequious, shaking hands and muttering something to their mother.

"Your husband is in the other room," he said, gesturing toward an open door, and something turned in Paul's stomach.

He followed into the room, and he saw against the farther wall an open black coffin.

He did not want to go closer.

"You come too, Pauli," his mother said. "It's only your daddy."

He approached, and he saw that his brother was standing and weeping quietly, and that his uncle was holding his mother's hand.

Then he saw something that was impossible.

Somehow the body had shrunk. Its skin was gray the color of flour paste, the kind you made when you were a child to glue papier-mâché, and its nose was arched and large. It looked like a bad reproduction in a wax museum.

Paul stood speechless above the coffin, unable to interpret what he was beholding.

"What happened to his eyes?" his brother asked. It was true, there seemed to be nothing behind his father's closed lids, just emptiness. Two holes.

"He donated his eyes," his mother said. "They also removed his brain," she added. "He donated that to science."

Matthew and his uncle nodded as if they understood all of this perfectly.

Paul looked again, and he could not comprehend what he was feeling, though he knew that part of it was fury. They had cut up his father in an amazing fashion.

Life had gone over him like a steamroller.

"He's at rest now," his mother said. She was speaking in a slow, controlled voice. "Poor Ed, he was so unhappy these last years, I guess it killed him. He was such a beautiful young man, such a golden boy—we fell in love the very first time we saw each other, before we had even met."

Paul had heard this before, but he listened now as if his mother's words contained some inestimable clue to life.

"He loved you two boys absolutely. Just last week he said, 'The best thing we ever did was to have the two boys.' He was a very good man—sometimes I thought he was too good. I got to the hospital just a few minutes after he died, while he was still warm, and when they left me alone with him I lay down next to him on the bed" (here she began to weep) "and embraced him and said goodbye for the last time, and I told him how much I loved him. Death is a part of life—I know that now. It's as natural as birth or growing up or any other part of life, it's all part of the same large cycle. I'm not afraid of it—and I don't want you boys to be afraid of it either. Now say goodbye to your father."

Paul realized that once he turned away he would never see his father again.

Matthew had taken his father's hand and was stroking his face, his tears falling onto the body.

"I love you, Daddy," Matthew said, words he had not spoken in ten years. "I love you."

Now all were weeping quietly—except Paul.

Paul put out his hand and then stopped. He was afraid to touch his father. He had loved everything about him, his smell, his warmth, the hair on his body, the sound of his voice, the shape of his hand. As a little boy he would watch his father shave, would shower with him, would snuggle into his warmth in bed. Now he was afraid to touch him.

"Touch your father," his mother said. "Don't be afraid."

He reached out, his hand hesitated, then he touched the coldness—the absolute coldness—of his father's cheek. Then he withdrew his hand.

Nothing that was happening was possible—and all of it was real.

The others had left, they had withdrawn toward the door, but he could not go. He felt he was choking, something was clutching at the inside of his throat. He had to leave but he could not—it was impossible that he would never see his father again.

Then he turned, he went halfway down the room, and then he was weeping. It was upon him before he knew, it was uncontrollable, he had fallen to his knees.

Paul Werth kneeled in the middle of that room and wept as if something inside had broken forever.

Their mother carried on stoically—and the boys took their lead from her. Numerous friends and acquaintances came to pay their condolences, details had to be attended to, life had to go on.

It was one of their mother's phrases—"Life has to go on." Paul was uncertain why this was so self-evident, but he didn't question its usefulness.

Something monstrous had happened—and no one

seemed to notice. No one but Matthew. All the time that life continued about one, the world was in fact flat, without dimension or depth—a mere scrim of appearance through which one could fall at any time. He had never noticed before—and no one else noticed now.

His mother had hung his father's wedding ring on a chain around her neck, and every time Paul saw this he choked.

"Do you see what she's done with Dad's ring?" Matthew asked with tears in his eyes. Paul merely nodded.

"God, I wish he could come back!" Matthew said. "If only he could come back for one hour! For one minute!"

"Where do you think he's gone?"

"I don't know. I swear, I don't have the slightest idea."

Matthew manifested a surprising sense of responsibility, shouldering as many burdens as he could. Their mother was plagued by telephone calls from services wanting to verify her credit. "How dare you ask me that at a time like this!" they heard her shout into the phone— and she wasn't a woman who shouted. "How dare you talk to me like that when my husband has just died!"

After that Matthew took to answering the phone.

That first night the family dined alone, only their uncle stayed.

"Do you know what I'd like to do?" their mother said. "I'd like to get out the pictures and look at them together. I'd like to remember all the good times. That's what Ed would have wanted."

They kept the pictures in a large box on the bottom shelf in the living room; for years their mother had intended to organize them, but this never happened. Now they got out the box and all sat about the living room looking at the pictures.

"Here's Maine—Jesus, look how young we look!"

"And here's Granny! What year was that?"

"That must have been 1954."

"And here's Dad with the canoe!"

"Here—let me see!"

There were some tears—but there was much laughter, and Paul and Matthew laughed especially hard. But Paul kept thinking, none of this can be true.

At nine their mother excused herself.

"You kids stay up if you want. I'm exhausted, I don't want to get run down."

Their uncle accompanied her to the foot of the stairs, and they could hear him talking quietly to her. When he came back he looked grim.

"Now, I don't want you boys being loud or boisterous, do you understand? Your mother's got to get her sleep."

The two brothers looked at their uncle without replying.

"I'm going to go in a minute, I'm done in—but I want you boys to clean up the house. You've got to take responsibility now that your dad's no longer here."

"Thank you, Uncle Austin," Matthew said. "We know what to do."

The boys cleaned up in the kitchen, and as they worked they talked.

"Uncle Austin sure is an idiot."

"He means okay," Matthew said.

"Where does he get off, telling us what to do?"

"He's just trying to help."

"Yeah—well I can do without his help."

"He'll go away soon—and then it will just be us. And then it will just be you, Paul, when I go back to Cambridge."

"Yeah," Paul said, "I know." And he was scared.

They went back into the living room and sat staring at the floor.

"If only I could tell him I was sorry!" Matthew said.

Paul didn't answer. He was absorbed by the thought that he should avenge their father's death.

"Do you think we ought to do something about that partner," he said, "the one dad hated so much?"

Matthew looked at him soberly.

"What could we do?"

"I dunno. Maybe we should hurt him somehow." In fact, Paul toyed with the fantasy of shooting him.

Matthew continued to look at his brother.

"I don't think that's such a great idea."

Then Paul heard a kind of a low whining, something like cats make before they begin to fight; he realized he had been hearing it for a while. He looked up and saw that Matthew heard it too.

"Is that coming from outside?"

"No—it must be the pipes."

They listened, and now the sound had changed, had become low and howling, and seemed to express the accent of pure unadulterated lament.

The boys looked at each other, and it must have struck them simultaneously what it was.

"My God!"

Paul felt his blood go cold.

They got up and went to the foot of the stairs. The sound became louder.

Paul started up the stairs and Matthew followed; he had gone white.

They stopped in front of their mother's closed door, and now the noise was wrenching and incessant. It hardly sounded human. The two boys looked at each other in disbelief and fear.

Two days after the funeral the brothers sat late at night in the living room. Their mother was asleep, the house was still, there were no sounds except the occasional distant hum of the city.

"I never understood him very well," Matthew said. He leaned forward toward his knees, rocking slowly, his voice expressing the intensity of his concentration. "He did love us, didn't he?"

"How can you even ask that?"

"I don't know. Don't you remember, he hit us with that belt?"

"He never hit us," Paul said.

"He hit me. He hit me across the legs."

"Not very hard. If he hit you at all, it wasn't very hard."

"No—that's true."

"And then you have to remember he was scared—we had run away."

"We hadn't really run away."

"We were gone for two hours, Matt. They thought we had drowned in that river."

"Yes—I suppose that's true."

"Of course it's true. Anyway, it's all so long ago."

Then they were silent, and Paul could hear the ticking of the house, low but perceptible, as if a large beast were breathing. Outside the night pressed against the windows.

His mother had called death *natural*, but in his opinion there was nothing natural about death. Death was a catastrophe, a violation, an absolute rupture in the order of things—and the fact that it continued about one daily, without comment or interruption, only added to the outrage.

"I don't understand what's happened," Matthew continued. "I don't understand how he could be here and then—disappear. Where has he gone, Paul?"

"I don't know."

"Do you understand what death is? I thought I understood, but now I find that everything we say is meaningless—literally without meaning. First we're here and then—poof, we've disappeared!"

Paul merely nodded his head.

He had not been this close to his brother in many years. When Matthew turned to him the need in his eyes was immediate and palpable, as if Paul might actually possess answers to his questions.

They had spent a lot of time laughing. It was unexpected that laughter should surround their father's death, but they had spent time reminiscing and dredging up memories from their childhood, and these had provoked laughter and even a kind of devil-may-care hilarity. But now they were again intensely serious.

"We'll have to try to help Mom," Matthew said. "We'll have to try to take his place."

The sentences filled Paul with anxiety.

"How can we do that?"

"I don't know. But I feel I've got to try."

"Those are pretty big shoes to fill."

"Yes," Matthew said, "yes, they are."

Then the two brothers were again silent.

"You don't think there can be any afterlife, do you?" Matthew asked.

Paul was shocked; his brother was the scientist, the rationalist.

"No—do you?"

"I don't know," Matthew said. "I never did before. But last night I thought Dad was standing by the end of my bed."

"That's just one of those feelings," Paul said, though he was spooked by what his brother had confided.

"Yes, I know. But still, it was spooky."

Paul went out to the garage to get the funeral program from the car; they had been discussing the ceremony, and he wanted to confirm the order in which events had occurred.

He paused, and he heard the creak of the night against the thin walls, as when wind creaks in the branches of trees, and suddenly he was certain that his father was outside looking in through the window.

The wind leaned against the garage, creaking, and Paul felt himself begin to shake. He knew he could believe or not believe. Keeping his eyes averted, he backed out of the garage.

Back in the light of the kitchen, Paul leaned against the counter, his breath coming in gulps. Even if the man he loved the most in the world were standing outside the window, he would be afraid to see him. He was cut off from his father forever.

9

When Paul returned from school he found his mother waiting for him with a letter in her hand.

"What is this all about?" She was chalky white and straight as a ramrod and her eyes were exceedingly dark.

He took the letter and glanced at it though he knew what it would contain: it was from the Bates committee concerning the inquiry about drugs.

He felt himself go white.

"It's all nonsense, Mom."

"What do you mean, nonsense?"

"I mean it has nothing to do with me."

She looked at him piercingly.

"Then why am I getting this letter?"

"It's all a mistake—a misunderstanding."

"A misunderstanding? Do you swear to me, Paul, that you've never had anything to do with drugs?"

"Yes," he said, returning her gaze, "I swear to you."

"No one in this family has ever lied to me."

"I'll never lie to you, Mom."

There was a long silence between them.

"All right," she said, and it was as if she had turned a

page. "So what do we do about this? I'll have to call the school."

"No, I can handle it. You have enough to worry about."

She looked at him carefully.

"This is a serious allegation."

"I can handle it," he repeated. "They have nothing on me, Mom. How could they? I've never touched drugs."

She sighed deeply, shaking her head.

"Do you want me to call Harriet English?"

"No, Mom—she's already on the committee."

"This wouldn't be happening if your father were alive."

His mother said to him, "Your uncle Austin would like to spend some time with you. I've asked him to come over on Sunday after lunch."

Since the death of their father, and notwithstanding the fact that he was notably ill suited for the part, their uncle had assumed the role of advisor to his sister's boys. He was a stolid, colorless man, not unintelligent but devoid of imagination and wholly devoted to the pursuit of money.

That Sunday, Uncle Austin appeared wearing a blue suit and a white starched shirt and a blue tie decorated with a marlin. His hair was thinning and his eyes sparkled and he cried hello to his sister and called Paul "boy," as if that were an especially endearing form of address.

"Well, Catherine, how are you—and how are you, boy? How are tricks?"

Paul allowed as how tricks were just great.

His mother gave him a sharp look.

"And how's your brother? What do you hear from the scholar up at Cambridge?"

"He's great too, Uncle Austin. Everything's just hunky-dory."

"Well, that's marvelous! I'm delighted to hear it!"

"Not as hunky-dory as all that, is it, Paul?" his mother interrupted. "I think you two should take some pie and go into the living room, where you can have a little chat."

"Without the womenfolk, eh, Paul?" And his uncle gave him a wink.

Paul picked up his pie, which he did not particularly want, and went into the other room.

When they were seated and his uncle had adjusted himself, pulling up the legs of his pants to relieve the tension at his knees and arranging his pie in front of him, he turned to Paul and exclaimed, "Well, now, isn't this dandy! Blueberry pie!"

Paul watched his uncle eat his pie. When his uncle ate fried eggs the yoke spread all over the plate. It stuck to the front of his uncle's teeth and stained the side of his mouth. It stained his napkin, which was then left egg side up by the side of his plate. Afterward Paul imagined he could smell egg on his uncle's breath.

"Well, Paul," his uncle said, putting down his plate and imperfectly wiping the blueberry filling from his mouth, "your mother and I are very concerned about you these days."

"Why's that, Uncle Austin?"

"Well, let me see if I have this right. If I understand what your mother tells me, you're not acting very happy."

"Happy?"

"Well, contented, then, if that's a better word. Now, I know you went through a rough spell, Paul, with your father's death and all—I'm not denying that. But it's time to turn a new leaf. We have to put that behind us, Paul. It's been over a year now."

"That long?"

His uncle looked at him and didn't say anything. He poked with his fork at the remains of his blueberry pie.

"Aren't you going to eat your pie?" he asked his nephew after a pause.

Outside Paul could see the young leaves along the branches. He remembered how his father would work in his garden while he stood watching. He would feel the love rising from his father's shoulders almost as if it were a mist, but he would say nothing, though he knew his love was palpable to his father too.

"I'm not very hungry."

"May I?" his uncle said, taking the pie. "Your mother sure can bake a blueberry pie!"

Paul watched his uncle eat the second piece of pie.

"You've got to look at the bright side of things," his uncle said, licking his fork and placing it thoughtfully by the side of his plate. "Life is like a kind of football game: you win some innings and you lose some, but you've got to keep your eye on the whole season."

"I see."

"So tell me what's bothering you. I'm not so stupid, you know. I've seen a thing or two. Is it your social life?"

"Yes, it's my social life," Paul said.

"Aha!" And his face lit up. "I thought as much. You know, when I was your age I had a devil of a time with the girls. I just couldn't seem to get the hang of what they wanted."

"What they wanted?"

"Yes. They're not much different from us, you know—not really. They want to see the big picture. They want to look at the bright side."

"And which side is the bright side?"

"Well, I'll tell you what isn't—brooding and hanging about and feeling sorry for yourself. That never won any prize that I've ever heard of."

Paul recognized this as the pint-size edition of the advice his mother dispensed, the brisk, somewhat stoical weltanschauung of her people, a philosophy not without its virtues though foreign to Paul's disposition.

"Now, I'll tell you what," his uncle continued. "You're worrying your mother and that won't do. She's got enough to worry about already. You've got to gird up your loins, as the Good Book says. You've got to act like a man." And here he tapped his nephew on the knee.

"Well, Uncle Austin, I certainly don't mean to cause Mom grief."

"You don't cause her grief, you don't cause her grief at all—that's not what I'm saying. She worries about you, that's all. It's not so easy for her either, you know."

"Yes, I know."

"Well, take that into consideration. You've got to be the man of the house, Paul—you and Matthew. You've got to take your father's place."

. . .

Paul hung about after school, wandering through the empty corridors, as familiar to him as a storybook from his childhood. Sunlight poured through the large windows, dappling the floors in pools of light.

He had seen Laura Kinski toward the end of that day in one of these corridors, and though he didn't admit to himself what he was doing, he hoped he might bump into her now. He hadn't spoken to her in days.

He knew she liked to take the sun in the upper field, and he drifted in that direction; climbing the hill, he saw the crane outlined against the sky. He skirted the construction site with care.

To his surprise he actually found Laura, sitting on a rock with her back to him, but she was talking to one of the seniors, a dark curly-haired boy who had been admitted to Yale on early admissions.

Paul could hear the distinctive sound of her laughter carry on the wind.

He watched as she bent forward, talking to the boy. Everything about her seemed to him lovely, the toss of her hair, the pout of her lips, the movement of her body.

He followed down the hill toward the train to the city, watching the sureness of her gait as she moved, the flow of her hips and shoulders.

He observed the conversation between them at the entrance to the train: the boy wished to accompany Laura but she didn't want him to, and though the exchange was bantering it offered Paul hope, for he saw that she didn't care for the boy.

He wondered if she was still angry at him.

Then she had disappeared, and he was alone. He

watched the late-afternoon sun beat off the tops of the trees and the tall distant buildings, and he felt a loneliness in his stomach, a forlornness which was now all too familiar.

Paul hadn't intended to go to Bobby Bower's party; he felt demoralized after his misadventure with Nicole, which had filled him with distaste. Nonetheless he found himself increasingly edgy as Saturday evening wore on.

His mother put her book down and watched him as he paced restlessly about the living room.

"It would be soothing to play a nice game of cards in the evening," she said, "bridge or canasta or something. But you don't like to play cards, do you, Paul?"

"Cards? I hate cards."

"It's your brother who's good at games. Of course, I can never beat your brother! You know," she continued, "I've been thinking that I might send the bankbook up to Cambridge for Matthew to balance."

He stopped and watched her as she adjusted her bookmark, lining it up evenly.

"Why would you want to do something like that? All you've got to do is add and subtract."

"Well, I wouldn't want to make a mistake, and you know how clever Matthew is."

"About adding and subtracting?"

"About anything to do with numbers."

"Jeez, Mom, I mean *I* could do the bankbook." But he let it drop.

"You know Matthew blames Dad for the heart attacks," he said after a pause.

"Does he?" She sounded thoughtful. "Well, that isn't right of Matthew. Anyone can have a heart attack. Still, it isn't good to be as angry as your dad was."

"Didn't he have cause?"

"Yes, but that's not the point. Matthew isn't right—but he isn't entirely wrong."

It irritated him to hear her siding with Matthew.

"I feel sorry for Dad," was all he said.

The light from the lamp fell on his mother's hair, and as he watched her he felt the old familiar contradiction of love and anger, need and frustration.

"I think I'll go out for a while."

"Oh—that's fine. Do you have someplace special to go?"

"Bobby Bower's giving a party. I thought I might go there."

"That's nice. How are Bonnie and Bobby, anyway? I haven't heard about them for a long time."

"Oh, they're okay," he said vaguely. He didn't want to be drawn into a conversation about the Bower kids, with whom he had grown up.

"Well, don't be too late."

"Don't wait up for me."

Paul went out the door and the wind was up; he could hear it blowing in the trees. His feet echoed on the empty pavement. He inhaled the dampness of the night air as he walked, and a riff from "Take Five" beat through his head.

He thought of Whitey but he tried to put that out of his mind.

He could hear music as he mounted the stairs to Bower's. The house was familiar to him from his childhood, spacious, with a terrace, a swimming pool, and a garden that extended for a number of acres in the back.

Kids were milling in the living room, dancing to the loud music. Paul nodded as he proceeded through the house and out the back door onto the patio, where more couples were dancing. Beyond them the garden rustled in fragrance.

Paul looked around, but there was no one there he cared about. He searched in vain for the trampoline from his childhood, long since disappeared. He wondered why he had come.

Wandering along the patio, he reached the end of the house where he stopped in the dark. He could see the stars overhead. Peering through a window, he saw kids in the lighted room, Doyle and Pursy, Bower and Peach's boyfriend, Bob Tucker, now back from Yale.

Just then Nicole entered; Paul could see her from where he stood in the dark. She was talking with Robbie Doyle, and now she had gone up to Bob Tucker and had taken his arm.

That was strange.

Paul stood outside the window in the dark, and the longer he watched, the stranger the scene became. There was something wrong with the way Nicole hung on to Bob Tucker. It was too close. It was too intimate.

After a while Paul turned away into the garden.

When he calmed down he went inside the house. The

rooms were even noisier and more crowded than before and people were sweating in the heat.

He encountered Bonnie Bower standing by the punch bowl looking hot and bored.

When they were growing up Bonnie had been a large, pretty girl who liked to ride and draw pictures of horses, which she sometimes showed to Paul. She had grown into a handsome young woman with large, prominent breasts and hips and a great mane of dark hair which she threw about like a horse. Now her face was flushed and she appeared to be looking for somebody.

"Hello, Bonnie."

"Why, hello, Paul! What breeze blew you in?"

"Hey, that doesn't sound very friendly."

"Oh, I just didn't *expect* you, that's all. I thought you'd be with *Laura Kinski* or something."

"What do you have against Laura?"

"Oh, nothing. She's all right, I suppose—if you like that type."

Paul let this drop. He didn't care enough about Bonnie's opinion to pursue it. Besides, he wasn't seeing Laura anymore.

"I see Bob Tucker's here," he said, trying to sound casual.

"Oh, yeah, he came with Nicole."

"Nicole? I thought he was Peach's boyfriend."

"Where have *you* been?"

"What do you mean?"

"You mean you really don't know?"

Paul looked at Bonnie.

"What are you talking about?"

"I thought everyone knew. Nicole's in love with Bob Tucker. I mean like in *love*. She's been that way for over a year."

Paul's throat had gone completely dry.

"But what about Peach?" he managed to say.

Bonnie merely shrugged. "Oh, Peach won't *speak* to Nicole. The two haven't spoken in months."

"I don't get it."

"Of course you don't get it. Nobody *gets* it. But those are the facts."

"And Tucker?" Paul forced himself to ask.

"Oh, Bob dates both of them." She shrugged again. Then, drawing closer: "He *sleeps* with both of them!" And she giggled. "Can you imagine?"

Paul didn't say anything. He felt as if someone had kicked him. At the same time the proverbial light had gone on in his head.

"Why do they put up with it?" he said finally.

Bonnie Bower merely laughed. "Put up with it? Don't you get it? They're *sisters!*"

Paul went into the living room, where the lights were off, and sat on the couch. He noted vaguely that Suzanne Pratt's blouse had come out of her skirt while she was dancing. It was hot in the room and Paul sat feeling the weight of the heat as if it were inside him struggling to get out.

After a while he got up and wandered back into the hall where the punch bowl stood. The punch was a concoction of fruit juice and ginger ale and rum and after gulping a first glass Paul poured himself another.

When Paul stepped outside the heat hit him like a blast furnace. His head turned and his feet seemed imperfectly connected to his body. He walked with care as if balancing something on the end of his nose, his hands thrust into the pockets of his sport jacket with ostentatious casualness, like his hero Jack Kennedy.

"Hel-*lo*, Paul!"

Paul turned and saw through cleverly focused eyes that he had been addressed by Jeb, who stood slightly above him on the lawn holding a highball glass in one hand.

"Hello, Sheb!" Paul cleared his throat as if to account for the mispronunciation.

"Damn fine party, eh?" Jeb said, staggering slightly.

"What's sho damn fine?"

"Well, the goddamn alcoholic refreshment, for one. It's the best goddamn alcoholic refreshment I've ever encountered, if you've got to know."

"I wouldn't know anything about it," Paul said with dignity. Just then one of his feet slipped for no apparent reason, though he caught himself almost immediately and brought himself back to attention with natural aplomb.

"You know what's wrong with you?" Jeb insisted, apparently not having noticed this imperceptible faux pas. "You're not an appreciator of the goddamn beauties of the world. I mean like the goddamn beauties of alcoholic refreshment, for example. You're some kind of a goddamn puritan or something, Werth. I mean like a goddamn *puritan!*"

The two boys stood looking at each other with sustained dignity.

"Jeb," Paul said after a moment, "it caushesh me pain to say this, but you are *drunk!*"

"I am not *drunk*," Jeb said with decorum. "I am intoxshicated!"

Paul stumbled into the garden and lay down among the rhododendron bushes. The earth felt cool beneath him. Already the party seemed distant; he was aware of the buoyant odor of grass and fresh leaves and observed far overhead the distant twinkle of the stars.

He closed his eyes, and immediately his head was a whirlpool pressing him into the earth. Panicked, he opened his eyes; the entire sky was a giant lid swaying off kilter. He sat up—too swiftly, and fell forward onto his hands.

He thought he was going to be sick.

Paul lay for a long time trying to gather his strength. He knew that if he closed his eyes the spinning would begin again. In his mind he could see Nicole standing too close to Bob Tucker but he dismissed this as something he would have to deal with another time.

He couldn't tell how long he lay there.

Slowly Paul sat up, moving with care. He hoisted himself to his feet. He stumbled through the bushes, and for a while he couldn't tell where he was. Then, obliquely, he heard a sound, and, looking, he saw the house: he had been moving parallel to it through the dark.

The sight of the house cleared his head. He came out onto the lawn, and now he was approaching the back of the swimming pool, lit like some weird astral emanation, a great glowing rectangle of aquamarine.

Kids were crowded about the pool. The sound of music blared at him as he approached.

"Will somebody please turn that goddamn music down?" Bobby Bower called. He was hemmed round by people and raised his arms to extricate himself from the crowd.

"Aw, Bower, don't be such a party pooper!"

"I'm not a party pooper, it's just that we're going to have the goddamn police!"

"Aw, Bower," Ned Hillman said, "don't be a pussy!" His shirt was open and his arm around Betty Rollins.

Bower turned to Hillman in annoyance.

"That's easy for you to say, Hillman. It's not your goddamn party. It's not your old man who's gonna go apeshit."

"Aw, shit," Hillman said in disdain. "Why throw a party if you're a pussy?"

Paul negotiated poolside and stood blinking in the light; he looked about him but couldn't see Nicole.

"You know what we're gonna do?" Hillman called. "We're gonna play JFK."

Bower regarded Hillman across the ripples of the pool, his face swollen in the heat.

"How d'ya do that?"

"Here's how," Hillman said, and with one arm he lifted Betty Rollins, no small girl, and dropped her into the water.

Paul made his way through the turmoil and into the house; he could hear splashes and screams as kids pushed and shoved one another into the pool. He paused in the hall; the entire living room seemed to be vibrating to "What'd I Say."

He went upstairs and sat on the landing. He was amazed to see that it was past 2 A.M.—someplace he had lost over an hour. A coolness drifted to him from down the hall; sounds came distant and muffled. For a while he rested his head in his hands.

When he finally stood up he wandered down a corridor. He peered into a room, but he saw only a pile of wraps, the scene suspended in a strange stillness as if the guests had thrown down their things helter-skelter and departed forever.

A second room, another bed, another pile of clothing, and—shoes and an arm. Paul's eyes adjusted: he made out Bonnie Bower, her head thrown back, her eyes closed, her knees pointing toward the ceiling. The shoes were the foreshortened legs of the boy lying between her thighs.

Paul backed away, but not before registering the image of Bonnie's naked breast, white and spilled like a pudding to one side.

Downstairs he paused in the hall. The music in the living room had subsided and heat emanated from the room as from an infection. He approached the punch table and poured himself another glass of punch.

The boy standing next to him was Philip Richards.

"Ah, *paeshano*," Philip said, his face flushed, the large vein on his forehead swollen and pulsing, "I greet you in the corridorsh of hell."

"Hello, Philip."

"*Hello, Philip?* What ish that? What ish that, anyway—the voish of fucking sobriety?"

"I was sick before."

"Ah, well, sick. Sick ish as sick does, eh? Whitey wash shick. Whitey was shick in the fucking *head*."

"Whitey was *sad*."

"Shad? Shad? You talk to me about fucking *shad*? Whitey was a loser."

With that the two boys looked at each other while

Richards frowned and nodded his head up and down with contemptuous certainty.

"I wash much disappointed in that lad," he said.

Just then a raucous blast escaped from the darkened living room and three figures staggered out: Suzanne Pratt, Bob Tucker, and Nicole Swann.

"Oh, I'm so hot I could just *die!*" Suzanne Pratt said. "I mean, it's like I just can't *breathe.*"

"My head is going *round* and *round,*" Nicole said. She leaned against the wall, and Paul could see the suppleness of her spine. "I need a *Coke* or something."

"Coke, Coke—who's got a Coke?" Bob Tucker chanted, staggering around the room and setting the girls off into giggles.

"Coke, Coke!" Suzanne Pratt repeated before subsiding into gales of laughter. "Oh, you crack me up, Bob, you just crack me up!"

"Oh, I'm a regular *nutcracker,* aren't I, Nicole? Aren't I a regular nutcracker?"

"Oh, you're a nutcracker all right," Nicole said, and she leaned her weight against the wall.

"You're a regular fucking idiot," Richards said.

Bob Tucker looked up and smiled; he hadn't made out what Richards had muttered.

"So, Bob," Philip continued, staggering forward into the light, "how doesh it feel to be the fucking hero come home? How doesh it feel to be the fucking Playboy of the Weshtern World?"

Bob Tucker looked at Richards and frowned in good-humored confusion.

"Who the hell are you?"

"Oh, that's just Richards," Suzanne said. "Philip, you're *so drunk!*"

"Oh, Suzanne," Richards said, "that's like saying, World, you're so round!"

Nicole Swann leaned against the wall and studied Paul out of large, inscrutable eyes.

"Does anyone have a Coke?" Suzanne Pratt asked. "I'm just *dying* for a Coke!"

"I'll get you a Coke," Bob Tucker said.

"No, don't leave," Nicole said. "I don't want you to go."

"What's wrong, Nicole?" Richards sneered. "You afraid someone might bite you?"

Nicole looked at Paul with a kind of brooding sadness. "Why is your friend so nasty?" she asked.

Paul didn't say anything. He studied Nicole for an instant, and he saw flash before him an entire school year wasted. Then his face hardened, and, turning, he quit the room.

He exited into the early morning. A small breeze rustled the foliage. He stood for a minute breathing the air.

O toi, qui vois la honte où je suis descendue,
Implacable Vénus, suis-je assez confondue?

"Why don't you forget about that chick?"

Richards had followed him outside. He spoke now out of the side of his mouth. "She doesn't do anything for you."

Paul looked at Richards but didn't say anything.

Philip shrugged. He took out a Pall Mall and lit it, flipping the extinguished match into the bushes.

"She's fucking that Bob Tucker."

"Who says she is?"

"Come *on*. Don't be a chump."

"What happened to Peach in all this?" Paul said bitterly.

Richards merely shrugged. "How should I know? They're two fucked-up chicks—especially that Nicole broad. She's fucked-up in the head, *bambino*—can't you see?"

Could it be true? Could Nicole be sleeping with *her sister's boyfriend?* Could he have been that *wrong?*

He thought about it for a moment, and he had to admit he saw the humor. What a joke! What staggering *intuition!*

Had he ever really been in love with Nicole? Or had he been in love with the heat of her dress, the slope of her back, the shine of her eyes, the sound of her name? Had he been in love with being in love?

At some level he already knew that love was a kind of game one played on oneself—a ruse to lift life out of boredom and loneliness, a sort of self-willed stupidity.

What is love, 'tis not hereafter!

He stepped down into the night, and suddenly he felt light-headed and directionless, as if he were falling through space.

Richards followed him into the shrubbery and, turning his back, pissed heavily into the bushes.

"Take that, you fucking swine. Fucking bourgeois swine, that's what they are." He stumbled forward, groping as he closed his fly. Paul noted that he had wet the side of his leg.

"Did I ever tell you about me and that Suzanne Pratt?" he inquired gruffly. They had come to a gazebo-like structure made of shaggy logs with a Dixie cup roof set on its top, and Philip sat down heavily inside, running his hands through his blond slicked-back hair.

"Listen," Richards continued. "Last September, Suzanne Pratt came to my apartment after a party. I mean, it was two A.M. or something and she was drunk as hell and she asked whether she could come back to my apartment to tell me something. I hardly knew the girl, but here she was sitting at the edge of my bed at two A.M.—so what do you think she says? I mean, Suzanne Pratt is *stacked* and everything, you know, with boobs out to here, and even though she isn't exactly my *type*, well, let's just say things were getting *interesting*. Because what do you think ol' Suzanne has to say? It turns out that Suzanne Pratt is worried she's *frigid*. Can you dig it? I mean, *Suzanne Pratt!* So before I know it she is lying on my bed and I am working over her like some kind of a lunatic, you see? I mean, I'm trying to make her *come*. And the truth is, Suzanne Pratt *is* frigid. I mean, I'm trying this and I'm trying that and she's closing her eyes and she's sweating and she's groaning a little but after a while she says to me—and she's just about crying—she says, 'You see, I told you—it's just no good!' And I think to myself, this is getting *serious*, because now my *honor* is at stake, and it's just at that moment that I find her *hot spot*. Dig it, *bambino?* Because now she begins to groan for real, and her back arches, and I can see those big boobs of hers grow hard as watermelons and those large titties stand up like cheerleaders, and suddenly we are marching to *clitoria*, baby, because this girl is going, going, *gone!*"

He stopped, and the two boys looked at each other a little dazed. Then Richards laughed.

"Well, that's my story, bubby, and you can believe it or not as you see fit. All you've gotta do is ask Suzanne Pratt!" And again he gave a laugh.

Philip lifted himself heavily from his seat and staggered down the stairs into the garden.

"Look at this fucking joint," he said. "Who do they think they are, anyway, the fucking French aristocracy? What is this, 1789 or something?"

He took a walking stick leaning against the gazebo and with a *swoosh* he beheaded one of the flowers.

"There, I'll give you 1789! What have flowers ever done for me, anyway—can you tell me that?" And walking over to one of the large earthen flowerpots that marked the end of the path, he beheaded another stalk.

"Jesus, Philip."

"*Jesus, Philip.* What's *that* supposed to mean?"

"I dunno."

"Yeah, I bet you don't. Here, I'll show you." And he began to chant a little rhyme of his own devising.

A was once a little ass.
Sassy lassy with your assy,
Why so smart and sassafrasy?

And with that he swung the walking stick against the side of the pot, cracking it open like a pumpkin. Then he staggered down the path.

B was once a brazen boy.
Oh, with joy that brazen boy
Stuck it to the hoi polloi!

And he swung again, cracking another pot.
"Philip, for chrissake! Those are *flowerpots!*"
Philip looked at Paul unpleasantly and smiled.

C was once a sticky cunt.
For a runt that sticky cunt
Sure could bellow, sure could grunt!

And again he swung, shattering another earthen pot.
"Philip, I'm not going to stay if you're gonna do that."
"Oh no? Well, don't break my heart, bubby. I mean,
you've gotta please yourself, *bambino*—that's what I'm trying to inculcate, dig it? I mean, that's my lesson for the
day—and it *is* just about day, right? And I've still got work
to do." And he proceeded toward the next pot.

Paul left Philip smashing flowerpots.

When he returned to the large house he could see a
lightening in the east. He felt tired and weak. A quicken-
ing breeze caused him to shiver and he turned up the
collar of his jacket.

The house seemed quiet as he approached. Then a
window was thrown open and he heard a burst of laughter and a head protruded and then withdrew and the window was again abruptly closed.

He mounted the lawn to the swimming pool, now de-
serted though still littered with the remains of the de-
bauch, including a number of wet bras and panties thrown
into a crumpled heap.

Inside, the house was quiet. Kids were slouched in chairs or sprawled on sofas, fast asleep. He continued to the foyer, where the punch bowl was overturned. From down the hall he could hear a kind of subdued ruckus.

Peering into the room, he observed people still dancing, though close to somnambulistic, as if they had been wound up and couldn't stop. One or two had reeled into a state of inanition: Pursy sat comatose on a chair, his large legs spread apart, his weight resting on his heels. Betty Rollins lay sprawled on a couch, her dress hiked up on one of her plump thighs so you could see her panties.

Paul walked home slowly through the morning light. He had never before stayed up all night and he felt tired and strangely light-headed, as if he were seeing the world for the first time.

Birds sang from the trees. A pigeon fell straight through the air, then bent its wings and curved abruptly upward in a sharp, graceful loop—the puff of a sail in high wind. Then the sun, a brilliant shield, rose slowly into the sky.

For the next few days the students at Highgate appeared chastened, as if recovering from a hangover. Paul avoided Philip. He noted that Nicole Swann was nowhere to be seen. And he looked in vain for Laura.

He was eager now to meet with the Bates committee and have it over. He didn't want to worry his mother more than he had already. He had gotten himself into a jam, but he relied on the fact that he was innocent. He had done nothing.

But before he heard from the committee, he heard from Feifer Kinski.

"Hello," somebody on the telephone said, "is this Paul Werth?"

"Yeah, this is he."

"Oh, hi, Paul! I'm not bothering you or anything, am I?"

"No, you're not bothering me. Who is this?"

"Oh—this is Feifer. You know, Feifer Kinski—Laura's brother."

"Oh, yeah—hi, Feifer. What's up?"

"Well, I guess I really shouldn't be calling you, Paul. I mean, my sister would kill me! But I thought I'd better call you anyway, if you know what I mean?"

"No, I don't really know what you mean. What's up, anyway?"

"Well, it's not like it's such a big deal. I mean, I wouldn't want you to get the idea that it's a matter of life and *death* or anything, okay? On the other hand, it's not so *far* from life and death either—if you see what I mean."

Paul was getting pretty worried by all of this, though mostly it just seemed a muddle. He was forming a picture in his mind of Feifer as some little runty kid with ink stains all over his fingers.

"I don't see what you mean, Feifer. What are you talking about?"

"Well, it's my sister. It's just that she—well, she tried to—you know—commit suicide."

"Jesus—Feifer! What are you talking about?"

"Yeah, I know—pretty stupid, right? I mean, like, it's no big deal—it's not as if she *succeeded* or anything. To tell the truth, I don't even think she *meant* it, if you want to know what I think. It's just that . . ."

"Wait a minute, Feifer—hold on! Please tell me what happened. Is your sister okay?"

"Yeah, yeah—she's fine. She just took some pills, that's all. She just like OD'd, you know? Only she left a note and everything so my parents would find out and she wouldn't *die.*"

And suddenly Feifer broke down; Paul could hear him weeping on the other end of the phone.

"Jesus, Feifer," Paul said in a weak voice. He felt sick.

"Are you okay?" he asked after a while.

"Yeah, I'm fine, I'm okay. It's just that I have this cold and everything, you know?"

"Yeah, sure. I'm sorry, Feifer—I mean, I'm *really* sorry. But the point is, is Laura okay?"

"Yeah, she's fine. I mean, she's resting and all, you know—but she's fine. But this is what I want to know—why did she do it? That's what I don't understand. I mean, why did she pull a crazy harebrained stunt like that? Do you know? Do you have any idea?"

"No, I don't. I don't know. Have you asked her?"

"Yeah, sure I've asked her. She says she just *felt* like it. She says it was just a *stunt,* for chrissake, to scare our parents. But, I mean, what kinda stunt is that? Half a bottle of sleeping pills!"

Paul whistled under his breath.

"Jesus!" he said. "Half a bottle?"

"Yeah."

Then both boys were silent.

"But what I wonder," Feifer said after a time, "is this: could you call her or something? I mean, I know she *likes* you. I mean, I know you're just about the only guy she *respects* or thinks is halfway intelligent or anything, or even is just like a *human being,* for chrissake, and not some kind of a stupid stud or something. I mean, I know that's the way she feels."

Paul didn't say anything.

"So what I wonder," Feifer continued, "is whether you might call her up. I mean, I know she'd like it, and it would cheer her up and everything, and maybe, just maybe, you could find out what's in her goddamn head? You know what I mean? I mean, Christ, we don't want her trying this goddamn stupid stunt again!"

"No, we don't," Paul said.

"So will you call her up?"

"You think she'd really like me to?"

"Yeah—I know it. I mean, like, she *cares* for you, you know? I mean she *respects* you and everything. She'd kill me if she knew I was telling you this. She'd kill me if she even knew I was calling you on the goddamn telephone. But the fact remains—I mean, this is just the plain goddamn fact of the matter, whether we like it or not—she tried to *kill* herself!"

"But why did you *do* it?" he asked.

It was night, and Laura and he were standing on the sidewalk in the early-summer heat by the side of her building, where she had agreed to meet him. Taxis and cars passed sporadically; a few night pedestrians were out walking their dogs or hurrying to some nocturnal rendezvous.

She seemed the same: the same slender, carefree body, the lines just slightly filled out with the health of young womanhood, the same dark, glossy hair cut short at the side of her face, the same slender, nervous fingers, the same long neck, the same ironic, amused expression with prominent nose and eyes kohled like Egyptian eyes and small mouth puckered in a grin.

"Oh, it didn't mean anything," she said, smiling. "It was just—a lark."

"A lark!"

"Yes—a joke. Don't you believe me?"

"How can I believe you? I don't know *what* to believe."

"Well, you'll have to believe what you want to believe—but I never meant to kill myself. I knew they'd find me."

"But what if they *hadn't?*"

"But they *did!*" And she laughed—but it wasn't a convincing sound. There was something snide and dismissive about it, as if she were laughing at the world.

"Laura—I don't understand you."

"Oh? I thought you had me all fixed in a formulated phrase?"

"No—don't be like that! Don't you know that I care for you?"

"Do you? You could have fooled me."

"But I *do*, Laura. You do know that! I want you to promise me you won't try this thing again."

"What is this—the Children's Aid Society?"

"Laura—don't!"

"Oh, okay, okay! I won't do it again, okay? Is that what you want to hear? Only—why not? I mean, why shouldn't I do it again? Can you tell me that?"

"Why not? Why not? I mean, my God, Laura, what kind of a question is that? Don't you get what you almost did? I mean, *death*, Laura! Don't you get it?"

The two stood looking at each other, their eyes staring in something very like desperation.

"What's the big deal?" she said after a moment, but her voice had changed, had faltered, become sadder, less defiant. "Who cares, anyway?" she said.

"Well, I'll tell you one person who cares—Feifer. I mean, that little guy was *upset*, Laura."

"Yeah—Feifer." And she smiled to herself. "He's sweet."

"Of course he's sweet. And he's your *brother!* How do you think he'd feel?"

"I dunno."

"Don't be stupid."

"Well, I *don't* know. I mean, it's all so stupid. So stupid! How can you stand it? How can *anyone* stand it?"

"Stand *what*, Laura?" he asked in real desperation. "I mean, that's *life*, that's what we get. You'll get the other flavor for a very long time."

"So maybe we'd better hurry up and get there."

"No!" he said angrily. "I mean, what in the name of God is the hurry? Don't you get it, Laura? That's *death!* That's the only other color it comes in. These aren't just *words*."

She was silent after that, leaning against the wall of the building while she studied one of her toes at the end of her long, elegant leg.

"I still don't see that it makes any difference," she said after a while.

He was desperate to know what else to say.

"Well, I'll tell you who else cares," he said after a moment. "*I* do."

She looked at him in the dark.

"Do you?"

"Yes, I do. I do, Laura!" But he could see he hadn't convinced her.

"Well," she said, and now it was she who was placating him, "you can set your mind at rest. I promise you I won't try to commit suicide again, okay? Only—I still don't see why not."

Lucius Bates had a habit of twirling his pencil between his fingers so that it struck the table with the eraser, then with the point; and he was now engaged in the pensive mode of this activity as he considered Paul Werth from under his brows.

"So let me see if I've got this right, Mr. Werth," he said slowly, consulting the notes that lay before him.

The room was filled with hot, uncomfortable afternoon light that blurred the three figures who sat at the front desks. Paul waited uneasily, bogged in a kind of fatalistic lethargy.

"You say you spent the entire evening of Laura Kinski's party with Philip Richards," Bates continued. "Is that correct?"

"Yes, sir."

"And at no time did you or Mr. Richards have congress in any manner with drugs."

"No, we didn't."

"You were alone, the two of you, I take it? I mean other than when you were at Miss Kinski's party."

"That's correct," Paul said. He didn't quite see where

this was going but he was eager to have it finished. Again trying to concentrate, he observed that Miss English was watching him intently while Mrs. Wagner stared, apparently in amusement, at the ceiling.

"All right," Mr. Bates concluded, striking the top of the desk decisively with his eraser. "I think I have this straight. Would either of you ladies care to add anything?"

"Would you like to change anything you've said to this committee?" Miss English inquired, leaning across her desk and looking earnestly at Paul out of her clear, intelligent, innocent Kansas eyes.

Paul swallowed. He wished he could change *everything* he had said to the committee, he wished he could tell them he washed his hands of the whole affair. But it was too late for that.

"No."

"You know, Mr. Vurt," Mrs. Wagner said out of the blue, "you got almost *all* the French homework wrong the utter day. Now, why was that?"

He couldn't believe she was saying this.

"I dunno, Mrs. Wagner. I guess I've got other things on my mind."

"Ah, yes—utter things! Vell vell vell—so cute and so stupid!"

He felt himself color to his eyes; he would never forgive her for that statement.

"Well, then," Lucius Bates said, clearing his throat, "if there are no further questions I think we may proceed. Miss English, could you ask the others to come in?"

This took Paul by surprise; he had expected to be dis-

missed. He watched with interest and then with mounting alarm as Berger and Philip Richards entered the room.

Berger presented his usual obsequious, smiling, defer-
ential self, bowing and scraping his way across the room.
Philip, dressed as ever in his blue suit with his hair slicked
to the back of his head, walked with perfect nonchalance
to a front chair and threw himself into it with evident
boredom.

"Gentlemen!" Lucius Bates said, and a half smile crossed
his handsome, saturnine features. "Thank you for joining
us today."

Richards looked at Bates but did not respond; Berger
smiled ingratiatingly.

"As you know, we've spoken to each of you separately,
but since there are some—should we say discrepancies?—
among your statements, we thought it expedient if we all
now met together. Shall we proceed?"

Berger kept his eyes on the ground, but Richards regarded Bates with a condescension equal if not superior to
the headmaster's.

"Let's start with you, Mr. Werth, shall we?"

Paul moved uneasily in his chair.

"Am I correct in stating that according to your testimony you and Mr. Berger did not spend the evening
together on the night of Laura Kinski's party?"

"That's right."

"I'm sorry, could you speak a little louder?"

"That's right," Paul repeated. He was looking at Bates
with hostility.

"Well, we *did* see each other at the party," Berger
chimed in, smiling ingratiatingly at the panel.

Paul glanced at Berger with distaste before looking away.

"Is that correct, Mr. Werth?" Bates inquired.

"Yes," Paul said.

"But you didn't spend time with Mr. Berger *after* the party, is that correct?"

"Yes."

"I see," Mr. Bates said, fingering his chin and twirling his pencil. The three adults were studying Paul intently.

"Now let's turn to *you*," Mr. Bates addressed Berger. "You understand that you've been accused of selling drugs outside Laura Kinski's apartment during and after her party?"

"I do, sir."

So that was it! Paul couldn't help looking at Berger again. The little swine!

"And what do you have to say to that?"

"I told you, sir, that it's not true. I've never taken any drugs and I've certainly never sold any."

"And yet the same accusation has reached us from a number of different sources."

"That doesn't make it true. I never had anything to do with drugs. As I told you before, I spent about an hour, an hour and a half, at Kinski's party, then Philip and I went home to his house. We were there before the party ended and we spent the evening there alone. We had nothing to do with drugs."

Paul knew Berger was lying since he had seen him outside Laura's when he left with Jeb. In addition, Philip had told him he had gone home that night alone.

"And now for you, Mr. Richards," Bates said. "What do you have to say?"

"I really don't have anything to say," Philip said loftily, drawling through his nose. "This entire inquisition strikes me as preposterous. So far as I can make out, you don't have a shred of evidence against Berger or anyone else."

"That remains to be seen," Mr. Bates said with a kind of twinkle, "but we certainly do have some conflicting testimony. Perhaps you might assist us."

It was not a question, and Philip did not bother to reply.

"Both Mr. Berger and Mr. Werth claim not to have seen much of each other on the night of Miss Kinski's party. They also claim not to have had anything to do with drugs. They also claim to have spent the entire evening— with you."

Philip stirred noticeably in his chair. He looked quizzically at Paul. Bates's face had assumed a Cheshire cat smile. He continued.

"Now wouldn't you call that conflicting testimony, Mr. Richards? Perhaps you can help us to see our way through this thicket."

Richards cleared his throat.

"Paul and I spent the evening together *before* the party," he said evenly. "I assume that's what you are referring to." He had regained his sangfroid and regarded Bates with a bored, expressionless countenance.

"No, I don't think so. Is that what you were referring to?" Bates asked, turning to Paul.

Paul, struggling for footing, perceived how lunatic it had been not to coordinate with Philip beforehand. Still, he couldn't believe that Philip wouldn't cover for him. He had said what he had said only to protect Richards. He *knew* Berger was lying.

"I spent the evening with Philip before the party. We walked home together afterward."

For a moment the room was silent. Berger was looking at Paul with a kind of smirk; Richards regarded him in lofty amazement.

"I don't believe Paul remembers this quite correctly," Philip said, and again he was drawling through his nose. "I don't see that it's of any significance, but in fact I went home with Berger. We left before the party ended, as Berger told you."

Paul could feel the eyes of Wagner and English studying him carefully. His color had come up in spite of himself: he was blushing. He felt as if someone had slapped him.

Berger was repressing a smile; Richards kept his eyes fixed haughtily on Bates.

And Paul felt a rising fury. How had he backed himself into this corner? He had lied only to protect Philip, who was now siding with Berger at his expense.

"Mr. Werth, perhaps you would like to comment on this discrepancy?"

"I have nothing more to say."

"Nothing to say?"

"Nothing. I'll say nothing more to this committee."

"I see. Then perhaps you had better leave."

Paul stood up so abruptly that he almost overturned his chair. Berger too began to rise, but Bates turned on him fiercely.

"You and Richards can remain, Mr. Berger. We've not quite done with you."

As Paul left he kept his eyes turned rigidly from Philip, who lolled nonchalantly in his chair.

Paul passed Berger in the hall by the locker room, where they were alone; Berger slinked to one side but Paul stepped in front of him.

"Hiya, Paul." Berger smiled.

"What's going on with you and Philip?"

"Whaddaya mean, me and Philip?"

"Just what I said. I saw you in front of Laura's place when I left with Jeb. You told us Richards had already gone home."

"Oh, yeah? Well, what's the big deal? Nobody told you to lie, y'know."

"I thought I was protecting Philip."

"Oh, yeah? Well, he doesn't need your protection, Einstein."

"Fuck you, Berger."

"Hey, Werth, why don't you go whack yourself off?"

Paul grabbed Berger and slammed him against the wall.

"Why don't you pick on somebody your own size?"

It was true, Berger was a shrimp. Paul let him go.

"Big man," Berger said, dusting off his rumpled dignity. "You think you know so much! Who told you to go sticking your nose into Philip's business? You think Richards can't look out for himself? You think he needs a jerk like you? Well, don't take it out on me, buddy. If you've got a gripe, take it up with Richards!"

．　．　．

"Hello, *paesano*," Philip said, affable and superior but with a steely edge to his voice; Paul hadn't realized how much he was resisting this meeting with Richards.

"We've gotta talk, Philip."

"Oh, yeah? Sure, why not?"

They turned into an empty classroom and walked to the far corner where they couldn't be observed from the hall.

The desks were made of a kind of blond wood that glowed with the afternoon sun, and Paul could hear from outside the window the sounds of students, raucous and carefree, as they departed for the day.

"Well, what have I always told you, *paesano*? That Bates is one schmuck."

"That's not what I want to talk about."

"Oh, yeah? Well, shoot—but make it quick. I've got things I've gotta do."

"Philip, why the hell didn't you cover for me? I mean, shit, man—you hung me out to dry."

"Whaddaya talking about?"

"You know what I'm talking about. I said we were together after the party, I covered for you—I gave you an alibi."

"Well, bully for you. I mean, who told you to do that, Werth? Who told you I *needed* an alibi?"

"That's not the point. The point is I did it for you, Philip. Then you simply left me hanging."

"Paul, Paul—you haven't learned a thing I've tried to teach you, have you? I mean, shit, man—I've got my own fish to fry."

"Oh, yeah? Which fish would those be?"

"Don't be so stupid. What did you think, anyway? Did you think it was a matter of *friendship?*"

This brought Paul to a stop; it hit him like a blow to the solar plexus.

"Yes, I guess maybe I did. I guess maybe I was that naive!"

Richards laughed derisively; it was more a snort than a laugh.

"Friendship!" he scoffed. "What does *that* mean? What does friendship even *mean?* You know, I had a friend once. He was our Italian gardener, can you dig it? I mean, he was the only person who ever *cared* about me. We used to go into the greenhouse on the top of the hill behind the house and he'd teach me the names of the plants in Italian: *margherita, calendula. He* was a friend! You know what happened to him? My old man fired him, that's what. For drunkenness! Can you dig it? I mean, my old man gets plastered every evening! But he fires Giovanni, the only *human being* I ever knew! That's your *friendship!*"

"Great, Philip. I mean, that's real tough about your Italian gardener and everything. But that's no goddamn reason for stabbing people in the back, especially when they go out on a limb for you."

"Aw, poor Pauli! Pauli's feeling all betrayed and brokenhearted, is that it? A little case of hurty feelings? Well, that's tough! Who told you to go meddling in other people's affairs, anyway? It was none of your fucking business!" And his voice shot up. "Next time you can keep your puppy-dog loyalty to yourself!"

"And what about Berger? What about *his* puppy-dog loyalty? You find his friendship less offensive?"

"Berger? Berger knows too much, Paul. It's as simple as that. It's a simple matter of expedience."

"Knows too much? What do you mean by that?"

"*Knows* too much, *capisce?* Too much! What's wrong, Paul—it's the English language, don't you understand? Berger *knows* too much!"

"What's to know?"

"You *are* a sap."

"I thought you said you had nothing to do with drugs."

"Did I? I can't remember."

"You told me drugs were for fools."

"Get with it, Paul. Get serious."

"I'm asking you, Philip. Do you have anything to do with drugs?"

"And I'm telling you, it's none of your goddamn business. Get it? . . . Come on, Paul, cool it. Get lost."

"I think I'm in heap big trouble," Paul said to Laura, and he saw her large brown eyes look at him and then flicker away.

"Why do you say that?"

"Because I've misunderstood everything. I think it's Philip who's been pushing drugs."

"Very likely," she agreed. "But how does that involve you? Surely you're not involved with that?"

"No, of course not. But the thing is"—he held fire for a moment—"you see, I *lied* for Richards. In front of the committee, I mean."

She winced noticeably.

"Why did you do a stupid thing like that?"

"Oh, don't even ask! I mean, it just *happened,* you know? I mean they were so *smug* and everything—and then I was so certain they were wrong. . . ."

"I tried to warn you."

"Yes, yes—I know. It's my own stupidity, of course. Only . . . well, you'd think Philip might have covered for me!"

"*Who'd* think?"

Then they were quiet while Paul tried to absorb this piece of information, though he wasn't entirely successful, for there was *still* something that drew him to Philip.

"Well, at any rate," he said after a time, "I botched it, and now I'm up the creek. The thing is, I don't know what it'll do to my mother—if I'm implicated, I mean. My only hope is Miss English. The other two will crucify me."

"Can't you go to them or something?"

"And say what? That I lied? Where will that get me?"

"Oh, Paul—what a mess!"

"Yeah," he said, "what a bummer!"

One afternoon when he returned from school he found a letter from Highgate addressed to his mother, and (something he had never done before) he pocketed it.

As he supposed, it was a communication from the Bates committee informing his mother that he must appear before them for disciplinary cause.

On Saturday, Paul sat for the SAT exam.

Administered in the Highgate lunchroom, the exam

started at eight-thirty and extended into the afternoon. Paul was one of the last to arrive; he felt queasy and exhausted and couldn't get his mind to focus.

"Oh, God, I'm so *nervous*," Brigit Bloom kept saying while she paced up and down, biting her cuticles and clutching a brace of sharpened pencils in her hand. "Oh, Paul, I just *know* I'm going to goof this, everything's gone out of my head completely. Can you remember the quadratic formula?"

"For chrissake, Brigit," Paul said, "knock it off, will you? You *know* you always ace these things."

They entered the large cool-smelling room and Paul sat at one of the long wooden tables and tried to adjust his thoughts.

What *was* the quadratic formula, anyway?

Lucius Bates stood at the head of the room and peered sardonically at the assembled students.

"Well, isn't this a lovely morning," Bates said, and he licked his lips. "Let me see, what do we have here?" He scooped up one of the exams from the box that stood on the table beside him and held it up to view. "The 1962 Scholastic Achievement Test. How delightful! I'm sure this shouldn't cause any of you any worry!"

He smiled at his own humor while a small sigh of nervous laughter rippled across the room.

"In a moment I am going to ask the proctors to pass out the exams. You should have no belongings with you at this time except your pencils. You *should* have your pencils." (Another tentative ripple of laughter.) "There may be *no* speaking during the examination. Keep your eyes fixed *solely* on your own paper. If you have any questions during the examination you may put up your hand and one of the proctors will attend to you. Is that understood? Good! We may now proceed."

The proctors passed down the aisles handing out the test.

Paul's stomach tightened; at the same time he was troubled by a kind of boredom, profound and disquieting—a floating disjunctive unconcern as if he weren't really there.

"Please write your names at the top of the examination booklet," Lucius Bates instructed.

Paul wrote WERTH at the top of the page and then stopped; he surveyed his handiwork thoughtfully. Bates was saying something else, but Paul was having trouble absorbing what it was.

The first part of the exam concerned reading comprehension and started with a section on the social and migratory habits of Canada geese. Paul struggled with the passages, trying to keep his attention focused, while another voice spoke disdainfully in his ear, pointing out the trick turns of phrase and the glutted statistics that provided stumbling blocks for all but the most retentive of readers. What kind of comprehension was this?

He answered most of the questions with reasonable certainty and concluded the exam before the end of the allotted time; but when he reached the last question he discovered to his horror that he had run out of rows in which to mark his answer. Somehow, somewhere along the line, he had skipped a number and marked an answer in the wrong box.

His hand shaking with nerves, Paul ran his eye over the

page to locate his mistake, but he couldn't discover where it was. The more he ordered himself to remain calm, the more nervous he became. He had to identify his error, erase all his subsequent answers, and translate them into the correct boxes in the column above; but time was running out.

Finally he found the mistake toward the middle of the exam, and, working madly, he began to erase all the following answers; but halfway through he stopped in horror, for if he erased all these answers he wouldn't know which box to mark in the column above.

By now he was thoroughly panicked and befuddled.

"One minute," Mr. Bates intoned. "One minute to go."

He would have to proceed answer by answer: erase a box, then translate the answer from the subsequent column into that column, then advance to the next column and erase that box—and so forth; but he didn't have the time.

He had fucked up.

"That's all," Mr. Bates called. "Please turn the page to the next part of the exam."

The next part of the exam was algebra and should have been easy for Paul but by now his mind was utterly confused; he didn't seem to be able to bring it to bear on the matter at hand, and it kept fingering over and over the simplest equations.

"The square root of x minus four, yes, I see, that's quite easy, the square root of x minus four is . . . yes, precisely, I'll have that in a minute, let me just see . . ." But all the while his mind was floating over the top of the numbers without taking hold.

And so he would rush on to the next problem.

"Let me see, let me just see—I'll find one of these in a minute, and everything will click into place, and then I'll go back and get the others, and then . . ."

But he could feel himself sinking into despair, for now he was fucking up the entire exam.

There was a ten-minute break after the first hour and a half. Paul's chest felt as if he was suffering from congestive heart failure. He could hardly breathe. He turned the exam over to the opening page, where he had left his name incomplete.

He filled in PAUL.

Getting up, he walked to the front of the hall, handed his unfinished exam to one of the proctors, quit the room, and left the school.

The day before Paul was to appear before the Bates committee the school was buzzing with the news that Pursy, Berger, and Richards had been expelled from Highgate.

Paul felt sick. He considered speaking with Miss English, but he didn't know what to say. He refused to get on his hands and knees and grovel. The truth remained that he had had nothing to do with drugs.

"So," Craig Lewis said to him, "I suppose you're sorry about Richards."

"And I suppose you're happy."

"Yes, I am. He was a bad apple, Paul. His influence was pernicious. For you too."

"You know what, Craig?" Paul said. "You're a sanctimonious asshole."

But he was sorry the minute he had said it. He was

shocked by his own language—by its coarseness and aggression; and he could see that Craig was too. And he felt ashamed.

The Bates committee convened the next morning at nine sharp.

Paul knew he had to do something to avert disaster but his stubbornness still made him reluctant.

"I want to say that I didn't have anything to do with drugs," he began. "Philip Richards was my friend—I won't say otherwise. But I didn't know anything about his dealings with drugs, if that's what he was up to—and I still don't. That's all I want to say."

"Well, Mr. Werth—if we thought you were involved in that manner, you would already have been expelled."

Paul swallowed hard; again he could feel himself sweating.

"There remains the question of your testimony," Mr. Bates pursued, and he didn't look friendly. "Not to put too fine a point on it, Mr. Werth, it looks to us as if you lied to this committee. The question is, what should we do?"

Paul looked at the three adults and he felt his heart beating. He considered apologizing, but looking at them he felt something harden inside himself and he decided to hold his peace. He tried not to appear hostile.

"I've got to tell you," Bates continued, "that the committee is divided about how to proceed. Two of us believe you should be disciplined—one feels otherwise."

"I see," Paul said. He glanced at Miss English and then

looked away, but for the first time he felt the breeze of a chance.

"Do you have anything you want to add?"

Again Paul swallowed hard; his mouth had gone dry.

"I never had anything to do with drugs," he repeated. "I'm sorry if I misled this committee, but I never had anything to tell you in the first place."

It wasn't very gracious, but it was the best he could command. He was breathing heavily.

"Well, then, if that's all you have to say, we had best proceed. My vote is that Mr. Werth be suspended for the rest of the term."

The room was silent. Paul looked at Miss English, who now constituted his only hope.

"Well, let's get on with it," Mr. Bates said dryly. "Ladies, how do you vote?"

"I have something to say," Miss English announced. She had drawn herself up very straight in her chair.

"I fear I haven't been able to disguise my partiality for Paul. He comes from a fine family, is himself one of the outstanding students in my class, and—if I may say so—is also one of the most likable boys in the school. I don't say this, Paul, to flatter you. I have thought long and hard about what I have to say, and I want you to hear it from my own mouth. I don't understand how a boy of your background could allow himself to become involved with the sort of people and events we have been investigating. Your behavior passes my understanding. We all make mistakes, Paul—but we then have to pay for those mistakes. You have been caught telling this committee a fabrication. Under the circumstances, I believe we have no choice but to suspend you."

There was silence in the room. Light played against the wall, rippling as through a fish tank. Paul was stunned.

Then Mrs. Wagner leaned forward and addressed Miss English.

"So I take it that you believe Paul was mixed up with the droogs?"

"No," Miss English said coldly, "I never went that far. I never believed that a boy of Paul's caliber would have anything to do with drugs."

"Precisely! Nor did you, Lucius, if I may speak on your behalf."

"That is the case," Bates said. "It was never the opinion of this committee that Mr. Werth was involved with drugs."

"So! But what is the *brief* of this committee? Is it not to look into the droogs?" She looked searchingly at her two colleagues. "What then is accomplished by suspending Mr. Vurt? Has this anything to do with the droogs? Would it help the problem of droogs in this school by one iota? I think not!"

"But Paul lied to this committee," Bates said.

"Lie lie lie! What does it mean? Because in a misplaced act of loyalty he said somet'ing on behalf of his so-called friend? Is that a lie? Did we believe him? Do you think Paul a liar? Look at him! Stupid, perhaps—but not a liar!"

Paul came out into the sunlight and for the first time in weeks he could breathe. Mrs. Wagner had prevailed—the committee wouldn't suspend him! He would be on strict probation for a semester—but what did that signify? He was home free!

But Mrs. Wagner! He was flabbergasted.

There was no way he could avoid his mother's finding out about the probation, but to his surprise she shrugged it off.

"They have some nerve putting you on probation! As if you had anything to do with drugs!"

"It doesn't matter, Mom. It doesn't amount to a hill of beans. After next semester it won't even appear on my record."

"Well, I should have spoken to Harriet English."

"A lot of good that would have done. She was for serving my head up on a platter."

"That surprises me. I wouldn't have thought that."

"*You* wouldn't have thought that!" And he laughed.

Paul ran a fever for the last game of the season: he could feel it coursing through him, a slight tremor, a light-headed excitement. He suited up and went down to the field.

For the first three innings he sat on the sidelines as he had for the last month. It was almost summer now and he could smell the grass and the odor of the heat.

The opposing pitcher was a long, gawky lefty with a high windup and a vicious fastball which no one could hit.

"He's a bitch," Doyle said after flying out. "He's got great control."

"Control nothing," Boom-Boom said. "I can't see the fucking ball."

From the bench Paul studied the pitcher carefully and he was confident he could hit him. His fever made him jittery and alert, and he knew that if given the chance he could hit this guy.

Scotty was pacing up and down in his usual fashion, swearing, his sweat pants bagged below his seat, and his finger gesticulating. He had a prominent Roman nose and dark eyes and his cheeks were pulled in as if he was perpetually sucking on something. His eyes looked slightly crazed.

Highgate had now fallen behind two nothing.

"Who can hit this left-handed bastard? Who the fuck can hit this guy?" Scotty turned and regarded his players with distaste as if they were a collection of puppies waiting for drowning; then he turned away, and then he suddenly wheeled back.

"Here, Werth, get in there and hit this sucker. Let's see you take this guy to the cleaner."

Paul sprang up from where he was sitting. He could hardly believe his ears. His dizziness caused him to lose his balance, but he righted himself immediately. He felt his heart pound.

He slipped his bat from the holder and strode out to the plate; he hadn't been in a game for a month.

The pitcher wound up and let the ball go and Paul immediately laced it down the third-base line—it was still climbing when it went foul.

All right, Paul thought, all right—I've got your number.

He took the next two pitches—a ball that missed on

the outside corner and a strike just slightly better placed. He knew what to do with this bastard; he had nothing but fastballs and a certain amount of control. He set himself and waited.

The pitch came just as he expected—a fastball on the outside; and, turning his shoulder, Paul went the opposite way and slapped the ball into the hole in right field.

As he rounded first he saw they were throwing home for the runner and Paul made it easily into second with a stand-up double. He had batted in a run.

It was the same play with which he had started his career.

At the end of the inning Scotty gave him the nod and he ran out onto the field and took his old position at second base; he had forgotten about his fever.

Wolf got the first batter out and then the redhead was up and clobbered the ball at Paul on a downward trajectory that stung into the ground just inches short of Paul's feet. Paul swept instinctively and had to look to see if he had the ball—and there it was, beautiful as an egg in its nest; even after the slight hesitation the throw to first was an easy out.

The next time at bat Paul sacrifice-flied to put Doyle into scoring position and then Bower tied up the game with a single.

At second the next inning he surveyed the infield. He couldn't believe the season was almost over, he wanted to play baseball forever. This was the very shape of happiness!

And then he was up at bat again and the game was tied

and the big guy was losing his stuff. Doyle was on second with the go-ahead run and the tall guy was getting wild.

Paul powdered the first ball foul—he had been out a little too late. Then the pitcher missed the next three—two on the outside corner and one low—and the count was three and one. Keith Firman glanced at the dugout, where Scotty was pacing, and then from the third-base line he signaled Paul to take the pitch: they weren't taking any chances—they were going for the walk.

Paul stepped out of the batter's box and swung the bat; he could feel the balance in the swing—he had his stuff back.

He stepped back into the box.

He's going to throw a fastball in the strike zone, he thought. He can't afford another ball.

Play Babits ball, he told himself.

The pitcher wound up and Paul timed himself against the kick of his leg; then the ball was coming and Paul had it in sight. He didn't take his eye off it as, against instructions, he lashed it over the second baseman's head, dropping it perfectly in midfield for an easy single.

Doyle slid in safe at home.

Paul could hear the cheering from the sideline. They were winning three to two.

"Didn't you read the signal?" Scotty asked dryly after the inning.

"Sure, Scotty—I thought I had the go-ahead to swing."

Scotty looked at him ironically and smiled out of the corner of his mouth.

"That's what I call being hungry."

. . .

And then Paul Werth fell ill: first he felt weak and then he developed a fever and then he lay in bed and couldn't move. And it was a relief to lie in bed like that! Final exams were approaching and it was high spring outside the window but Paul had ceased to care; despite the weight of the fever it was a relief just to lie in bed.

But what did he have? At first the doctor, a firm, fat old gentleman who had been their physician since they were tiny, expressed alarm because the symptoms suggested— leukemia! But the second blood test proved mononucleosis, the kissing sickness, though Paul knew he hadn't contracted the illness through any kissing.

"He doesn't sleep at night," he heard his mother explaining to the doctor on the phone. "He stays up all night reading."

Well, he wasn't reading now. He lay on his back and slept while through his head whirled the fragments of his life. His fatigue was so oppressive that it assumed the shape of pain, a physical presence pressing him down into his sweated sheets; he would lie in a stupor of sleep and waking, gasping for breath, the sun a great orange thumb smearing his eyelids.

'Twas many and many a year ago in a kingdom by the sea that he was climbing upward. O he was climbing upward because you see there was no tree he couldn't climb no rock, he could stand at the edge of a cliff and see Orion Draco Cassiopeia although only a dumb son of a bitch would sell drugs. Hardly had the trip started when he became seasick. I'm depending on you. He'll probably kill himself with anger since only a jerk would permit exploratory surgery surgery surgery. You don't have to be afraid! O afraid said the maid in the shady ambuscade! A kingdom by the sea. A school for turkeys although you have to stay within yourself, gobble gobble gobble. That's not what I mean by staying within yourself! You've got to be hungry—with a hard gemlike flame! I won't forget you. O with a flame with a flame that will frame your precious name! A school for turkeys. One dollar an answer five dollars a set why should I get caught we're the leaders of the class (although she doesn't want us in the house alone) she's crazy, my mom, if you come for dinner he'll drill you something terrible, Adams Jefferson Madison Monroe Mickey Mouse Van Buren (I bet ya forgot that one!) Van Peeble Van Pooble Van PooPoo Bates Madison Washington (I cannot tell a lie) Whitey Farrino is he a president? (You don't have to be afraid!) Where is there an end to it the wailing! the Greeks didn't have a word for gobble gobble gobble you should read Emerson. Five dollars a set. Hardly had the trip begun when he struck out you're such a shithead! I can't see you anymore you're making a mistake very likely. What's the difference if I have a reefer in the privacy of my own room you're the only one who knows hey wait a sec what's going on here you mean to tell this committee those are *damn* pigeons? The first theorem of hooky. Cassandra! A hard gemlike flame! It's all so meaningless so stupid I heard you got high it reminds me of Faulkner by an idiot full of sound and fury gobble gobble gobble. I wouldn't be so keen on him if I were you but he's my friend is that your statement before this one hip higher than the other a game of canasta. O Whitey he's a loser he's a boozer he's a daddy doesn't want us to make a fuss. It's just *darkness* isn't that just *fascinating?* Fascinating while you're waiting I'm debating. In my kingdom by the Charles in Cambridge O for chrissake Mother! His hands with veins I've been here before. Been here been here been here. It isn't good to be as angry as you don't have to be afraid. I won't hurt you. I'm depending on you, depending on you, depending . . .

He sat in the library propped on his father's leather sofa with blankets tucked about him—but decidedly on the mend. When he slept he experienced long, vivid dreams peopled with his parents, his grandmother, his brother, his teachers, his friends. And it seemed that he was working out the algebra of his life in a particularly lucid and original manner, though when he woke he couldn't for the life of him translate this mathematics into waking terms. But the dreaming itself satisfied and intrigued him, and he plunged back into its warm stream as into a commodious novel—and this also was peculiar, for he usually hated his dreams.

Sometimes he would hear his mother moving in the other rooms of the house, and this touched him with a sense of security and satisfaction, as if he were still a boy, which he now knew (now perhaps for the first time knew) was no longer the case; and his love for her surged back forcefully, immovably, as if it were, after all, the primal thing.

Laura Kinski sat on the edge of his bed in the middle of the week when no one else was at home, and the sun beat against the wall and framed her where she sat.

"But won't you get in trouble with school?"

"Oh, what do I care? I'll write an excuse and sign my mother's name. I couldn't go without seeing you, Paul. It's been two weeks." And she took his hand. "Are you feeling better?"

"Yes, much. But for a while there I thought I was going to die."

"Are you being serious?"

"Well, not really die."

"Don't die." And she squeezed his hand. "I don't want you to die." And she bent over and kissed him lightly.

"Watch out—you'll catch my disease."

"Oh, I'm not afraid."

And she laughed and tossed her head.

She turned to her leather satchel and took out flowers, music (a new recording by Charlie Mingus), and brownies, which she laid on the bed table next to him.

"These should brighten your day. Where can I get a vase?"

"There should be one down in the kitchen somewhere on the shelves over the sink."

"Your mother won't mind?"

"Of course not."

He sat propped in bed eating a brownie while she went to fetch the vase.

"These are terrific! Did you make them?"

"Of course!" She was arranging the bright tulips by his bedside.

"You're a terrific cook!"

"I didn't make them, silly! I'm lucky if I can make an English muffin."

"Well, you fooled me!"

"That's not hard to do."

And they laughed together.

"So tell me—are you really feeling better?"

"Yes—really. I'll be all better in another week."

"Good—because I can't stand school without you. I've grown accustomed to your face."

Then she sat and looked out the window and held his hand.

"Paul," she said after a time, still not looking at him, "you don't think I'm *bad*, do you?"

He sat up and took her by the shoulders.

"Of course I don't think you're bad!"

"Because I'm not, you know. I'm really not." She lowered her head. "What I told you that other time was true—I've never been with a boy like that—never."

He held her against him, and the intoxication of holding her dizzied him.

"I believe you."

"Oh, God," she said, "let's run away together! We can go anywhere you want."

"Is that what you want?"

"Yes—completely!"

They lay next to each other while she nestled into the side of his neck and he could feel her heart beating against him.

"Oh, Paul, let's just skip town!"

"What about Vassar?"

"Oh, I'll do a year at Vassar—what difference does it make? I can be back every weekend. And then I'll transfer wherever you're going. I'll go anywhere you want—I'll go to Australia!"

"Australia?"

"Sure—Greenland, Newfoundland—I don't care. I'll go

wherever you go. Oh, Paul!" she said. "I promise I'll love you to bits!"

And she leaned and kissed him.

He was caught up in her excitement, intoxicated by her beauty as she lay beside him, her hair tickling his nose.

"You give me fever!"

"Yes, yes—I've got to be good! I forget you're a valetudinarian. Isn't that the right word?"

"Well, I hope not."

"Well, a sicky! I've got to take care of you—you've got to get better."

"Listen, Laura," he said, "I've been thinking while I've been sick. I've been wrong about so many things! It makes me ill just thinking about it! I think my sickness was a kind of coming to terms with that—with my *wrongness*, I mean. It's as if my sickness was really in my head or something. Oh, I don't know what—I'm probably not making much sense.

"But I seem to have gotten everything wrong! I mean, I was certain about Philip—certain he wasn't behind the drugs, certain it was Hillman and that bunch—and yet I was dead wrong. And I was wrong about Wagner and Miss English and about so much else besides! I was even wrong about baseball. I mean, I wasn't supposed to care about baseball, it was just something I did; and yet the only things I care about at Highgate are baseball—and you!"

"There's something else you got wrong."

"Yes! Precisely! That's what I'm trying to say!"

Then they were both silent while Laura picked thoughtfully at the blanket.

"I'm not very good at this," she said, "this looking into life, I mean. I'm not sure it's worth it. Maybe it's better just to skim along the surface—for me, at least. Sometimes I think that life is like peering down into water: when the sun shines you see the surface and everything is beautiful, but when a cloud passes you see down and down—and I don't always like what I see down there."

After that they were again silent. Beyond the room Paul could hear the silence of the house surrounding him, holding him, present always, laden now with his own familiar ghosts.

Small white cabbage moths fluttered like scraps of sunlight across the descending hill, and as they walked, the knee-high grasses swayed before them in the wind. It was a surpassingly beautiful day, with high clouds floating westward and a light, scented breeze that brought with it the promise of summer. She laughed as she walked, and she held his hand.

Laura had lured him out into the sunlight though he was still weak, and he leaned on her as they descended the meadow—the same he had come to as a boy when he had wandered from home that summer.

He could see the river moving beyond the trees, a great, broad, sinister expanse hunched and mud-colored and stamped with the bronze of the sun. The water rose and fell like the muscles of a prizefighter, dirty green in the distance, dun and tawny brown closer to shore; but throughout it carried the dangerous, swift authority of something living and guileful and beautiful beyond human measure.

Laura was wearing a dark wraparound skirt tied at her waist and an Italian silk shirt open at the throat, and she smelled of her heady familiar perfume.

"Run with me," she said. "Run!"

"I can't run, my legs are made of rubber."

"Run, you sissy, run!"

And she pulled at him till they were running downhill, his feet misstepping on the uneven invisible potholes beneath the grass, both of them now whooping as she pulled and stumbled before him, the hill steeper than they supposed, until, their knees buckling, they collapsed into the tall grass, their lungs aching with laughter and excitement.

She lay on her back gathering her breath.

"You sicky."

"I'm not a sicky!"

"I can't even kiss you—I'll catch some nasty disease."

"Isn't it a little late for that?"

And he leaned and kissed her on the mouth.

He kissed her for a long time, tasting her lips. She was a small island riding beneath him, sweet-smelling and hidden by the grass. It was marvelous to be lying there with the sun beating about them in diaphanous fire at the center of the world.

Butterflies are white and blue
In this field we wander through,
Suffer me to take your hand,
Death comes in a day or two.

"Are you feeling better?"

"Yes—much. It's great to get out of the house."

"You see—I'll be your doctor, you'll have to do whatever I say."

"Will that be good for my health?"

"Oh—very!"

She rolled away from him, but not far, and, propping herself on one elbow, she studied him while she chewed a stalk of grass.

"I won't be able to go to the dance with you," she offered dispassionately.

"Oh? Are you jilting me already?"

"Don't be stupid."

"Well, what is it, then?"

"I'll be out of town—my uncle's birthday. A family gathering, no less. God help us."

"It sounds like fun."

"Yes—like drawing and quartering. You go without me—I trust you."

"You're a wacky kid," he said impulsively.

"Wacky?"

"Yes—with all your intensities and opinions. I never know which way you're going to jump. Aren't you afraid of anything?"

"Oh yes!"

"What are you afraid of?"

She thought about that for a while.

"Of Whitey's suicide," she said. "That frightened me."

"It frightened me too."

"You?" She was surprised. "Why did it frighten you? You've never thought of suicide, have you?"

"Thought of it? Who hasn't thought of it?"

"But you've never thought of *doing* it, have you?"

He laughed, but without humor. "No, not really. But don't you know that suicide is the philosophical question of our age? Someone once told me that."

"Oh, I don't know anything about that."

"You'll never try it again—will you?"

"No, of course not. Not anymore. I never meant to do it anyway. But Whitey meant it. Whitey really meant to go all the way."

"Yeah, I know. It gives me the spooks!"

"Me too!"

She sat up and tucked one leg under her so that from where he lay he could see up the firm plumpness of her thigh.

"Here," she said, "I'll show you how to blow grass." And splitting a stalk down the center, she held it between her two thumbs while she blew into it, producing a shrill, high-pitched screech that caused them both to laugh.

"Lovely!"

"Here, smarty—you try."

But he could produce only a feeble piping, much to her delight.

"You see—everyone has his talents. But tell me, what happened to your friend Richards?"

"I dunno—he disappeared."

"Oh, yeah? Well, it's a small loss."

"You think so?"

"Yes, I think so. He was no friend of yours."

"I think he was—for a while."

"No, he wasn't, Paul. Because he doesn't know what it is to be a friend."

"Something went wrong," was all he would say. "I'm not sure what. But he was my friend."

She merely shrugged.

"And what about that other girl?" she asked after a pause.

"What other girl?"

"You know—I'm not going to say her name."

"She doesn't count."

"Don't you still love her?"

"I never loved her."

"Never loved her—is that true?"

"Yes, it is. I loved the *idea* of loving her. It's something I talked myself into. I never loved *her*. Not that particular person. She was just a coatrack on which I hung my coat."

"God, that sounds terrible!" And she laughed. "And me—am I just a coatrack too?"

"No, you're a bed of sweet-smelling grass."

"Am I?" She looked at him with amusement.

"Yes. No one could help loving a bed of grass."

"It doesn't sound very hard to come by."

"A bed of grass? Well, harder than you might think. Most people are just—a bed of concrete."

"A soggy mat."

"A whisk of rotten hay."

"Well, if I'm a bed of grass"—she laughed—"don't you want to lie on me?"

As he kissed her he seemed to become invisible as the air. All life seemed insufficient to exhaust this continent that stretched beneath him, deep and expansive as Africa. *Where the bee sucks there suck I.* And soon there was no mind at all, only hand and lip and eye, the world contracted to that small circle where there again there was enacted the quotidian wonder for the first time. And as they mounted higher and higher he thought it must continue forever until suddenly it could continue no longer and he was falling, darkly and unheedingly, until, tragically, he had landed, he was again in the field with the wide world all about him, with Laura rumpled and moist beneath him like young grass.

He rolled off and lay staring at the sky.

"No, don't," she whispered, and she snuggled against him.

"Oh, God!" she said. "That was so *perfect!*" And she buried her face in the side of his neck.

"I saw flowers," she said. "I saw little pink flowers."

He stroked her, and he was moved again by her beauty, but there was a sadness to him now, a heaviness, as if in coming down he had landed too hard, and he had to force himself to attend, feeling unattached though responsible.

He noticed, however, that there had been no blood.

"Did you know I was crazy about you?" she said.

"Are you?"

"Oh yes—since the first time I met you, I think. I knew you were mine."

"Yours?"

"Yes—meant for me. Is that strange?"

"I dunno."

"It wasn't that way for you, was it?"

"No, not exactly."

"What was it?"

"I guess I was afraid."

"Afraid?" She offered a little laugh.

"Well, not exactly afraid. I liked you immediately—but I didn't know it was *you*. I mean, I thought you were somebody else—somebody different—even though I never *met* that other person, only this you whom I talked to and laughed with and liked so much. Does that make any sense?"

"Not a lot—but I think I know what you're saying."

Again he kissed her.

"Was it the first time for you?" she asked.

"Yes."

"For me too." He looked at her carefully but he didn't say anything.

"Oh, Paul," she said, "why can't we be like this always?"

"What about your going to Paris and taking lovers?" He was joking with her, but there was an edge to his joke; he still wasn't certain who she was.

"There'll be no lovers," she said. "Only you. You'll be my lover."

"But what about all your plans—all the things you talked to me about?"

"Why can't we do them together? Why can't we do all of them together?"

It made him uneasy when she talked this way, he didn't know how seriously to take her. She seemed to shiver with intensity, and her beauty dazzled him.

"Oh, Paul!" And she put her arms around his neck. "You don't have to be like everyone else, you can be different—you can just be yourself!"

He could see the grass ripple beside her. She seemed to

him herself an extension of the grass, beautiful and sweet-
smelling and warm.

Suffer me to take your hand,
Suffer me to cherish you
Till the dawn is in the sky.
Whether I be false or true,
Death comes in a day or two.

10

The Quad in the summer heat was decorated with Japa-
nese lanterns, against which the moths, careening, col-
lided with an audible ping. The hill moved up into darkness; but where the couples moved to the beat of the
music, the light filtered from the lanterns in shifting pat-
terns that caught the shoulders and hair of the dancers in
momentary phantasmagoric glamour.

There was no wind, and the heat of the night brought
the odor of cut grass and of the perfume, warm and
heavy, which the young women, dressed in evening
gowns, their shoulders bare and their slender throats glit-
tering with their mothers' jewelry, had liberally applied.
The music pulsed soupily, lost its beat, found it again in a
long ululating whine. *There Goes Cathy's Clown.*

Paul Werth stood at the side of the Quad watching. He
hadn't been certain whether he would come, and now he
wandered from place to place observing his classmates
with affection and disinterest as if he were a traveler returned from a far country.

"Hiya, Paul—you feeling better?"

It was Boom-Boom Teller, the shortstop, with his arm about Bonnie Bower, the two apparently a couple since the night of Bower's party.

"Yeah—I'm fine."

"What was it anyway—mono?"

"Yeah."

"Tough about that. You've gotta watch that kissing!"

Boom-Boom offered his jock-boy laugh. Bonnie, on the other hand, wheeled partly away and refused to look at him.

"Well, glad you're back on your pins, jocko!" And Boom-Boom hit him playfully but too hard on the shoulder.

"Well," Jeb said to Paul, addressing him in a deepened voice, as if practicing some thespian part, "this is a grand evening."

"Hello, Jeb."

"I have good news."

"Do you? What's that?"

"Mr. Bates says the prognosis for Yale is good if I keep up my present grade point average."

"That's terrific, Jeb. Congratulations!"

Jeb frowned and lowered his head and seemed to suck on an invisible pipe as if in preparation for his sojourn at New Haven.

"But where's the beautiful Laura Kinski?"

"She couldn't make it tonight."

"Ah! So you and Kinski are really a thing?"

"Yes, I guess so. Yes, we are."

"Ah, Laura Kinski! Do you remember that night?"

"Sure, I remember."

"You've come a long way since then, I suppose!"

"I suppose so."

"But how did you do it?"

"Do what?"

"You know—how did you *Laura Kinski*?"

And the two boys laughed.

Paul guided Brigit Bloom up and down the dance floor, and as they maneuvered he watched his classmates moving about him. Brigit was stiff in his arms, but he could feel her breasts against him and he liked the healthy protein odor of her hair. He was happy dancing with Brigit and rubbing shoulders with the kids with whom he had grown up, but he was still aware of some underlying loneliness. He wished Laura was there.

"Are you and Laura Kinski going together?" Brigit asked.

"Going together?"

"Well, you know—a couple."

"Yes."

"I've always liked Laura."

This implied numerous things: that Brigit knew about Laura's reputation and overlooked it—or perhaps that she would overlook it for Paul; that she didn't disapprove of Laura, or perhaps even that she envied Laura her popularity. Mostly the sentence meant that she, Brigit, forgave Paul for the fact that he still hadn't turned to her—that in fact he would never turn to her—but that she still wanted to be friends. There was doubtless some further reference to Nicole, who remained Brigit's confidante, though, whatever it might be, Paul didn't care. Paul was aware of these implications but chose to ignore them; what he chose to understand was how much he liked Brigit. He pulled her closer to him, and he wished he could be many people with many lives.

"So how did you do on the math final?" she asked, bringing him back to earth.

"Jeez, Brigit—don't ask me about that now! I mean, who gives a damn?"

"I'm sorry." She sounded genuinely contrite.

"Don't be sorry, just don't forever *worry!*"

"I can't help it—that's who I am."

The plaintiveness in her voice moved him, and again he offered a small hug.

"That's all right, Brigit. For chrissake, I'm a worrier too! But that's why we shouldn't always *talk* about it! C'mon, let's get something to drink."

Teachers congregated behind the punch table, including Lucius Bates, bored and superior, and Eva Wagner, dressed in her habitual brown suit, though adorned for the occasion with a corsage, her brown intelligent eyes amused and ironic, her mustache aquiver in the golden light. Paul wanted to thank her but didn't know how and he turned away in shyness.

"You guys want something for that piss?" Robbie Doyle asked conspiratorially, revealing a flask hidden beneath his sport jacket.

"Sure," Paul said.

He followed Doyle into the shadows away from observation, where Robbie produced a fifth of rum.

"Here, this'll freshen you up."

Paul heard the sound of the rum pouring into his cup and smelled the sweetish odor of the alcohol.

"This party sucks," Doyle observed. "You wanna go to Hillman's later?"

"I can't, Robbie. I'm still not right on my pins."

"Yeah? That's tough. That was one helluva game, though."

"Thanks, Robbie."

Paul drank the rum and wiped his lips while Robbie drank from the bottle.

"You want some more?"

"Yeah—that'd be good."

"Tough about Pursy."

"Yeah—tough. What's he going to do?"

"I dunno. He's all right, that Pursy. Here, y'need some more of this?" And Doyle held out the rum. "Take the rest, it's almost finished anyway."

Paul accepted the rum with thanks.

"Well, I better be pushing along. Maybe I'll see you later."

"Yeah—maybe."

Paul stood by himself and breathed the night air. He drank the rum, and as he drank he experienced a strange familiar mixture of exaltation and aloneness that seemed to him one with the vast lonely beauty of the night.

He ambled back to the Quad, and now the dancers were a single huddled mass swaying beneath the whine of the music. It was getting late.

Suddenly Paul stopped in his tracks. He knew before consciously recognizing the slouch of the shoulders, the curve of the back, the set of the jaw; and, halted, he stood watching in the heavy air under the swaying discs of light.

Nicole Swann was dancing with Jack Wheeler.

She leaned against him, her eyes partially closed, her cheek resting against his shoulder, while he held her with expert proprietary assurance, as if she were a small sailboat he had leased for the summer.

So Wheeler is now her cover, he thought. And immediately it came to him that he didn't care. He could watch Jack Wheeler embrace Nicole Swann with no more concern than if she were the fat lady in the circus.

Whatever it was that had held him was over.

He turned, and now he was eager to leave. Something had come to an end.

But at the bottom of the stairs he ran into Keith Firman, distraught and wild-eyed.

"Did you see her?" Firman demanded. "Did you see her with Wheeler?"

"Hello, Keith—what's eating you?"

"Don't give me that shit. Did you see Nicole?"

"Yeah, I saw her. What about it?"

"With Wheeler," Keith almost cried, "with Jack Wheeler!"

"So what? What's the big deal?"

"So what? You don't care about anything, do you? You don't let anything get to you."

"Come on, Keith," Paul said. He started to walk past but Keith shoved him back violently.

"Come on," Keith challenged, unhinged with rage and despair, "come on, you wanna fight?"

Paul looked at Keith in dismay. His face crimson and

his fists clenched, Firman was snorting and pawing like a bull.

And suddenly it came to Paul that he didn't have to fight Keith. He could simply leave. He didn't care about Keith's anger. He didn't care about Jack Wheeler. And he didn't care about Nicole Swann.

That was the truth.

"Come on, Keith," Paul said again, this time sadly. And he walked away.

As he passed the Arch someone called to him from the shadows.

"Hey, boss! This way! Come here!"

Paul looked, and it was Berger.

"What is it, Berger?"

"Someone wants to speak to you."

"Oh, yeah?"

He kept walking, and soon he saw someone standing in the shadows, hidden in the darkness where he couldn't be seen.

"Hey, *paesano*," Richards said, stepping into the half-light. He was dressed as usual in his blue business suit with his hair slicked back. "How's my fair-weather friend?"

"Hello, Philip—how are you?"

"Me? Never been better. But I hear you've had a touch of something—TB or something, eh?"

"Yeah, that's right. So what brings you here, Philip?"

"What, do I need a special invitation to visit my old alma mater? Love brings me here, bubby—love and justice. It just so happens that some people owe me a thing or two. I've come to collect."

"Owe you?"

"Yeah—IOUs, that sort of thing—you know? You too, Werth—you owe me."

"I?" Paul was genuinely surprised. "What do I owe you?"

"Let's just call it tuition fees, okay? But I never thanked you for sticking up for me like that, did I, *bambino*? You sure did do us all a great big favor."

"You lied to me."

"I lied to you? Oh, that's rich. That's really rich!"

The two young men stood staring at each other tensely. Then Richards shrugged and snorted.

"Listen, hotshot, I'm going to tell you something you haven't heard before, it'll be my last lesson before I disappear into thin air, dig it? You think life's so big and glorious, right?—full of all sorts of possibilities. But I've got news for you, *bambino*—all those great things you think are going to happen, all those changes and shit—like waking up a great man or something—well, forget it! I mean, like, man, that's Disneyland! It doesn't amount to zilch. Because whatever you are *right now*, that's what you'll always be—and not one iota different. And whatever's already happened to you—that's all that can happen to you for eternity, get it? I mean, like, it's eternal recurrence time, baby. No exit. The room doesn't get any larger. We're trapped like this forever. So make the best of it, *bambino*, because that's all that's coming your way. They're not going to teach you this at Highgate—or anywhere else you go—not in the land of the free and the home of the brave. No way, dollface. You have to come to me, ol' Richards—I'm the only guy who tells it like it is. No pie in the sky—just you forever. And that's tough, baby! That's hell!"

"I'm sorry for you, Philip."

"Sorry for me? Fuck you, buddy. You haven't understood anything I've said."

"No, I'm not sure I have."

"Well, tuck it away in the back of your head for a rainy day. The sky's the limit, right?" And Richards gave a sour laugh.

Paul Werth was climbing upward. He couldn't say when he had started to climb, it had been automatic, as if the crane had been placed behind the school precisely for him, and he was partway up before he gave thought to what he was doing, moving upward into the night.

It seemed to him an absolute good to be climbing the crane. Below him, far away, the Quad was a pool of darkness cut by moving shapes of light that swayed idly in the night breeze. The dance was over, a few last couples drifted away into the night, their voices trailing after them like gauze. He was alone.

He was alone except for the stars twinkling above him in the clear night, distant sparks rising into nothing.

"That's Polaris, the North Star. That's Orion's belt."

It seemed to him an absolute good to be sitting alone, clutching the cold steel between his knees, the night wind lifting the hair from his perspiring forehead. He had wanted to do this forever. *"You haven't understood anything I've said."*

Perched on top of the crane, he felt the rum in his bloodstream, and he knew that if he had to live that year over again, he could not do it.

He wanted to stay where he was forever, out of it all. Around him lay the suburb of his childhood, a small nest of sleeping humanity. He stared into the tops of the trees, through which an occasional light pointed. Farther, he could see the world curving into darkness.

"I will give you all this, all the kingdoms of the earth. They're yours for the taking."

"How's that?" Paul removed his eyes reluctantly from what he was seeing.

"All you have to do is to cast yourself down."

It was true, the world was a great and remarkable place, beautiful and without price, but it was also, when all was said and done, just a small globe whirling in space. Trivial, really.

Paul thought of that year, and of his father, and of his death, and of Laura, and of Nicole, and of Whitey, and of Richards, and of his mother, and of baseball, and of Harvard, and of his brother, and of the night.

And suddenly a fatigue overcame him, an exhaustion, as if the whole venture were indeed useless and petty; and he wondered whether Whitey hadn't been right, and whether Laura hadn't been right—and whether it wasn't all meaningless.

Paul Werth swung one leg off the crane the way you might dismount from a horse. *To cease upon the midnight with no pain!* He tried to think, but he wondered why he had to think. All he had to do was to let go.

And in that instant he remembered his father.

. . .

Paul's father was lying in the hospital with an afghan pulled over his legs. It was a week before he died.

The afghan surprised Paul, for it was an heirloom from his great-aunt and had been in the family for as long as Paul could remember. Composed of colored rectangles of wool crocheted loosely together, it usually inhabited the bottom of the chest that stood by his parents' bed. As a child Paul had often wrapped himself in it on special occasions when he was ill or when he took a nap in his parents' room, and it had assumed a kind of talismanic power, like some species of shamanistic garb that bore an all but magical significance.

Now as Paul entered the room his father was lying in half-light with his eyes closed. Paul approached quietly, and his heart smote him with foreboding.

"Oh—Paul! Is that you?"

"Hi, Dad."

He came and stood by his father's side.

"How are you feeling?"

"I'm fine, son, I'm fine."

Then for a moment there was silence while Paul breathed the fetid hospital air.

The older man cleared his throat.

"I want to talk to you, son."

"Yes, sir."

"I don't want to see you deal yourself out, Paul."

Paul was taken aback.

"What does that mean?"

"I'll try to explain. I wouldn't speak to you like this if I didn't love you."

"I know that, Dad. You don't have to say that."

"I've always had a special feeling for you, Paul. Perhaps I shouldn't say this. In some ways Matthew is very like your mother."

"Yes, I know."

"But you've always reminded me of *me*. It's not a question of love, you understand."

"Yes, I understand."

"I think we all love each other equally. But things can be equal and still be—different."

Paul didn't say anything. His father lay studying the afghan on his knees in front of him where his handsome, clever hands lay useless.

"That's what makes me talk to you this way. I don't want you to have to learn through hardship what it took me half a lifetime to learn. I don't want you making the same mistakes I made."

"What mistakes, Dad?"

"The French have a saying: *Il faut jouer le jeu.* Do you know what that means?"

"Yes, I guess so."

"There's a lot of wisdom in that saying."

"Is there? What does it mean?"

"The saying?"

"Yes, what does it mean? That I should have a suburban ranch house with a cookout patio?"

He was sorry as soon as he had spoken; his father's mouth turned down in deprecation.

"That's not what we're talking about," he said quietly.

"What *are* we talking about?" Paul demanded, and he realized his blood had come up and he was slightly out of control. "Going to Harvard? Is that what we're talking about?"

His father's green eyes came up and looked at him levelly.

"Harvard, if you want. There are a number of good schools."

"Great, Dad. That's just great!" Paul felt hollow with disappointment. It seemed to him that the world was a small dirty hole into which he had fallen.

His father looked at him steadily.

"You're disappointed, Paul. You think there's a great secret to be passed along. There's no great secret, son, only a collection of tawdry little ones. But they are worth passing on anyway. *That's the secret.* That's what I'm trying to say.

"Listen, Paul. The world's a large and exciting place— no doubt about it. But it's something else as well. The world will knock a man down and kick the stuffing out of him—not just occasionally, but whenever it can. Do you understand? If I could make it otherwise I would, but since I can't I'm telling you the way it is."

"I know all this, Dad."

"Do you? Let me continue for just a minute—I won't be much longer.

"You're not a child anymore, Pauli. You've got to go out and make your way in the world just like everyone else. And there's only one world in which to make your way. You've got to have the tools, the stamina, the guts, to hold the world at bay. That starts *now*, Paul. The decisions you make now will be with you for the rest of your life. The ramifications will be with you. I can't allow you to deal yourself out, son. Not if I can help it."

Paul Werth's hand slipped—and he fell forward into nothing. He gripped convulsively at the crane, and his entire being shuddered: he was hanging one hundred feet above the school grounds.

He pulled himself back to the crane; his limbs were shaking, he had broken into a cold sweat.

How had he gotten here!

Slowly he began to climb down from the top of the crane. He was nauseated with vertigo, his confidence with heights had left him forever.

Carefully he made his way, his hands working dumbly in the dark, his limbs clinging to the steel as he descended. A sickness of dizziness assaulted him every time he looked down: the earth spun and he broke out in perspiration. He thought he would never be off that crane.

Finally he reached the ground—and his legs collapsed beneath him. He sat on the earth and pressed his palms against it until they stung.

He rolled onto his side and lay on the ground feeling the earth beneath him. Slowly his head stopped spinning. He could hear the insects now, the stirring of the grass, a distant car, the rustle of leaves. Home!

And a great heartfelt swell of love passed over him. He ran through his mind the names and features of everyone he knew, and it seemed to him he was disposed to love them all!

He rolled over onto his stomach and pressed himself

full-length to the ground. How he loved life! He had to
laugh at his pitiable state—for these thoughts welled his
eyes with tears. He lay like that, breathing deeply under
the suburban stars, gulping with thankfulness for the
mere immense improbable good luck of being alive.

The world lay all before him.

Nothing would turn out as he expected.

ABOUT THE AUTHOR

John Herman grew up in New York City and received a Ph.D. in English from Berkeley. After living in Paris, where he taught at the Sorbonne, he returned to New York and worked as an editor and publisher in the publishing industry. His first novel, *The Weight of Love,* was published in 1995. He lives in New York City.